THE
FIDDLER

Books by Beverly Lewis

The Tinderbox • *The Timepiece*
The First Love • *The Road Home*
The Proving • *The Ebb Tide* • *The Wish*
The Atonement • *The Photograph*
The Love Letters • *The River*

HOME TO HICKORY HOLLOW
The Fiddler • *The Bridesmaid* • *The Guardian*
The Secret Keeper • *The Last Bride*

THE ROSE TRILOGY
The Thorn • *The Judgment* • *The Mercy*

ABRAM'S DAUGHTERS
The Covenant • *The Betrayal* • *The Sacrifice*
The Prodigal • *The Revelation*

THE HERITAGE OF LANCASTER COUNTY
The Shunning • *The Confession* • *The Reckoning*

ANNIE'S PEOPLE
The Preacher's Daughter • *The Englisher* • *The Brethren*

THE COURTSHIP OF NELLIE FISHER
The Parting • *The Forbidden* • *The Longing*

SEASONS OF GRACE
The Secret • *The Missing* • *The Telling*

The Postcard • *The Crossroad*

The Redemption of Sarah Cain
Sanctuary (with David Lewis) • *Child of Mine* (with David Lewis)
The Sunroom • *October Song*
Beverly Lewis Amish Romance Collection

Amish Prayers
The Beverly Lewis Amish Heritage Cookbook

www.beverlylewis.com

THE ℱIDDLER

BEVERLY LEWIS

BETHANYHOUSE
a division of Baker Publishing Group
Minneapolis, Minnesota

© 2012 by Beverly M. Lewis, Inc.

Published by Bethany House Publishers
11400 Hampshire Avenue South
Bloomington, Minnesota 55438
www.bethanyhouse.com

Bethany House Publishers is a division of
Baker Publishing Group, Grand Rapids, Michigan

Printed in the United States of America

Library of Congress Cataloging-in-Publication Data
Lewis, Beverly.
    The fiddler / Beverly Lewis.
       p.   cm.—(Home to Hickory Hollow)
    ISBN 978-0-7642-0987-1 (alk. paper)—ISBN 978-0-7642-0977-2 (pbk. : alk. paper)—ISBN 978-0-7642-0988-8 (large-print pbk. : alk. paper)
    1. Women violinists—Fiction. 2. Amish—Fiction. 3. Amish Country (Pa.)—Fiction. 4. Domestic fiction. I. Title.
PS3562.E9383F53 2012
813'.54—dc23   2011043956

Scripture quotations are from the King James Version of the Bible.

This story is a work of fiction. With the exception of recognized historical figures, all characters and events are the product of the author's imagination. Any resemblance to any person, living or dead, is purely coincidental.

Cover design by Dan Thornberg, Design Source Creative Services
Art direction by Paul Higdon

To
Julie Klassen,
sweet friend and former editor.
May you write many more
bestsellers!

Prologue

Late-afternoon sun blinded me as I threw open the back door and stepped onto the porch, duffel bag in hand. The screen door caught my foot and dug deep into my ankle, and I dropped my bag with a thud.

Despite my anger, I took a deep breath and wondered if I should just suppress my urge to run off, and stay put in Hickory Hollow. But *Daed's* stinging words were fresh in my mind. *"You've got one foot in the world and the other in the church, Michael. Go on with ya—and don't come back till you decide!"*

At the height of this latest spat, *Mamm* winced and fled the kitchen for the next room, her prayer *Kapp* strings flying. I'd like to have fallen in step right behind her, to reassure and comfort her somehow. Yet what could I tell her that wouldn't break her heart?

No, I wouldn't turn back. I hurried down the road to my Mennonite uncle's place, where I kept my car, and sped away toward his cabin, not far from here. Far enough, though, to find some solace from this latest wrangle.

Soon, though, once I calm down, I'll be a fugitive on my knees praying, not only for wisdom in dealing with my ill-tempered father, but for my future. And it wouldn't hurt if I put Marissa Witmer out of my mind, too.

Awhile there, I'd actually thought she might become Amish for me, which is the worst reason to join any church. But it's mighty hard competing with a girl's *"first love,"* which is just how she put it to me months ago on our final date. There, near the old covered bridge in Gordonville.

Shortly after that, Daed started pressuring me to settle down . . . and marry. *"What's a-matter with our girls?"* he'd asked.

But getting hitched in the Amish church would mean giving up my computer and other fancy gadgets, as well as my car—especially my car!—in order to commit to the People. *"A lifer,"* some of my former Amish friends describe it.

Sure, I'm expected to honor my parents and obey the fifth commandment; I know that. But when you've had a taste of higher education and the Internet, how do you go back to reading the *Farm Journal* and relying on the Amish grapevine?

I considered all this as I sped away, my foot heavy on the gas, gravel spraying up after each stop sign. Cranking up the car radio, I relished the feel of the booming bass in my gut. Bishop John Beiler had taken me aside more than once to warn about my interest in worldly music, shaking his finger in my face. Not because I'm a baptized church member, but because I'm approaching twenty-five and still balking about bending my knee to make the church vow. *"A mighty poor example for the young folk,"* the bishop said recently, his face clouded with disapproval. *"Especially your niece!"*

Bishop John's words hit close to home, considering that

Elizabeth—my parents' only granddaughter among many grand-sons—was charging down the path of disobedience. Since she's always looked up to me as her favorite uncle, I couldn't help but wonder if I really am to blame. Doubtless Daed thinks so.

Things might seem less futile now if I hadn't lost my fiancée prior to all of this. The memory of Marissa's infectious smile and, *ach*, those adorable blue eyes is still before me. There's no denying she stole my heart away.

"*I'm so sorry, Michael*," she said with tears rolling down her pretty face. It was all I could do to keep from holding her till she came to her senses. Surely she would.

Surely . . .

But last I heard from her cousin Joanna Kurtz—our bishop's niece—Marissa had not changed her mind. "*She's followin' her heart*," Joanna told me, eyes shimmering.

Sure isn't following me . . .

Now I was holed up in this small cabin hidden away in the woods, miles from home so Daed couldn't come looking for me by horse and buggy. I had plenty to keep me busy, including work for my online course of study, wrapping things up for an associate in arts degree. Not that I needed a degree in anything, really, what with all the work I'd already been doing for several years now, drafting blueprints for custom houses and even a stately colonial-style church.

What a way to spend a summer vacation, I thought as I worked offline on my laptop. There was no access to the Internet in this remote cabin.

After a time, I wandered to the small washroom on the other side of the room and studied my reflection in the mirror over the sink. Clean-shaven . . . blond hair cropped just below my ears, with the usual old-fashioned bangs. I glanced down and took stock of my bare feet, my black "barn door" trousers, beige suspenders, and long-sleeved blue shirt. I looked like all the other young Amishmen I knew. And it made me feel even more lost.

Deserting the mirror, I went to kneel beside one of the bunks in the main room. "Hear my prayer for guidance, O God," I whispered, feeling guilty as I was reminded of my disobedience to the wishes of my parents. Could I expect my prayers to reach past the ceiling?

A single gas lantern brightened the gloom. There was really no need for the lantern when the cabin had electricity, but seeing it there gave me a semblance of comfort. It reminded me of the very thing that had brought me to this momentous day. Because I knew full well if I continued to walk the fence, I might end up on the other side—the outside, looking in.

I inhaled deeply, knowing my father would want me to pray for forgiveness, too. But I didn't honestly believe that driving a car and listening to music from someplace other than the *Ausbund* was a bad thing, even in God's eyes. Yet the Old Ways ran deep in me, so I pressed on, spending more time on my knees before rising.

Then, eyeing the small table where I'd put my duffel bag full of clothes, CD wallets, and fresh batteries, I attempted to shrug away my melancholy. Music was my consolation . . . but I wouldn't give in to the craving just yet. I'd wait till sundown.

After a long sprint through the woods, I returned to the old log cabin and stood in the doorway, staring out. The truth began to sink in—what I should've realized all this time. Marissa was never going to have second thoughts no matter how much I'd cared for her. Her new path was firmly set.

I watched the sun slowly fall over the secluded woodlands. And in the stillness, the psalm my father read aloud that morning came to mind. *Even the night shall be light about me.*

It wasn't easy to push away the painful past; I knew that. But it was high time. I breathed in the spicy scent of pine, aware of distant thunder.

We know the truth, not only by the reason,
but also by the heart.
—Blaise Pascal

Chapter 1

Amelia Devries stood waiting in the wings, her well-polished fiddle tucked beneath her right arm, bow in hand. The rhythmic vibration of guitars and a banjo buzzed in the floorboards of the outdoor theater, beneath her stylish boots. No matter the venue for her performances—classical or country, indoors or out—she often experienced a slight twinge of nerves before a concert. Normal stage fright, nothing more.

The preshow jitters had begun on the day Amelia played her first violin recital as a precocious five-year-old. But as time passed, she learned to trust the moment—the instant she raised her bow and drew it across the strings. *Just get me there* became her mantra.

Tonight she was the guest fiddler for a small country band—one of the warm-up gigs to Tim McGraw's featured concert this sultry mid-July evening at the Mann Center in Philadelphia's West Fairmount Park. And she had an impressive performance planned.

The tall blond master of ceremonies, Rickie Gene, brushed

past her to make his way to center stage, wearing a black tux and blue shirt. *He's fired up,* she thought, remembering the first time she'd met him a year ago at a fiddle fest in Connecticut . . . unknown to Byron, her longtime boyfriend back home in Columbus, Ohio. Or to her father, a former violinist himself, stricken with early onset Parkinson's disease.

Rickie Gene cast his winning smile like a fishing line to the crowd. "It's Thursday night at the Mann!"

Loud cheers rose from the crowd.

"Are ya ready to welcome the best little country band this side of the Alleghenies?"

The roar of delight filled the park, where thousands of people sat in either the covered seating area or farther back on the lawn, picnicking on blankets. The smell of popcorn and honeysuckle hung in the humid air.

"Help me give it up for . . . the Bittersweet Band!"

Fans seated all over the grounds applauded and cheered.

Rickie's appealing chuckle reverberated through the sound system. "Ladies and gentlemen, we have a fabulous surprise tonight." He paused dramatically. "Right here at the Mann . . . I give you none other than the winner of this year's New England Fiddle Fest—Miss Amy Lee!"

Wouldn't my parents just cringe? Amelia thought at the sound of her stage name. She breathed in slowly, willing away the jitters, and took to the stage.

"And . . . it's . . . *showtime!*" Rickie announced, promptly making his exit.

Amelia planted her russet boots center stage and curtsied in her flowing vintage dress. More deafening applause.

Though still anxious, she was eager to play her heart out in this well-known open-air setting. Quickly, she brought up her fiddle and cradled it under her chin . . . bow ready.

Almost there . . .

And then it began to happen. Always, always, an indescribable something transpired the instant her bow touched the strings. Oh, the glory, the sheer magic of connecting this way with a receptive audience. She felt at one with the band, the stage, and her adoring fans. All the years of performing for a crowd converged in that moment.

Despite the venue, deep inside she was the same petite virtuoso darling her father had groomed for solo work on the concert stage. Beginning her instruction at age four, he had meticulously taught her using the Galamian method, following in his own footsteps. Within four years, Amelia had auditioned at the Oberlin Conservatory in Oberlin, Ohio, where she began preparatory study with master teacher Dorothea Malloy. From then on, Amelia and her doting parents made weekly commutes on weekends.

In an attempt to give their little girl a normal life—apart from her recognition and celebrity—Amelia's mother planned for her to live at home while attending the best private schools. So Amelia kept busy with homework and exams and all the typical school-related activities while her father filled her leisure hours with practicing scales, arpeggios, thirds, and octaves. Only rarely had she missed a day of practice.

Between lessons in Oberlin, young Amelia played in professional recitals and soloed with regional orchestras, first in her hometown of Columbus, and then, when she was twelve, with the big orchestras.

Once she finished high school at seventeen, Amelia made her debut recording, as well as enrolled in college courses at Oberlin, all while traveling on the weekends. But after the years of the insane touring schedule, Amelia began to voice her frustration to her father, whose "serious music only" mentality had begun to annoy her.

"It's normal to feel the pressure—comes with the territory." Her father always downplayed Amelia's frustrations. *"When you're at the top, you'll appreciate the effort required to get there."*

By the time Amelia had celebrated her twenty-first birthday, she was weary of his hovering. She loved the music but disliked the expectation that she travel and perform in her leisure time, after college classes . . . and then, following her graduation. For a period of time, she rarely slept in the same bed two nights in a row, and she yearned for a more normal life—and the possibility of marriage and her own family someday.

One night while spending time at her parents' vacation home in Madison, Connecticut, Amelia read about a fiddling contest. Intrigued, she slipped out of the house and attended her first-ever fiddling festival in Manchester. Immediately, she was enthralled by the country style and the happy-go-lucky sound and, self-taught, eventually began playing in the East Coast's lineup of up-and-coming fiddlers.

And so, a country fiddler was born . . . her secret life.

Amelia drew her bow across two strings simultaneously, creating a harmony in one masterful sweep: double-stops. Leaning into the fiddle, she began to play "Pretty Polly Ann," Ozark-style fiddling and her first in a set of three crowd-pleasers. She loved this one, and the crowd had an uncanny way of drawing the first rousing song out of her, egging her on. *So liberating . . . just what I need!* They adored her, and she felt the love.

After two curtsies the crowd quieted, and she began to play

"Bumblebee in the Gourdvine," made popular by the legendary Texas fiddler Benny Thomasson. *My hero,* thought Amelia.

She had learned how to work an audience during her solo concerts, saving the best and showiest for last, just as she did with classical encores. So when it came time for "Orange Blossom Special," she played her licks with reckless abandon. The raucous tune brought smiles to the entire front row of concertgoers, she noticed; because of the brilliant spotlights, she was unable to see much farther back. Oh, she was in fiddle heaven with all of the string plucking and harmonic slides that mimicked a train whistle. The piece was a fiddle player's national anthem. Focusing only on the exhilarating number, she played as fine as she ever had.

But now she was coming to the middle section she adored. Sonny Jones, the banjo player next to her—a soft-spoken older gentleman—picked the strings like the seasoned musician he was, their resonating sound irresistibly warm and down-home.

Stepping back on the stage, Amelia let the guys do their picking and strumming, embracing every fabulous moment. Bobby, James, and Lennie—the best mandolin player and two guitarists she'd ever encountered, bar none.

She kept up her fiddling at a furious pace, her mind flitting to her father, whom she assumed was relaxing in his plush office, feet resting on his leather hassock, dissecting DVDs of big-city stops on her recent concert circuit. *Like a football coach, analyzing plays.* He would be dismayed if he knew she was goofing off instead of practicing her classical solo repertoire.

So would Byron . . .

Still, plenty of talented concert violinists also excelled in fiddling. *I'm not alone in this.* Amelia justified herself with the knowledge that the best violin concertos ever written incorporated advanced fiddling techniques—the third movement of the Bruch violin concerto, for one.

And as she played, she visualized Byron's text message just before she'd made her entrance tonight. *You're ignoring me, Amelia. . . .*

Her eyes roamed the first row again, these devotees of country music. Their faces were alight with pure joy, the same beaming response as classical music lovers in a very different kind of venue. The same meshing of minds and hearts, though no one here was dressed to the nines.

Why, Amelia wondered, did she feel this way when she mixed it up with the Bittersweet Band, removed from the serious music embedded in her soul? What was so terrible that she had to conceal this side of herself from the ones who loved and knew her best?

Two more measures and the lead was all hers again—and the fastest, showiest part of the piece. She'd come to know it like her own breath, and she moved back into the spotlight, standing now only a few feet from the edge of the stage. Her heart was on her sleeve as she took the piece to its rousing finale—bringing down the house.

Amelia gratefully acknowledged the responsive audience, all caught up in the excitement of her performance. Then, after curtsying again, she hurried confidently offstage, where she waited in the wings, still taking in the thunderous applause.

After an appropriate length of time, she gave her first curtain call amidst shouts of "A-my Lee . . . A-my Lee!"

Again and again she curtsied for the wired-up crowd. Their reaction was phenomenal—surely word would travel about her appearance tonight.

A prick of concern touched Amelia. *How long before I'm found out?*

Chapter 2

Four more messages had arrived since Amelia stepped onstage tonight. *Even when he's texting, Byron sounds like an English professor,* Amelia thought while standing backstage after her best fiddling performance to date. She was weary of the quotations Byron kept sending. *Give all to love; Obey thy heart.* . . . Penned by Emerson.

And then another: *We are most alive when we're in love*—John Updike.

"Hmm . . . no kidding," she muttered.

Nevertheless, she owed Byron some explanation for her silence. After all, they were practically engaged, and she had essentially stood him up.

Of course, she didn't dare reveal where she'd gone; instead she left a casual text: *Needed some time off.* Quickly, she tacked on an apology and pressed the button to darken the screen.

"Aren't you staying for the rest of the concert?" asked Jayson, one of the stagehands.

"Not this time."

"Really? I wouldn't miss it for anything."

She laughed at his joke—he *had* to stay, he was being paid to.

"I'd better get going. It's a seven-hour drive back to Columbus," Amelia told him. But the truth was, she wanted space after having given it her all. The nerves came prior to the concert, then the sweet spot—the performance itself—followed by the need to recuperate from the spotlight.

Turning, she literally ran into Rickie Gene. "Oh, sorry . . . didn't see you there."

"Trying to walk and text at the same time?" he teased. But his smile faded quickly. "Uh, someone's at the back entrance, demanding to see you."

Demanding?

Rickie handed her a business card. "Know this guy?"

She cringed as she immediately recognized the card. "Sure I know him. It's my agent, Stoney Warren." She sighed, touching Rickie's arm. "Thanks for the tip."

"Do you wanna slip out another way?" he asked.

She considered it briefly. "I think I'd better face the music . . . literally."

Nearly twelve years ago her father had handpicked Stoney Warren. In a matter of months, Stoney was grafted into the family tree, a top-drawer agent who oversaw her career like a caring uncle. Between Stoney and her father, Amelia had been escorted to every classical musical event since.

She shifted the case where she kept her fiddle and bow, nothing like the fancy case she used for her expensive and much better violin back home. Walking over to Stoney, she forced a smile, despite the wince in her stomach. "Imagine meeting *you* here."

He eyed her boots and vintage dress. "Amelia, honey . . . what's with your—"

"You don't like my Alison Krauss look?"

"Your hair—it's down."

Her mother, who wore pearls with almost everything, preferred Amelia to wear her long hair up whenever she performed. *"More professional,"* she said.

Stoney's eyes were earnest. "What are you *doing* here?" The lines around his mouth were more pronounced than she remembered and his brown hair windblown. She guessed he'd driven quite a distance to find her. But the question remained: How did he know *where* to find her?

"I'm taking a little time off." She pushed her hair away from her face. "I just warmed up for Tim McGraw. Pretty impressive, eh?" She scrutinized Stoney's body language. His shoulders were stiff . . . he was definitely not impressed. And not in the least amused.

He shook his head. "What do you suggest I tell your dad?"

She shuddered. "Don't tell him anything." Amelia stared at the ground. "He wouldn't understand."

"Neither do I."

"Let it be our little secret." She pled with her eyes.

"You're impossible, you know that?" Stoney offered her the crook of his arm. "Have you forgotten what the *Chicago Tribune* published two weeks ago? 'Amelia Devries plays with disarming buoyancy and an angelic sensitivity. Her rendition of the Brahms violin concerto exudes romantic passion.' End quote."

She drew a long breath. "Fiddling's just a hobby, okay?" She looked away, willing herself not to tear up. "It's relaxing."

Lightning zigzagged across the sky as they walked toward her car. "Well, don't fiddle in public. You have a class-act reputation, remember?" Stoney shook his head. "Do you really think Itzhak Perlman made a name for himself playing in fiddling contests?"

She shook her head slowly. "No."

"You have to mimic the greats to become like them, Amelia."

"I only fiddle in my spare time."

"Amelia, there's no such time for musicians like you. You're a star in the heavens. Why throw away everything you've worked for?"

"Is that what you think I'm doing?"

He pushed his hands into his pockets, silent for a moment. Then he searched her face. "How long have you been known as Amy Lee?"

She opted not to answer that question and paused, weighing her next words carefully. "If you want the truth, some days I can hardly wait to return to country music and these really wonderful people."

"And what does Byron think about all this? Or doesn't he know, either?"

She shook her head. Her boyfriend would share her agent's shock.

But Byron wasn't here. Maybe there was still something to salvage, if only Stoney agreed to keep this secret.

When they reached her car, Amelia opened the back door and placed her fiddle inside, next to her overnight bag. "How'd you find me here?" She closed the car door and leaned against it.

"That's beside the point," he said. "We have bigger things to talk about."

"What do you mean?"

"My dear, you have an important decision to make." Stoney

began to present what he called an amazing opportunity. "Nicola Hannevold—only a few years older than you and touring with the top orchestras in the world—anyway, she's taken ill. She's undergoing surgery and must cancel her seventy-day European tour."

Amelia had been preparing for a big tour, as well, but it was more than a year out and not finalized as of yet.

Stoney's eyes pierced hers. "This is a gold mine, Amelia. A real boon. But you have to sign on the dotted line by the end of next week or we lose it."

She groaned. "Stoney . . ."

"I need at least a verbal commitment from you. Right now."

"How can I possibly be ready in time?"

"You're ready now," he assured her.

She looked away, struggling.

"Another violinist will happily preempt you, I might add. She'll step into this readymade tour in a heartbeat."

"Well, if someone else wants it so badly—"

"That's entirely out of the question!" Stoney shot back. "Have you forgotten your picture on the cover of the *Strad?* I mean, really, Amelia . . . you're the next big thing."

"Stoney . . . I—"

"This is a windfall, Amelia. And I won't let you trample it under those ridiculous boots." He grimaced as the next act's lilting music drifted through the evening air. "If you were thinking clearly, you'd weigh the consequences of your actions and see my logic."

"I understand." *He treats me like a child!*

But Stoney was still making his case. "This can put you over the top—take you to the next level and beyond. But you can't afford any distractions, Amelia. You have to grab this *now.*"

Was this truly about her, or was he really saying that *he* couldn't afford for her to snooze this opportunity? The financial reward had to be an enormous draw for him.

"Amelia, I need your answer."

She swallowed. "Does Dad know about the tour possibility?"

"Yes, and he assumes you'll do it. He *expects* you to."

"Well, I need time to think."

"Think?" Stoney looked away, shaking his head. "What's to think about?"

"It's just so . . . sudden."

"Listen, if you let this go, your father will be crushed. Especially if he were to find out you're playing fiddling gigs in your so-called free time, kiddo."

"Why does Dad have to know?" She did not want to displease her poor father, afflicted as he was.

"This tour is a gift dropped in your lap. It's everything your father's dreamed of for you. *You*, Amelia . . . the singular shining light in his life."

She nodded and suddenly felt drained. "Well, nothing has changed. Everything is going to be fine."

Like always . . .

He folded his arms over his slender frame, quickly regaining his composure. "Good. You had me worried."

"I wouldn't disappoint you . . . or Dad." She gritted her teeth. *Or Byron.*

Stoney smiled, removed his wallet, and took out a twenty. "Get yourself a nice *venti* cappuccino for the drive," he said.

She accepted the money, even though she had plenty of her own.

"And think hard about your future . . . *Amy Lee*." He shook his head. "Pretty cheesy, hon. Don't tell me you prefer it over Amelia."

"Of course not."

Stoney squeezed her shoulder. "And maybe there's no need to trouble your father over any of this after all."

"Thanks," she whispered.

"Why don't you get a hotel room somewhere and get some rest, instead of driving home tonight? Playing fiddle in a twangy band isn't exactly relaxing."

She nodded.

"Keep your phone charged up, in case I need to get ahold of you. And answer my texts, okay?"

Amelia forced a smile, but it felt weak and dishonest.

"We'll talk more when you get home." Stoney waved nonchalantly. "Tomorrow is soon enough." He glanced over his shoulder just once as he walked to his silver coupe.

Amelia started her car and backed out, aware of Rickie Gene near the building's exit, standing and watching her. She opened her window and pulled forward, stopping the car to talk to him.

"You okay?" he asked.

"You know how it is . . . agents."

He grinned. "It was great having you here, Miss Amy. See ya next time!"

"Thanks." She waved. With that, she headed out of the parking lot toward I-76, resisting the urge to cry.

Chapter 3

Less than ten minutes into the trip, Amelia's ringtone signaled another text. She assumed it was from Byron and decided she would reply later, when she stopped for gas.

Glancing in the rearview mirror, she was suddenly struck with the significance of today's date: July seventeenth. "Oh great," she groaned aloud. "How could I forget?"

No wonder Byron had been so insistent about reaching her tonight! She glanced at her phone lying on the console. Having dated him exclusively for three years, she should have remembered the anniversary of their first date. *He'll be seriously disappointed.* They had planned to meet in Columbus for dinner at the Worthington Inn—classy, romantic, and very intimate.

A few minutes passed, and now her phone was ringing. *Who but Byron actually uses his cell to call?* She much preferred texting and email to talking by phone.

Amelia clenched the steering wheel, knowing she had to come clean with him now that her agent knew her secret, yet dreading Byron's potential response.

Her phone rang again, the first ten notes of Purcell's "Trumpet Tune."

Definitely Byron.

Slowly she breathed and reached for the phone. "Hey," she answered. "Happy anniversary."

"Where *are* you, Amelia?"

"Driving."

"Well, I happen to be sitting at a candlelit table for two. . . ."

"Oh, Byron, I'm so sorry."

"You . . . forgot?"

"I'll make it up to you somehow."

He was silent for a few seconds, and when he spoke his words were strained. "Is it too late to drop by later?"

"I'm really pretty tired." She didn't say she was still in the vicinity of Philadelphia, many hours away from her townhouse in the northern outskirts of Columbus.

"Pretty is right," he said, flirting. "I'm missing you right now." Byron had a way of sweet-talking her back to reality after her furtive trips to fiddle fests or stints with the Bittersweet Band. Hearing his mellow voice almost made her want to apologize. Almost.

Amelia had to change the subject or come out with the truth. "I feel just terrible," she said. Then something about the balmy twilight encouraged her to reveal all. Didn't he deserve as much?

"I'm driving west through Pennsylvania," she ventured.

"Good night, what are you doing there?"

"Don't laugh." She sighed. "You will . . . I know you will."

"Are you all right? You sound, well, rather strange."

She breathed in some courage. "I had the opportunity to play in a warm-up band for Tim McGraw tonight. So I ran with it."

Byron laughed, harder than necessary. "Seriously, what were you doing, Amelia?"

"I *am* serious. I played at the Mann tonight—it was wonderful."

He was stunned—she knew it by his prolonged silence. When he found his voice, his words were soft. "You opened for . . . whom did you say?"

"The amazing Tim McGraw."

"Amelia, I don't understand. Why would you do something like that?"

"For fun," she said, wondering if he could relate to the idea of doing *anything* for fun. Byron was one of the hardest-working musicians Amelia knew—a first-chair trumpeter. They'd met four years ago, when she played as a guest soloist with the Cleveland Orchestra, and months later he'd started pursuing her, at first mostly from afar. In time they had hatched a plan for their future—well, *he* had. The plan involved spending days and weeks apart as they reached their goals, yet staying connected as best they could. At some point in time, when it worked into their professional schedules, they would marry, but having a family was out of the question until they were much older—if at all.

"I didn't even know you liked country music," he admitted.

"Yes . . . I actually do."

He didn't skip a beat. "Aren't you preparing for South America— next year's grand tour?"

"I am."

"But how is that possible?" He sounded confused. "This is such a . . . a . . . departure from your goal."

He'd meant to say *our goal*; she was almost sure of it.

"Am I the only one in the dark about this?" Byron asked. "Surely your parents don't know."

She made herself answer. "No."

"Oh, Amelia . . . Does your *agent* know?"

She inhaled slowly. "Everything's cool, Byron. You don't need to worry." She paused, waiting for him to jump in and fill the silence. Surprisingly, he did not. "I just needed . . . a little distraction."

"All right," he replied, sounding reassured. "No more fiddling around with your future, okay?"

Amelia sighed. Byron, although immensely talented, had pulled himself up through the ranks of musicians by sheer determination and sacrifice. She had always admired him for his grit. He once told her that if she worked as hard as he did, she could be the *greatest* female violinist of her day. But instead of feeling elation, she'd cried herself to sleep. *What if I don't want to be the best?*

"Remember, we have a plan."

"Yes, of course, and I'm trying to follow it." Immediately Amelia realized she'd said the wrong thing.

"*Trying?* Listen, I want what's best for you, and for us," he said. "Do you doubt that?" She could hear the hurt in his voice.

The all-too-familiar lump filled her throat. Not from sadness but exasperation.

He breathed into the phone. "Look, we're both tired."

"And you're understandably upset that I skipped out on our anniversary dinner."

"Well, it's hard to imagine you'd forget."

"I know . . . and I'm so sorry." She sighed. "We'll talk tomorrow."

"I'll look forward to that." His tone was softer now, but she still detected a note of tension. With a brief good-bye, Byron hung up.

He's right; I have no choice, Amelia thought as both Byron's and Stoney's words pounded in her head—and worries of her dad getting wind of this. *I have to go ahead with the European tour.*

At the Morgantown turnoff, Amelia stopped for gas at the Turkey Hill Mini Mart on Main Street. When she finished pumping in the self-serve lane, the wind suddenly became gusty, followed by heavy rain. In a few seconds, visibility became nearly non-existent, and Amelia was completely disoriented as she turned left out of the gas station and headed toward Twin County Road.

Later, when she realized what she had done, she tried to retrace her path at the interchange but couldn't in the torrential rain. One small blessing, though—she'd changed out her old windshield wipers just yesterday and had a full tank of gas for the drive. If only she could circle around and find her way back to I-76 again. But she simply could not see well enough to navigate it.

She squinted and leaned forward, gripping the steering wheel and whispering a prayer. But she had no idea where she was until a glimpse of a road sign gave her a clue: *Welsh Mountain Preserve Ahead.*

"There's a mountain . . . here?" She could not believe how dense the woods had become, closing in on her and the thin ribbon of road. Was this a long-lost piece of Penn's Woods?

Amelia groaned. *How did I get so lost?*

Given the present deluge, Michael Hostetler was glad there was far less lightning than was typical for a summertime storm.

He marveled at the drumming sounds overhead and might have suspected the cabin's roof of being tin if he hadn't known better.

Going to the table, he turned up the volume on his CD player, hoping to drown out the jackhammering rain. He sat at the table and booted up his laptop, anxious to put his father's words behind him. Was that even possible? Daed's expectations and directives were etched on Michael's eyelids. *"That's what fathers are meant for,"* his youngest uncle once told him, after overhearing a heated exchange between Michael and his father. That night Michael's cheeks had burned with mortification . . . and guilt. Now, though, he refused to let any of this latest debate derail him from the task at hand.

He read the instructions for his business coursework, ready to move forward with a test in statistical analysis.

After a time his focus for his studies began to fade. Michael pictured his family sitting around the front room on comfortable chairs and the upholstered sofa Daed had purchased for Mamm a few years ago. Without a doubt, Daed was reading in German from the Luther Bible. Mamm sat to Daed's right, her eyes fixed on the heavy *Biewel*. Sometimes his father read two full chapters, sometimes more, *"for good measure,"* as he liked to say, his eyes alight.

Michael's married sisters, Sallie and Betsie, and their husbands might've stopped by, caught in the sheeting rain after coming for an impromptu visit, as they often did. In Michael's imagination, his mother poured meadow tea for everyone, and dishes clattered as the family gathered in the dining area of the large kitchen for homemade ice cream. The babble of voices undoubtedly filled the air . . . and Sallie and Betsie prattled on like they hadn't seen each other in weeks. *As always.*

Shaking himself, Michael forced his attention back to the test, determined to finish tonight. How timely that his vacation from work had coincided with this most recent dustup with Daed. *Did I unconsciously set it up?*

Meanwhile, rain poured relentlessly, and the hoot owl Michael knew resided in a lofty tree behind the cabin had no chance of being heard, there in the deep woods of lonely Welsh Mountain.

Chapter 4

Never in her life had Amelia driven in such a tempest. Rain blew in horizontal sheets across the road, silver-white in the headlights, resembling a blizzard. She watched the road closely, well aware that the wind and rain might mesmerize her. She turned up her radio even louder and tried to keep her gaze riveted to the ground.

Driving past a mobile home park, she wondered how safe the residents were there. One of the fiddlers in the Connecticut contest last year had told Amelia she'd grown up in a trailer and never acclimated to the width of a typical hotel room. "*Everything seems too big,*" the girl had insisted. Amelia hoped the other contestant was safe and snug on a night like this.

But am I safe?

Farther up the road, a lone sign read *Jesus* in large black letters. It reminded her of the Sundays she had attended her maternal grandparents' church in rural Ohio—and the weeks she'd spent riding their horses as a young girl. And of happily memorizing Bible verses at summer church camp.

Unfortunately, these days she more often heard the Lord's name spoken with disdain than love or reverence, not that she was a prime example of spiritual devotion. *I need to pray more,* she thought, missing her grandmother's own dedication. Her parents believed, as well, but her grandmother's relationship with God had truly been something special.

Turning onto Gault Road, Amelia kept her eyes alert and slowed her speed to ten miles per hour, noticing on her GPS that the road would eventually lead her back to the main highway. There was no hope of turning around on this thread of a road, especially without a single streetlight . . . and the driving rain coming harder by the minute. She'd heard of monsoons associated with hurricanes, but there had been no weather alert on her phone's weather app. Perhaps this was only a freak storm and would eventually blow itself out. Yet she knew a mere cloudburst would have ceased by now. And this wind was ferocious.

Large amounts of water had collected on the road, causing her to drive even more carefully. Now and then she tested her brakes, recalling her father's instruction back when he'd first taken her out driving. In the chaos of the present moment, she realized he and Mom had taught her nearly everything she knew—about music *and* life. Her mother, who preferred to take a backseat when it came to the limelight, had always offered her own loving support, but Dad had been the more influential when it came to Amelia's career.

Especially after he became ill. Amelia had never forgotten the first time she'd observed his hand tremors, years ago. She brushed away the painful image, wishing something could be done to reverse the debilitating disease that had snatched away his radiant yet short-lived career. The image of her dad holding his violin under the crook of his chin, standing with perfect posture—the hair of the bow suspended over the bridge—was fixed in her brain.

Her mother had often stood in the doorway of the music studio, watching them with pride. *Yet music was mostly Dad's and my thing,* thought Amelia, wishing to include Mom even more in her life. These days, her mother busied herself with writing a novel. And while Amelia had no idea what the book was about, she assumed it was a way for Mom to cope with Dad's diagnosis.

Amelia drove through a heavily flooded area, and water sprayed forcefully under the car and out from the sides, catching her off guard. For a moment, the vehicle was hydroplaning.

As her wheels took hold of the pavement once again, Amelia experienced momentary relief—then she heard a whishing *pop,* and the car jerked hard to one side out on the remote Pennsylvania mountain. Just barely, she managed to creep forward and make a left-hand turn onto a dirt lane, thankfully getting the car off the main road.

A flat tire . . . tonight?

Moaning, she leaned her head on the steering wheel, heart pounding. She had an emergency spare tucked in the base of her trunk, but even if she could change the tire in this storm, she didn't trust the small spare on the flooded roads. And the rain? By the sound of it, the violent weather was here for the night.

She sat there, surrounded by the darkly sinister woods and the rain. What would Dad say to do? *"Why not practice, Amelia?"* he might suggest if he were here. *Not one to squander a single moment,* she thought.

Despite her situation, she chuckled wryly at the thought of practicing in the middle of a downpour. She turned to look over her shoulder at her fiddle and overnight bag, the pitch-blackness closing in. There was no room to play her violin in the car!

The road behind her cut through the forest, and yet she had not seen a single house light. "Dear God," she whispered. "I'm seriously lost. Please help me find my way back home."

Amelia picked up her phone. No coverage.

What did I expect?

If she got out and tried to walk for help—but where?—she might be blown away . . . certainly soaked to the skin in a matter of seconds. But getting wet wasn't her biggest concern. She was alone in the middle of nowhere and feeling increasingly more frantic.

The constant beat of rain on her car drowned out any hope of hearing the radio, so Amelia turned it off, not wanting to wear down the battery.

Still trembling, Amelia reached for the iPod in her purse, choosing a recording of her own performance of Prelude no. 5 by Rachmaninov. *Nice and slow*, she thought, hoping the lovely melody might soothe her . . . somehow.

Lillianne Hostetler glanced at the day clock hanging high over the sink in Ella Mae Zook's cozy kitchen. "Ach, *yuscht* look at the time," she said, sitting with her cup of peppermint tea at the small table. "I best be goin'."

Ella Mae waved her hand, blue eyes shining. "Stay as long as ya like, Lily. Goodness knows, you need a breather ev'ry now and then."

White-haired Ella Mae wasn't known as Hickory Hollow's

Wise Woman for nothing. Lillianne tugged on her apron, looking down at her still half-full teacup. "How do ya get your tea to taste so *gut?*"

"It's all in the steeping. Three minutes and no longer . . . and raw honey from over yonder." Ella Mae motioned toward the bishop's farm.

"I'll remember that."

Ella Mae reached across the table and placed her gnarled hand on Lillianne's wrist. "Remember something else, too, won't ya, dear?"

Lillianne half expected this. She knew her neighbor and good friend well enough to realize the Wise Woman couldn't just let her get up and leave without one final bit of insight.

"Your son ain't punishing you and Paul by up and leavin'."

Lillianne nodded her head. She knew. Oh, she knew.

"And something else." Ella Mae's eyes were moist in the corners. "Your boy loves ya, he does."

"Well, he took his clothes along . . . and plenty of food, too. So how's that figure?"

Ella Mae smiled, showing her dimples. "But you offered the food, didn't ya?"

She had indeed. "*Jah.*" Lillianne's lip quivered. "Honestly, I couldn't have Michael goin' hungry, could I? What sort of mother—"

"You're a *wunnerbaar-gut Mamma,* and don't ya forget."

Lillianne swallowed, refusing to cry. "Do you think he'll ever come back home? Oh, Ella Mae . . . will he?"

"The Lord knows all 'bout that." Ella Mae's little head bobbed up and down. "And I daresay Michael will know soon enough, too."

"I just pray his heart's not too awful pained. His father can be harsh at times—still blames him for Elizabeth's leavin', ya know."

"Well, prayin's the best thing for any problem, even for your granddaughter. Mighty powerful, 'tis."

Lillianne agreed. "Guess I just needed to ramble some, is all." She rose to stand near the doorway, watching the wind rustle the tops of the trees. "Sure looks like rain's comin'."

"Smells like it, too." Ella Mae got up and shuffled over and stood there by her for a moment. "The Lord sees into your boy's *gut* heart, Lily. You can trust that."

Nodding, Lillianne looked fondly at the elderly woman who'd seen her and many of the People through plenty of struggles. *Like Katie Lapp's shunning.* Lillianne shivered at the memory of it.

"*Denki* ever so much," Lillianne said.

"My door's always open." Ella Mae patted her arm. "Don't forget."

Lillianne smiled and stepped onto the small white porch. A clap of thunder echoed from the north, loud enough to startle the sleeping German shepherd lying on the back stoop.

Michael, my son . . . are you safe tonight?

Chapter 5

Amelia watched the rapid raindrops dance on the windshield as time dragged on. She chose the first Paganini caprice next on her iPod, listening closely to Sarah Chang's fabulous rendition, taken anew by the unexpected phrasing and expressions as she sat, a captive audience.

It was one thing to be thought of as a *"wunderkind"* when she was little, Amelia thought, and quite another to compete with other adult violinists your own age. Continually Amelia endeavored to put her own special stamp on the tried-and-true concert pieces, just as the top performers did.

She thought of the recent *New York Times* review: *Devries' performance was a perfect blend of poetry and fury.*

All for you, Dad, she thought, leaning back in the driver's seat to stretch her neck, enjoying the piece.

After a few minutes, she looked in the glove box for her small flashlight, thinking it wise to keep it handy. *In case of what?* But she knew there was a real possibility she might be stuck there all night.

The wind and rain swirled, a mocking reflection of the storm in her soul—Stoney's finding her out—still maddening! And Byron's shock at hearing she loved country music—even performed it—hurt even now.

The worst is still to come. Amelia cringed at her father's inevitable disappointment. All of it plagued her. There was no keeping such a secret forever. And once he did know, Dad would plead with her to stop. Once again, she would end up feeling as though she had no say at all.

Despite everything, Amelia refused to disappoint him. Not the way he suffered . . . and not considering he'd put all of his hopes and dreams into her talents. *She* was his trophy and had been given every opportunity to develop and excel.

How can I think of not *doing the European tour?*

More minutes piled up, and just when Amelia was sure she'd end up sleeping in her car all night, the rain slowly began to let up. Even the wind was noticeably retreating.

She stared off to the left, through the trees, and saw what looked to be a glimmer of light.

She leaned forward and squinted to see more clearly. There, a few hundred feet away, she thought she saw a cabin tucked back in a clearing.

Waiting and fingering the flashlight, she saw that while the rain was still steady, it was no longer lashing as before. "Now or never." She opened the door and got out, still holding her flashlight.

Her cell phone landed in the massive puddle near the car, completely submerged in the murky water. Irritated, she pointed the flashlight down and fished around to retrieve it.

I'm toast!

Putting her soggy phone inside the car, she hoped it might dry out. Amelia shook her head, perturbed at not having paid more attention.

What else can go wrong?

"I need to slow down," she muttered, closing the door and locking it out of sheer habit. Then she zeroed in on the faint light in the near distance and sloshed through the water and the mud, glad she'd worn boots.

As she drew closer, she heard loud music and perked up her ears. Was it coming from the cabin? Approaching the small residence, she recognized it to be country music.

She quickened her pace—weren't country music lovers typically kindhearted? She smiled at her oversimplification yet certainly hoped so in this case. Amelia really had no idea who could be living up here in the boonies.

The light from the cabin's interior shone out as a welcome as she strode toward the pebbled walkway. A baritone voice inside belted out the melody as unreservedly as someone singing in the shower.

Amelia walked to the entrance, but despite her flashlight, didn't notice so much as a doorbell. She knocked on the door and the music coming from inside stopped abruptly. Suddenly, she was thrust into a brassy spray of light. And, blinking her eyes in the stark brilliance, she saw a good-looking young man standing at the door. His blond hair had been oddly cut, almost as if someone had plopped a bowl on his head and chopped around the edges. Bangs fell across his forehead. If Amelia hadn't known better, she would've guessed from the clothes he was wearing that he might be Amish.

Is he alone? Can I trust him?

"Hullo?" he said, a frown on his suntanned face.

She realized she must look like a nearly drowned rat. "I got a flat tire in the storm. My car's parked at the end of your driveway." She turned and pointed toward the end of the dirt lane. "Sorry to bother you."

"Ach, miss . . . let's get you out of the rain," he said, his blue eyes showing concern. "You're soaking wet."

"Thanks. I really hate to intrude."

"No, no . . . that's all right." He sounded convincing enough, and his face seemed kind, even innocent. He beckoned her inside, then left her standing just inside the doorway, mud caked on her best cowgirl boots as he disappeared into a tiny bathroom, calling over his shoulder about getting her a dry towel.

When he returned, he handed it to her with a shy yet concerned expression. "Pardon my bad manners." He offered to shake her hand. "My name is Michael Hostetler. Some of my English friends call me Mike." His smile was warm and unassuming. "What's yours?"

"Amy Lee," she said, giving her fiddler name without a second thought. "Thanks so much for the towel . . . and the shelter." She patted her thick hair and then wrapped the towel around her like a shawl, letting it absorb some of the dampness from her clothes. "Do you happen to have a phone handy?" she asked, glancing about the cozy cabin, not moving her feet an inch.

"Just my cell phone, but coverage up here is spotty at best."

She considered this and wondered how to reach her family and Byron. She knew all too well her boyfriend would worry even more if she said she was marooned in the Pennsylvania mountains. "My own phone's out of commission," she explained to Michael.

"Oh?" He stood there awkwardly, as if not sure how to make her comfortable. She *was* fairly drenched.

"Silly me, I dropped it when I got out of the car—into a puddle, no less." She'd heard that putting a waterlogged phone in a bowl of uncooked rice overnight could draw out the moisture, but she wasn't going to ask Michael Hostetler for additional favors.

"Maybe it will dry out, jah?" His face reddened at his Dutch and he apologized quickly. "Sometimes the Amish in me just shows up."

So he *was* Amish. She wondered why he'd want to hide it, if that's what he meant. Shrugging, Amelia thought her lack of a phone might not be a terrible thing, at least for a little while. A respite from the bombardment of texts and calls from the disgruntled men in her life. Looking at it that way, she welcomed the break.

"Would ya want to come in . . . and sit awhile?"

Pointing to her boots, she grimaced. "Not sure I dare."

"No problem. I can help you with that." Michael hurried to get a wad of paper towels and laid them out on the floor, where she removed her boots and set them on the towels. "The mud will harden," he said.

Then he showed her into the small space, complete with a corner kitchen at one end of the room, where she noticed a table with a CD player and a laptop—obviously where he had been sitting and working. And singing with gusto.

It began to rain harder again, clattering on the roof. She glanced at the ceiling and caught Michael doing the same. "Normally a flat tire wouldn't be such a problem, but in this weather, well . . ."

"Oh," Michael said, furrowing his brow as if considering her predicament. "I'd be glad to take a look at it once the rain stops. Unless you're in a hurry."

She smiled and shook her head. "I really hate to put you out."

He waved nonchalantly. "Not to worry—I've got plenty of time." He pulled out one of the wooden chairs at the table, and she accepted. Going to the fridge, he offered some cold root beer. "Homemade," he mentioned, then caught himself and asked if she'd rather have something warm to drink.

"Hot tea sounds perfect, thanks." Even though it was a balmy night, she felt chilled.

Quickly, he filled the teakettle—one just like her grandparents had years ago. Michael showed her an assortment of tea bags in a wooden box, similar to ones she'd seen in quaint restaurants. Was it handmade?

She looked about her as he stood at the small stove. "Do you live here year round?"

"*Nee*—no . . . just visiting." He offered her sugar from a bowl on the narrow counter. "There's some half-and-half, too, if you'd like."

Smiling, she said, "My mom takes her breakfast tea with a few drops of milk." Amelia checked herself; she couldn't believe she'd just told a virtual stranger her mother's personal habits.

When Michael poured the boiling water into her cup, she was aware of his steady hand, unlike her father's.

"Didn't I hear music earlier?" she asked.

Michael's face flushed. "You heard that?"

"Actually, it helped me find my way to your door."

He grinned, and the combination of his smile and the perfectly even bangs framing his face made him look boyish. "Do ya like country music, then?" he asked as he sat down across from her.

"Do I ever." She considered mentioning her warm-up gig to-night, but she was not and never had been a name-dropper. "I play the fiddle sometimes," she said. "It helps me unwind."

His eyes brightened. "That's wonderful-*gut*."

He seemed so overjoyed it caught her by surprise, and she told him about the fiddle tucked away in her car.

"Ach, really?"

She nodded, unable to keep her smile in check.

"I've often wished I had learned to play a musical instrument, but my people tend to frown on that."

"I could play for you, if you'd like."

"That would be just great," he said.

"Sure . . . once the rain stops," she said, surprising herself. Already she felt oddly at ease with Michael.

She was thoroughly enjoying the relaxed moment in this re-mote little getaway, despite the steady rain—and the nagging frustration that she needed to get back on the road. If she didn't check in soon, her father, her agent, *and* her boyfriend were likely to call out the National Guard!

I'm fine, she thought, smiling back at the handsome young man across from her. *Actually, never better.*

Chapter 6

Michael made a conscious attempt not to stare at the pretty young woman. Her cologne smelled wonderful, and her blue-gray eyes sparkled as she engaged in conversation—everything about her was appealing. And he was especially intrigued by her long, dark hair and her fine features, all of which bore a strong resemblance to his niece, Elizabeth. Even the way Amy Lee held her cup, with the handle on the opposite side, reminded him of his wayward Amish niece. Yet there was nothing Plain about Amy.

He watched her sip her warm tea, her damp hair falling against her cheek, then glanced toward the window, not wanting her to think he was gawking. "If ya don't mind . . . where are you heading on such a stormy night?"

"Back to Ohio."

He chuckled. "Well, I think you're more than just a little out of the way, don't you?"

She smiled, her eyes and overall expression animated even as she explained how the poor visibility had caused her to make a wrong turn. "But I have to confess I'm pretty surprised to find someone, um . . . Amish living up here in the woods," she said. "That is, *if* you are."

"Yes," he said, wondering how she knew about the People. "Have you met other Plain folk elsewhere, maybe?"

"My grandparents owned a dairy farm near Berlin, Ohio, so I saw Amish teenagers tending their roadside vegetable stands, or coming and going in their buggies."

"You visited your grandparents often?"

"Every summer for several weeks during my elementary and middle school years. I was an intense child; my time there was supposed to help calm me down."

"Why'd ya quit goin'?" He blushed—was he asking too many personal questions? Although he had met a few fancy girls through the years, he'd never spent much time getting to know any of them.

Amy shrugged. "Oh, I just got busy doing other things," she told him, sounding as if she regretted not seeing them more. "When they passed away, I missed them terribly." She set her cup down and looked away. "I still do."

"I understand that." He thought again of spunky Elizabeth, very much alive but lost to those who loved her. The People's great loss was his own doing. Surely it was.

"I craved those visits to the farm," Amy said softly, looking back at him now. "And spending time with Papa and Grammy . . . and their Plain neighbors."

Michael nodded. No wonder she seemed familiar with Amish.

"But that was a long time ago. And . . . I'm not sure how I ended up here tonight, at your door," she finished quietly.

Her words struck a chord and he bowed his head. Then, very

gradually, he raised his eyes to meet hers. "Well, Amy, to tell ya the truth, I don't know what I'm doing here, either."

"Sorry?"

He shook his head. "It's just the way things are, I guess."

Amy tilted her head demurely, motioning to his laptop. "Looks like I interrupted your studies."

Once again he assured her it was no trouble. "I'm mighty glad I was here to give you shelter," he said, realizing how much he meant it.

Mighty glad . . .

"Well, I appreciate it," she replied. "I don't know what I would have done otherwise."

He smiled back, attempting to be casual in his response. And trying *not* to think about Elizabeth . . . yet wondering where she was, and if *she* was safe.

"Maybe it was Providence that we met," he said. Instantly he felt ridiculous. *What a dumb thing to say!*

Amy looked at him quizzically, then down at her tea, quiet now.

"Not sure why I said that."

But she raised her head and smiled warmly, meeting his eyes. "Actually, I was thinking you might be right." She shrugged shyly and bit her lip.

Clearing his throat, Michael looked away, suddenly eager for a distraction. But despite his effort to appear nonchalant, her words soared through him, affecting him in a way he hadn't known since before Marissa broke off their engagement.

Amelia was surprised at Michael's eagerness to talk so freely. The Amish she'd encountered in Ohio were more reticent, as she recalled, but perhaps he was merely killing time until the storm blew over.

He seemed especially interested in telling her about his schooling, what he referred to as "higher education." He'd managed to get his GED after a period of years of study. "Since then, I've been taking classes at a community college while I work two different jobs," he explained. "One part-time for Nate Kurtz at his dairy farm, and the other as an apprentice for an architectural drafting firm in Lancaster—*Englischers*, of course. My path has been anything but normal for someone from my community—Bishop John is staunchly opposed to pursuing learnin' past the eighth grade."

The bishop? So the Amish church dictated what a person could or could not do education-wise? Amelia found this curious but didn't question it, letting Michael continue to share about his strict upbringing and the expectations of the People as a whole—and his father in particular.

"Believe me, I know how fathers can be," she said.

At that, Michael looked thoughtful. "I don't know why I'm tellin' you this. Guess it's because I can't speak openly to most folk about such things. So many of them are baptized Amish."

He went on again as though he had been deprived of a friend. He backtracked to his work as a draftsman, telling of his passion for creating blueprints and describing the repertoire of homes he had worked on and helped build. "And a beautiful colonial-style Mennonite church, which I drew up plans for, stands not too far from here."

Mennonite. She'd heard the word numerous times. "Aren't Mennonites Anabaptist, too?"

"Jah." He hesitated. "I was actually engaged to a girl from that church."

"Sounds like you have a lot of building experience already."

He folded his hands and leaned forward on the table. "As a boy, I was always constructing things—mostly out of mud or bits of leftover wood."

Amelia listened. "And your fiancée was Mennonite?"

"Yes," he stated, looking uncomfortable.

"Sorry, I guess I shouldn't have asked."

"No, it's all right. We just . . . weren't right for each other."

Based on the way Michael said it, Amelia wasn't convinced. Had the girl's family—or the bishop—opposed the relationship? From what she knew of the Plain tradition, most Amish couples married within the confines of their own or a neighboring church district. And Mennonites rarely married into the Amish church. Typically it was the other way around.

Loud thunder rolled across the sky, and she stiffened as more rain pelted the roof, seeming to increase in intensity. She was definitely thankful for this refuge . . . far better than sitting alone in the car.

Michael looked at the ceiling. "The rain's not letting up. And I should warn you, Amy. Up here, the rain sometimes lingers for days on end."

She studied his face. "I hope you're kidding."

"No, I'm serious. Weather systems can hang around, believe you me."

His comment didn't make her panic, which surprised her. *I should be dying to get home.*

"What do you suggest?"

"I could check on your car—change out the tire."

"In this storm?"

He shrugged. "Or I could drive you somewhere, but the nearest hotel is a long way from here."

"And the roads were beginning to flood earlier," she added.

"In that case, maybe it's best we stay put."

Then, astonishing her, he offered the extra bunk for the night. "There's a curtain you can pull closed, of course. Tomorrow, when it's light, I'll change the tire and you can head out."

"That's . . . really generous of you," she said softly. "Thank you."

"Say, I have an idea," Michael said, changing the subject. He got up from the table and pulled out a chessboard from beneath one of the beds, along with a drawstring bag of chess pieces. "Would you care to play?"

"Sure," she said. "It'll help pass the time." Amelia hoped she didn't sound impolite.

Michael closed his laptop and moved it off the table. Then he laid out the chessboard and the game pieces.

Even though she had little choice but to accept his offer, Amelia couldn't believe she would consider such a thing. The real mystery, however, was that she felt quite comfortable and not at all concerned for her safety. She would never have trusted a stranger anywhere else in this sort of situation. But Michael reminded her of the gentle, soft-spoken young people in Ohio who smiled kindly beneath their straw hats and offered assistance at the bakeries and the farmers' auction there. Certainly there was nothing dangerous about them.

"My father would have a fit if he knew I was entertaining an English girl . . . alone here," Michael said suddenly.

"Mine wouldn't be too thrilled, either."

Amelia tucked one bare foot under her and helped him set

the pieces on the board, glad they weren't going to just sit and talk, face-to-face. Texting had become so ingrained in her, she felt nearly at a loss without her phone. On the other hand, Michael's apparently effortless way with words reminded her of how things used to be. *Not so long ago.*

As they set up the chessboard, she relished the peace of the cabin, despite the howling rainstorm.

I don't remember the last time Byron and I simply sat and talked. Lately, Amelia had preferred being alone after a long day of rehearsals or concertizing to hanging out with Byron, even though they had shared many good times together. *Why don't I rush back to him after each concert anymore?*

For tonight, she was in a completely different world. Stumbling onto this cabin was a real gift—a true blessing, her grandmother might've said. She was fascinated by Michael's choice of words, the way he talked . . . even his wide-eyed sort of wonderment. Despite his laptop and CDs, he seemed somewhat untouched by modern society.

"I don't mean to say this out of disrespect," Michael said. "And I don't want to mislead you, Amy. You see, I'm not here for a little summer vacation, like you might think." He looked at the white king and the black rook in his hand. "I'm here because . . . well, I ran away." His shoulders rose and fell. "My father gave me an ultimatum just today. Shape up or *gut* riddance . . . and ya know what? He's quite right."

Amelia saw the frustration on his face and felt a degree of empathy. Then, wanting him to know she understood on some level, she cracked the door open. "Well, my dad might soon be saying the same thing to me."

"To you, Amy? But . . . why?"

She wasn't ready to divulge that. Too painful; too complicated.

"My boyfriend has already stated his opinion, however." *And not so long ago.*

Michael tilted his head. "Well, I hope he was kind about it."

She shrugged off his comment, not going there. "Are you required to make a decision—to answer your father?" Suddenly, she wished she hadn't asked. This was getting too personal, too fast.

"At nearly twenty-five, I should've already joined the church—'least by most Amish standards." He explained that a son's rejection of the Old Ways was the worst possible blight on a man—and on a family. "Truth be known, I'm leaning away from what the bishop and my father want for me." He bowed his head. "Hard to say it, but I honestly want to go fancy—become English."

"Do they know?"

"That's just it—what I want doesn't count. What the *Ordnung* decrees matters most . . . and that's my problem right there. I've tried, believe me. But I can't come under every single rule of the ordinance. I don't even think God expects it of me. Therefore, I cannot become a church member."

One broken rule and you're out?

Amelia shivered, still damp from the rain. Michael seemed to notice and rose from his chair, going to a large armoire and pulling out a man's shirt and pants. Returning quickly, he gave them to her and insisted she put on something dry. Looking first at the clothes, then at Michael, she said, "Are you sure?"

His winning smile was the answer, and he motioned toward the small room on the other side of the cabin. She assumed it was the bathroom, amazed by his unusual thoughtfulness.

Amelia carried the pants and long-sleeved shirt—*his clothes*—into the bathroom and closed the door behind her.

Chapter 7

A short time later, Michael offered to run out to Amelia's car and get her luggage, along with her fiddle.

"I wouldn't think of asking you," she protested, eyes wide. "It's still raining hard."

"Well, it's not all that unselfish of me," he admitted. "I'd really like to hear you play. Besides, you'll want a change of clothes tomorrow, jah?" He was downright determined to do this for her, no matter how bad the weather. Still, he couldn't help noticing how mighty cute she looked in his shirt, the sleeves rolled up, exposing her dainty wrists and a thin gold bracelet.

She reluctantly agreed and went to get her car keys from her purse, confirming what he already hoped—she trusted him.

He smiled as she dropped the keys into his hand. "Be back in a jiffy," he said before darting out the door.

The rain was startlingly cold and pierced through his clothes as he ran through the trees. Michael could scarcely see as he hurried to the car and opened the back door on the driver's side. Quickly, he reached for the fiddle case but noticed a program stuck between the cushions of the backseat. Midway down the front page, he saw the words *Presenting Amy Lee*.

"Amy Lee?" he muttered. "A performer?" Hadn't the brunette stranger introduced herself earlier by just that name?

Curious to know more, he climbed into the car and closed the door, the fiddle case resting on his knees, the program still in his hands. Michael stared back at the cabin, then looked again at the program. *Is she famous?*

His own mother had caught him listening to fiddling several times on the radio. Yet as exhilarating as such music was, he'd never imagined a fiddler so pretty . . . nor so friendly. Michael peered again through the rain-streaked window, toward the cabin. "Unbelievable."

Pushing the program back where he found it, he opened the door and ventured back into the rain.

This time Michael ran cautiously through the woods back to the cabin, mindful of the musical instrument he carried. His pulse pounded with anticipation at hearing Amy Lee play. What would she think if she knew music, especially fiddle music, had the power to set him right when circumstances around him baffled him and compounded his guilt?

Amy met him at the door holding a bath towel, ready to offer it to him, just as he had for her.

"Denki—er, thank you. Whew! Is it ever wet out there." He set both the overnight bag and her fiddle case down carefully. Then Michael accepted the towel and excused himself to the washroom, where he willed his heart to slow its beating.

Amelia promised to play for Michael once her fiddle became acclimated to the cabin's environment. She opened the case and tightened the horse hairs on the bow, then sat down at the table to return to their chess game.

"So, out by my grandparents', there were a lot of Amish dairy farms. Do you live on one?" she asked, hoping to make further conversation.

Michael shook his head. "My family raises heifers, so milking's not Daed's focus. But now, our neighbors, the Kurtzes—dairy is their livelihood. And I bet you'd be surprised at all the 'modern' contraptions they use. For one thing, the milk is kept fresh in refrigerated bulk tanks powered by a diesel engine," he added. He also went on to describe the vacuumlike diesel-powered milking machines.

She tried to visualize what Michael had described. "Interesting," she said. "My grandpa always said there was more than one way to skin a cat."

"That's the truth," Michael said, telling her of a young man in the area who'd rigged up a way to recharge batteries for buggy lights with solar panels—down in Gordonville, not far from there. "Some of the older ministers aren't too keen on it, though."

"Really?"

He shook his head. "Newfangled things are eyed with skepticism . . . at least at first."

"And then what?" she asked, making her move on the chessboard.

"Sometimes a handful of folk slowly begin to see the light, although most hold a hard line in the direction of the Ordnung."

When it was his turn she didn't talk, letting him contemplate his move in silence. As well as Michael was playing, he had undoubtedly planned his strategy from the start. Amelia knew that Byron also liked to play in a calculated, competitive manner.

Michael remained quiet as he reached across the board, his hand still poised on the queen. Even when he finished his play, Michael still did not speak. She didn't want to ask if he was all right; it wasn't her place. But he *had* shared some surprisingly personal information with her earlier, so he must view her as harmless . . . if not a friend of sorts.

As they alternated turns, Amelia enjoyed the leisurely pace of the game, and eventually, Michael began to talk again . . . slowly at first. Church membership still seemed to be heavy on his mind. That and his father's irritation over Michael's reluctance to join.

"Tellin' the truth, my father's put out at me over several things," Michael volunteered.

"Have you considered leveling with him?" she suggested. "Or just letting him know how you see things?"

He folded his arms. "Some. But Daed's only part of it. My mother is such a good woman, I hate to . . ." His words trailed away.

Amelia thought of her own mother. Writing well enough to be published had been Mom's priority for a number of years. And while Amelia longed to read what she was working on, she didn't dare ask. "You hesitate to upset your mother, right?" asked Amelia more softly.

"It would be an unbearable distress for her." Michael explained that a son or daughter who had been raised Amish was expected to follow in the footsteps of the devout parents.

"Right . . . I get that. Lots of parents want to see their children grow up to embrace their belief system. That's only natural."

"Well, it's more than that." Michael's eyes were serious. "To leave the People would not only reflect poorly on my parents—my father, especially—but my family believes it would condemn my soul to an eternity separated from God. I'd be considered lost, destined to an eternity apart from God."

"Why? Because you didn't become a member of a particular church?"

He nodded slowly. "Amish beliefs are to be passed on . . . embraced by the next generation. The People would say I'd accepted the world as my standard for livin'." He sighed. "*If* I left . . ."

"Really?"

He offered a quick smile. "But I wouldn't be shunned, since I'm not a church member."

"What would happen if you did join, and then left?"

"I'd be excommunicated and eventually put under the *Bann* for life."

"So now would be the best time to leave, right?" She slipped a strand of hair behind her ear. "Listen, Michael, not to be tactless, but lots of groups believe they have a corner on redemption."

"Oh sure. But it doesn't change my situation in the least. Fact is, the People believe I will die in my sins if I leave the community for the world."

"Well, what do *you* believe?" she asked gently. "Does leaving the Amish community have to mean leaving your faith, too?"

He ran both hands over his head but didn't answer. "The Ordnung sure isn't the Bible, no. But all the same, my walking away is not that simple."

Given his laptop and his interest in secular music, Amelia assumed he already had one foot in the English world. "How long can a person walk the line between the Plain and the fancy?"

"That's just it. I've been on the fence for a good five years already." Michael shook his head, apparently struggling. "And Daed's mighty peeved. He wants me either in or out."

"So then, you'll choose to stay because you refuse to hurt them?" She so closely related to his dilemma.

"I figure I haven't jumped the fence yet, so why not just muddle through somehow." There was a sudden futility in his voice. "For the rest of my life."

Michael, you don't mean it. In that moment Amelia felt she could see into his heart.

"I s'pose I ought to fast and pray about it, like Moses of old—demonstrate my humbleness to God," he said quietly.

"And . . . to demonstrate how serious you are?" She looked at him, completely understanding what he was going through. He was both torn yet longing to break free, just as she was. "You know what I think? At the end of the day, you'll follow your heart. I'm sure of it."

His eyes flickered with recognition, as if he wanted to say, "*You understand, and thanks.*"

The hour was growing late. Michael briefly closed his eyes, then opened them, smiling faintly. "I've even confided in the Wise Woman about this, something out of character for me. Mostly she's one to counsel the womenfolk."

Wise Woman?

Amelia was immediately captivated; she could hardly contain her questions. Her mind conjured up a highly respected woman whom everyone ran to for advice. "This is someone in your community?"

"Jah, our gentle sage in Hickory Hollow. Some folk think more of her than even the bishop."

How interesting!

"What does this woman suggest you do about joining the church, may I ask?"

He rubbed his neck. "Well, she's rarely told me what to do."

Like a good counselor.

"She once quoted a Bible verse from a psalm to me: 'Delight thyself also in the Lord: and he shall give thee the desires of thine heart.' Then she went on to explain that when our lives line up with God's will, the desire referred to means *Him*. The Lord himself." Michael paused, eyes brighter now. "It's not so much that we desire things or circumstances to change, she says, but that we've always desired our heavenly Father. He is our first true love."

Amelia considered that. "And all other loves are inferior . . . and send us running to Him, longing for His perfect love." She parroted her grandmother's own words.

Michael agreed and looked toward the door.

"Your Wise Woman sounds rather unorthodox," Amelia added.

"She's a cross between a Dutch uncle and the sweetest grand-mother ever," Michael said with a chuckle. "You'd like her, Amy. I know you would."

She laughed. "Well, I doubt she'd know what to say to the likes of me."

"You might be surprised." His face beamed. "She has a way about her."

Amelia looked at her watch and gasped. "Hey, it's almost midnight." *How'd that happen?*

Michael seemed equally surprised at the late hour, but she was the one who suggested they call it a night. "Oh, wait . . . I didn't play my fiddle for you."

But being the gentleman he was, Michael insisted she get some rest. "I can wait," he said with a disarming smile.

Then, curiously, he insisted they leave the chessboard up, which surprised and secretly pleased her. So, he *did* hope she might stay around long enough to finish the game. For the first time tonight, Amelia found herself actually looking forward to tomorrow.

Chapter 8

Amelia could not see her hand in front of her face as she lay quietly in the spare bunk. The night sky was pitch-black and filled with the singular sound of rain, rain, and more rain.

Still glad for the small flashlight, she placed it next to her pillow. As she stretched out on the narrow bunk, she felt surprisingly keyed up. It had been an exceptionally long day—first the exciting gig at the Mann in Philly, then being found out by her agent, telling on herself to Byron, and getting lost on the Pennsylvania mountain. On top of everything, it was also quite impossible to dismiss Michael's pressing issues, so like her own.

Running her hands over the light sheet, Amelia thought of her comfortable townhouse. And of all the nights she had spent mentally "practicing" her classical pieces as she tried to fall asleep, especially the demanding encores and curtain calls for her performances.

But when had she ever felt so comfortable in an unfamiliar place? Amelia questioned her initial impression of this out-of-the-ordinary encounter—here in this Amish stranger's haven against his own world. She knew that if she had made the correct turn in Morgantown, she would be nearly home by now.

How ridiculous is this . . . ending up here in the woods?

She tried to shake off Michael's weighty family concerns. He had more or less shared with ease, considering what he was up against. He'd even maintained that he had never talked about his thoughts so readily with anyone. Most men would never admit such a thing. And as for Michael's former fiancée, Amelia guessed Marissa had been the one to break up with him. At least from clues in his demeanor, it would seem that way.

Why didn't he fight for Marissa?

Rolling over, Amelia slipped her hand beneath the pillow, glad she could not see even the outline of the next bunk, only a few yards away. *On the other side of the curtain.*

But she *did* hear what sounded like whispering in Pennsylvania Dutch. She wondered if Michael was praying.

The rain continued to fall, steadily but slower now. "A *soaker*," Mom would call it. Thinking of home, Amelia hoped her parents wouldn't worry—*if they even realize I'm gone.* Considering Stoney's recommendation to spend the night somewhere, Amelia guessed he had also informed her father, at least, of the possibility of her arrival back in town tomorrow. She wasn't sure what scenario Stoney might spin to cover for her, however.

Just so he doesn't say he bumped into me at the Mann! It was tough to imagine his keeping her fiddling secret. Although if he said he would, she shouldn't have reason to doubt. *Trust is a big factor between agent and client. . . .*

And between friends. She thought of Michael again—yet did she really consider him that so soon?

In the near distance, an owl hooted loudly. A vision of her

father, disappointed, came to mind. Hurting him was the last thing Amelia wanted to do. Anything . . . anything to keep the slightest displeasure from creeping into his hazel eyes.

I'm losing control of my life, Amelia thought, trapped between her heart and everyone else's expectations. No one knew her private hopes, and no one seemed to care.

Amelia pulled the sheet up to her chin. *This weather matches my mood,* she thought, dreading going home. It would mean giving in to her need to please her father and Stoney. She sighed, thinking also of Byron. Was he more in love with their "plan" than with her?

Tears trickled down her face, and she dried them with the hem of the pillowcase. *I'll leave at dawn,* she thought, momentarily forgetting she was at the mercy of the elements. But Michael had said he'd take a look at her car in the morning. From the sound of it, he could fix most anything.

Well, not everything . . .

⋯ ≻ ≺ ⋯

Lillianne rose after midnight, glad for the steady rain—"*gut* for the crops," she muttered as she padded down the stairs to the kitchen. She poured a half glass of milk, fresh from the cow just yesterday.

Yesterday . . .

She recalled the zeal-turned-anger on her husband's part. Paul was sometimes known for his swift temper, in a near-constant battle to curtail it. Her sleep this night had been disturbed by unsettling dreams of Michael . . . gone. *Where?*

She ran her fingers through her waist-length hair, wishing she might braid it for sleeping, like Old Order Mennonite women sometimes did. But such things were mere wishes here in Hickory Hollow. More important was Michael's leaving. There was no doubt in Lillianne's mind that he was in need of paternal nudging as opposed to a firm hand. Even Bishop John must've thought so, stopping by last evening to talk straight to poor Paul.

Lillianne inhaled slowly and went to sit in her mealtime spot at the table, feeling ever so tense. She'd heard tell from Rhoda Kurtz, Joanna's mother, that Michael's former sweetheart was getting along with her studies and hoped to go to Uganda as a missionary in due time. And that Marissa had been the one to break things off with Michael last January.

No wonder his heart is all torn apart.

What could *she* do to help her son? Especially now that he'd fled? Lillianne didn't entirely blame Paul for running him off, but she knew in her heart of hearts that Michael would be sound asleep under his father's roof this very moment if Paul hadn't hollered out his ultimatum. Michael never would've up and gone away otherwise. Now it was much too late to retract all that.

Still, maybe what had happened was for the best. Maybe their *ferhoodled* boy would finally make the right choice and agree to follow the Lord as his kinfolk had done, clear back to their immigration here. Their Swiss ancestors had longed so dearly for the freedom to worship the Lord God and live Plain lives here in Penn's Woods.

Or, come to think of it, it was very possible Paul's aggravation would only push Michael to flee to the English world, just as their son's present leanings seemed to indicate. Truly, Lillianne feared what Michael might do. Oh, had her husband pushed him to the brink?

There were always a handful of youth in any given church district who struggled to make the decision to "stay in the faith." Some even felt coerced into making the permanent vow. Not many, but when it came to teenagers and church baptism, there were some parents who were unbending. The wiser ones—like Lillianne's own—permitted their children to experience *Rumschpringe* for as long as necessary, encouraging them to make their lifelong decision with joy and devotion. And entirely on their own, lest they join too early and regret it later in life. She knew firsthand that some parents lamented the day their grown children had ever knelt for holy baptism, only to change their minds later.

Through the years, Lillianne had noticed that thoughtful words worked far better with Michael than any spoken too quickly. She had always read this son like a book!

To his credit, Michael had proven to be financially self-sufficient since he was grown and had willingly given a good portion of his earnings to his father for room and board. He had earned his keep working as a draftsman. But to a harness maker like Paul, their son's aspirations pointed squarely toward a modern life-style.

She recalled what a good little Amish boy Michael had been, sitting so still next to Paul on Preaching Sundays, over with the menfolk. He was as obedient as the day was long. The early years he'd worked as a hired hand for Nate Kurtz were good ones, too. But his latter teen years till now had taken a toll, particularly his going after higher education and Michael's work as a draftsman, where he rubbed shoulders with Englischers each and every day. The world had pressed in and all but snatched him away.

May this phase soon pass, O Lord.

She peered at the darkness outside, unable to see the rain, though she heard its persistent patter against the windowpane.

She finished drinking the milk, remembering all the nights she and Michael had happened upon each other right here, pouring a glass of cold milk and eating a cookie or two. As recent as a few weeks ago, she'd found him listening to music on his radio—both forbidden. Alas, she, too, was drawn to the lively fiddle music. She'd never think of revealing the times she'd crept into Michael's room when he was away at work and listened to his battery-powered radio. Not to her husband, and certainly not to Michael, for fear he'd misunderstand and think she was condoning his defiance. Truth was, she and her youngest seemed to gravitate to the large, empty kitchen while the house slept, better able to converse at such a late hour.

Lillianne sighed again, wishing there were some way to roll back the events of yesterday and let Michael know he was sorely missed. And dearly loved.

O Lord, please look after my son.

Michael stared into the darkness after praying longer than usual. *What guy wouldn't give his eyeteeth to get to know a pretty country fiddler like Amy Lee!* He felt anew a sting of guilt for spending so much time with her alone in the secluded cabin.

Even so, he justified that in his mind. After all, she'd arrived soaking wet and clearly needing shelter. And then if they hadn't talked nearly like old friends from the moment she arrived! Yet, despite their unusual affinity, the thing that was most appealing was her trust in him. Considering the peculiar, even awkward circumstances, it surprised him. No, it shook him up. He'd never expected such a thing to happen. Not to him, of all people.

Never in a million months of Sundays . . .

Chapter 9

Amelia awakened with a start Friday morning. Stretching, she managed to get her bearings. *Ah yes.* She remembered the storm last night and the unfinished chess game. . . .

She strained to hear any activity in the small cabin, but all was silent. Out the window, the sky was clearing in the east, although still mostly overcast. Nearby, birds were chirping happily. "I crave sunshine," she whispered, getting out of bed. She'd had it with the gloom and the rain. It added fuel to her dismal mood—and her sheer frustration at feeling so helpless. But then, Amelia was often a little out of sorts upon waking, or so her father had pointed out to her back when she was juggling violin practice with her private school or traveling tutor. *Very little time for anything but music,* she recalled now, having felt somewhat isolated at the time. Her best friends were her parents and her instructor . . . and a handful of school chums. Beyond that, there was really no one she'd confided in. Not even Byron Salter knew her heart.

Pondering all of that, she made her way to the small bathroom to wash up and dress for the day. Though bleary-eyed, she couldn't miss seeing the speckle of whiskers in the sink. She wondered why Michael would bother to shave. *Why . . . up here in the boonies?*

Glad for some fresh clothes from her bag, she dressed quickly and then ventured over to the screen door. She spotted Michael at the end of the dirt lane, crouched beside her jacked-up vehicle. *So that's where he went.*

What if there's something wrong with the spare? she thought suddenly, holding her breath. *Would that be so bad?*

Chiding herself, she shook off the ridiculous thoughts.

As she turned away from the door, she had an impulsive idea. What better way to show her gratitude than to cook a nice hot breakfast? Years ago, her dark-haired mother had taught her to break an egg without getting shells into the yolk. In her recollection, she still heard the sound of her father practicing his violin in the background as Mom mixed onion and a little milk into the eggs. Everywhere, classical music was woven into the embroidery of her childhood. Every scene, every home activity . . . it was always, always there.

Presently, while Amelia looked for the eggs, bacon, and bread for toast in the tiny kitchen, she was once again aware of a deep sense of frustration born of the very real prospect of a European tour in her immediate future. And certainly by now she must have numerous voicemail and text messages from Stoney on the subject, and from Byron, as well. It wasn't right to keep Byron—or her parents—in the dark about her location. She needed to contact them as soon as possible.

If only pay phones weren't nearly extinct. Everyone owned a cell phone now—even Michael, she recalled, seeing him coming this way, through the trees, his face beaming.

Quickly, she opened the cupboard, where she discovered cereal and oatmeal and looked for a box of uncooked rice, thinking of her possibly defunct cell phone. More than likely, it was irreparable by now. *My own carelessness.* But just as she wasn't in a hurry to leave the serene setting, Amelia also did not bemoan the loss of her phone.

When Michael reached the cabin, he looked surprised. "I'm making breakfast," she announced, beginning to fry the eggs and bacon.

He, in turn, declared that her tire was changed and ready to go. "There's a place in Morgantown where ya can stop and get a full-size tire, but the car's purring like a contented barn cat."

After dishing up the eggs and carrying them to the table, she took her seat across from him. Michael asked to give a silent blessing, and she bowed her head quickly. At his amen, he reached for the salt and pepper and began to talk again of Hickory Hollow. Each time he spoke of the place, his blue eyes twinkled.

"You must really love it there," she remarked.

"No matter what, it's always been home."

They ate without speaking for a time, and she was aware of an unexpected undertow of tension between them. Amelia sensed he was mulling something as he worked his jaw. He kept looking over at her.

"Listen, I've been thinking." He leaned forward, his eyes fixed on her. "This might sound peculiar, but I came to this cabin to pray for guidance and . . ." He stopped for a moment and smiled quickly. "You know, Amy, I'm beginning to wonder if God sent you to get me thinking outside the box."

I've never been anyone's answer to prayer before, she thought, glad she hadn't said that aloud. "I've always heard that there can be a real mystery in the way God orchestrates things."

"Right, and time and again the Bible shows that." He rose to get a jar of peanut butter from the cupboard and spread it thickly on his toast. "I've been torturing my parents needlessly."

"Have you decided what you're going to do?"

He stared at his plate, knife in his hand. "I know you're right— what you said last night. I would never want to hurt my folks, 'specially my mother. She has such a tender heart . . . she alone has helped keep me in the fold, all this time."

"But is Amish life really what you want?"

Even now, Michael's concern clouded the cabin, just as the rain had the skies last night. He did not respond.

She drew a breath, reluctant to hit the road for home, though she must. "You've been most kind, Michael, giving me a place to stay." She paused, already missing the quaintness of the cabin. "And thanks for changing my tire. I really appreciate it."

"Not a problem."

For the first time in her life, she groped for the right words. "Well, thanks again." Then she backpedaled, offering to clean up the mess she'd made cooking breakfast. But he wouldn't hear of it. She even went over to the small area near the bunk where she'd slept and looked about for . . . what? She'd brought very little—an overnight bag, purse, and her fiddle case. Nothing more.

"You haven't played for me yet." From where he sat at the table, Michael looked at the still-open fiddle case.

He's stalling, too. . . .

"It'd be a shame if I didn't get to hear you in person, Amy Lee."

The recognition in his eyes told it all. He must be aware of her country music stints. But how?

"Okay, I'll come clean. I should've said something before."

He looked too serious. "I saw a program in your car with your name on it."

To her surprise, she felt herself blushing.

"So, would ya mind doin' the honors before you go?"

She nodded. *Just great, he thinks I'm a celebrity.*

She placed the fiddle case on her bunk and opened it. She tightened her bow, placed the instrument under her chin, and quickly tuned the strings. Why should she care what an Amish guy thought of her?

Michael leaned back, seeming to listen intently as she began to play the first few measures of "The Mason's Apron." Halfway through, Michael began bobbing his head in time to the music. His gusto—and fabulous smile—encouraged her, and she flipped it into high gear, pushing the tempo. That got his feet going as he sat there, nearly dancing in his seat.

Maybe I was wrong, she thought, thoroughly enjoying his response. *He genuinely seems to love fiddle music.*

She played one last song, not a fiddle tune, but one she'd always loved: "Somewhere Over the Rainbow." A song of hope and promise, the perfect encore to end their serendipitous meeting here.

When she finished, he clapped so long she felt embarrassed. "Thank you," she said, putting the fiddle and bow away again.

"You have a gift, Amy Lee. Really, you do."

She smiled and acknowledged his appreciation. "Thanks, you're very kind."

"No, I'm honest." His eyes searched hers. "You know, I was thinkin' while you played: Why don't you come with me to Hickory Hollow?" Michael paused for a second. "You could meet some of the people I've been talking 'bout."

It was then she saw something other than admiration in his eyes. *Maybe he just needs a friend . . . or moral support.*

"What do ya say, Amy?"

She considered the idea. But no, what was she thinking? "It's very nice of you to invite me . . . but I really have to get going." She considered her dad again, and how he must feel if Stoney *had* spilled the beans.

"Listen, if it would help, you could drive down the road a ways and use my cell phone," he offered, looking crestfallen. "Two miles south of here, I usually get reception."

"That close?"

He nodded.

"Well, it's not like I need to call home and get permission," she said, laughing softly but liking the idea of checking in with her father.

Michael had already turned to get his cell phone from the little bureau in the sleeping area between the two bunks. The space where she'd slept so peacefully last night. *First time in months.* She accepted his phone and assured him she would return with it immediately.

"Take your time . . . really."

"Thanks," she said as she headed for the screen door. Amelia looked back only to see that a smile had returned to his handsome face.

Chapter 10

Her parents' phone rang repeatedly until Mom picked up, right before the voicemail would have kicked on. "Devries residence," her mother answered.

"Hi, Mom—just want you and Dad to know I'm safe and sound." Amelia paused, not sure what else to add, not wanting to say where she was in case Stoney had kept his word and hadn't blown her secret.

"So good to hear from you, Amelia. Stoney relayed to us you would be in town sometime today, dear. We'd love it if you could stop by on your way home."

Amelia held her breath, wondering exactly what Stoney had told them. But when her mother changed the subject and commented on how very warm and rainy it had been yesterday, Amelia breathed a sigh of relief. "Sure. We'll talk real soon, all right?"

"Thanks for calling, honey." She visualized her tall, slender mother holding the phone in her left hand, her dark chin-length hair thick and shiny.

"I love you both."

"We love you, too, dear. I'll let your father know you called."

"Thanks, Mom. Good-bye." She pressed the button to end the call.

A flicker of a sweet memory crossed her mind—she was only seven and had been sick with the flu and a high fever. Concerned, her mother sat up all night with Amelia, putting cool cloths on her forehead and holding her hand. It was the year before she'd auditioned at the Oberlin Conservatory. She marveled at the sacrifices her parents had made during those earliest years of her musical study . . . one of the reasons she didn't want to disappoint them. She again thought of the overseas tour, resisting the urge to get emotionally bogged down.

Amelia dialed Byron's number next, hoping to catch him at home. No doubt he would be waiting for her call.

He answered on the second ring. "Byron Salter speaking."

"Hey again," she said.

"Amelia?"

"Yes . . . has my voice changed overnight?"

"Well, I saw the name Michael Hostetler on the caller ID and assumed it was a wrong number."

She gulped—she'd forgotten she was using a different phone. "I had to borrow one," she explained, trying to sound composed. "I had a little accident, and my own phone landed in water." She didn't say where or why, hoping he might think it was the bathtub at a hotel.

"I take it you're not home as of yet."

"No, still in Pennsylvania." *It's a long and very strange story,* she thought. But she said instead, "I got caught in a bad storm." She hoped he wouldn't ask where she'd spent the night.

"Are you on your way home?"

Quite unexpectedly, the image of Michael running through the dense woods to her car, getting drenched just so he could hear her play her fiddle, came to her. It shook her up enough to disorient her for a moment.

"Amelia? Are you there?"

It crossed her mind to just start talking again and then simply hang up on herself. Let Byron assume she'd lost service—a polite sort of way to terminate a difficult conversation. But she wasn't a quitter; she would tough it out . . . and choose to be honest. "I'm taking a little detour today," she told him.

"I'm sorry; I thought you said you were making a detour."

"I did."

"But—"

"I'll be home eventually, Byron." She didn't wait for him to say more. "I really don't know exactly when I'll be back."

"What's going on?" He was silent for a second. Then, "I don't understand."

"I just need some time, Byron—that's all. Good-bye for now." And she hung up.

When Amelia arrived back at the cabin, she thanked Michael for loaning his phone.

"Anytime, Amy . . . really," he said, and she wondered if all young Amishmen were so accommodating.

"And if your invitation still stands—" she stopped, wondering how what she was about to say would go over—"I think I *would* actually like to visit Hickory Hollow with you."

He looked momentarily stunned. "You want to?"

"From everything you've told me, I feel like I already know some of your neighbors there," she added.

"Wonderful, then. Why don't you follow me there in your car? We can stop quick in Morgantown on the way to get a new tire."

She wasn't having second thoughts, but she wondered aloud, "I should ask you—will the People be okay with this? I mean, are they typically all right with visits from outsiders?"

"Ach, most will welcome you." He nodded, grinning now. "We are plenty interested in Englischers, and don't let anyone tell ya different."

We? He still thinks of himself as one of them. . . .

Michael seemed exceptionally cheerful as he busied himself packing the food he'd brought, as well as his clothing—far more than she'd realized. Obviously he'd planned to stay here longer than for a single night.

Later, when Michael was ready to go—before she got into her car—Amelia turned and looked back at the rustic little cabin. Feeling strangely nostalgic, she memorized the sight of it, tucked away from the narrow road, in the heart of Welsh Mountain.

Amelia had done plenty of driving recently, but not without her GPS. Having tested her phone earlier that morning, she had decided it was not going to revive itself. No sense hoping it would dry out now. In some ways, this turn of events felt astonishingly good. It was a change from feeling absolutely tethered to the Big Three: Dad, Stoney, and Byron.

No longer, she thought, knowing she would have some explaining to do once she returned home. But Amelia was determined to enjoy her day in Amish country.

Letting go of her stress, she followed Michael to Morgantown to purchase a permanent tire and change out the spare. That done, they headed to Highway 10, down past the rural towns of Honey Brook and White Horse. She drove west on Route 340, toward Intercourse Village, just skirting the rural edge of town before turning south on Cattail Road, taking the back road leading to the most peaceful blink-and-you'll-miss-it town she'd ever encountered.

Amelia enjoyed seeing the hitching posts and white silos, and the horse and buggies, too. "So this is Hickory Hollow," she said and parked her car behind Michael's in the paved driveway that led to a beautiful old farmhouse. *Mr. and Mrs. Jerry Landis*, the mailbox read.

She remembered what Michael had told her about this special parking arrangement with his Mennonite relatives. *Where he hides his car.*

Turning off the ignition, she spotted a stout woman with cherry-red cheeks—certainly Michael's aunt—waving from the front porch, her hair in a severe bun as she called a warm greeting.

Amelia waved back and when Michael came over to her car, she asked, "Is this your private parking spot?"

"I guess you could say that. I've been using it for years now, since near the start of my Rumschpringe." He gave her a quick glance. "You know about Rumschpringe, right? It's the stage of Amish life when young people sixteen and up are permitted to 'run around.' Some of us try on the world for size."

"So, do your parents even know you own a car?"

"Oh, they know." He nodded as they began to walk toward the road. "Not that they're any too pleased about it."

"Well then, why do you hide it?" she asked, matching his stride.

"Most young men who have cars keep them away from their parents' property out of respect." Michael removed his straw hat and held it in one hand. "Of course, most youth never stray as far as that."

"Like you have?"

"Well, owning a car *is* a big deal, and I don't much care to flaunt it. I don't want to trample on the Old Ways. I'm not doing this out of rebellion, though it might look like that to the People."

She grasped some of what he said, but the idea of allowing young people to experiment with the outside world after being sheltered so long seemed risky.

"Let's head to Nate Kurtz's dairy farm," he said, changing the subject.

"How far away?"

"Less than a mile." His voice suddenly sounded thinner. "Oh, and while we drove here, I was thinkin' it might be best if you don't go with me when I talk to my Daed."

"I didn't expect to," she said, looking ahead, enjoying the landscape. "Do whatever works for you."

"Denki—thanks." Michael glanced at her a second time, then looked away.

"What about your Wise Woman . . . any chance I might have time to meet her?"

"I'll see to it." He gave a nervous chortle. "I might actually need to talk to her myself."

Amelia wondered if he might need the comfort that only the Wise Woman could offer. *Someone who is Amish.*

"Should we make an appointment with her?"

He smiled, yet she'd been serious. "No need for that, really," he said.

"Okay." Amelia swung her arms and took a deep breath—the air was fresher here, she realized. And it felt good to let her hair blow free, away from her face. The farmland was a lovely departure from big-city living.

"Nate milks forty head of cattle, twice a day," he said. "I've worked for him part-time since I was thirteen."

She recalled the first time she had milked a cow by hand, with her dear grandmother's help. It had been one of the happiest days of her life.

Why did God take Grammy so soon? Amelia recalled how stunned and helpless she had felt when news came of the massive stroke that had so suddenly claimed her dear grandmother's life. Her grandfather's death had come years later, but he let it be known that his sweetheart's passing had all but broken his heart.

Walking this farm country made Amelia feel closer to her grandparents. So many cherished memories! She soaked in the serenity as they passed thousands of rows of corn in a landscape dotted with farms and adorable barefoot children dressed like mirror images of their parents. She was surprised by the profound effect all of it had on her. And to think she was experiencing this with an Amishman by her side!

She looked again at Michael and he caught her smile. "It's truly beautiful here."

"The garden spot of the world, ya know." His face remained serious.

"Should I even ask if you're nervous about returning home?"

"You mean, so soon after I left?" He was quiet for a moment. "Yes and no. I think I just needed a good kick in the pants is what." He paused as though considering further. "I mean that . . . and I'm grateful to you."

She looked down at her boots and dress. "Maybe I should go barefoot while I'm here."

"Why not be comfortable? I'll carry your boots for ya."

She surveyed the road ahead. "On second thought, I'd better keep them on."

"Afraid you'll burn your feet?" He chuckled, surprising her. "When was the last time you walked on gravel without shoes?"

Surely she didn't have to tell him that she always wore shoes outdoors. "I'm a city girl, remember."

"Could've fooled me." There was that same twinkle in his eye she'd seen at the cabin.

It was interesting that Michael was so relaxed again when he was soon heading into the thick of the fray. Was she giving him the support he needed? Was that it?

But his mood changed as he pointed out the one-room Amish schoolhouse. "Bishop John's farmhouse is just beyond the playground and the boys' outhouse. A long stone's throw . . . and then you'll see a sandstone house, built in the mid–eighteen hundreds. It's a striking place—that's our closest neighbor, Samuel Lapp. Believe me, there are oodles of Lapps round here, including Samuel and Rebecca's sons, all married now."

He sounded wound up. "Are you all right?" she blurted without thinking.

He gave her a sidewise look. "To be honest, it won't be easy to say what I must to my father."

Now Amelia felt guilty for urging him to return.

"But it's not because I plan to talk to Daed. Not really," he added quickly. "Don't take this wrong, Amy. I'm just wonderin' if I should've brought you here."

"I hope I won't get you in hotter water."

He didn't look at her. "It just might send the wrong message to my parents."

It would to mine! she thought. She felt like a tagalong. Maybe she really shouldn't have come. "I'd hate to upset your parents or anyone who thinks we're—"

"A couple?"

She blushed, shocked that he guessed what she was thinking. "Well, I'd hate to cause you further trouble."

He seemed to contemplate that as he moved across the road to the shaded side, and she followed.

When they rounded the bend, the sandstone house came into view, and past that, she saw an equally stunning stone house. "Is that your house?" She pointed. "It's gorgeous."

"Jah, it's been in the family for five generations."

Five?

"My married brothers' children are the fifth."

"So your great-grandparents lived there?"

"They did."

She wondered if he was supposed to have inherited the place, had he planned to stay Amish. She did not ask, aware that his hands had become clenched fists.

"Just about to the Kurtz farm. Joanna will enjoy showin' you round the place . . . while I go and talk to my father."

"Okay. Sounds good," she said, looking forward to meeting the young woman he had spoken about last night.

"Say a prayer for me, will ya, Amy?"

"I can do that," she agreed, sensing his distress—and wishing him well. But Michael had no idea how very few prayers she'd prayed lately. *If so, he might not ask me to pray at all!*

They took their time getting to the treed area. Once there, she

85

removed her boots and socks and savored the grassy coolness. It was then she noticed her boots were free of the caked-on mud. Michael must've cleaned them earlier this morning before she awakened. Marveling at this, she glanced up at him. "You're full of surprises," she said, pointing to her shoes. "Thanks for scraping the gunk off my boots."

"The pleasure was all mine," he said comically as they made their way past his parents' home, staying near the side of the road so Amelia wouldn't have to walk on the gravel. And all the while, he carried her boots—one in each hand.

A swarm of bees buzzed overhead, and she wished for her slouchy hat. Then she thought better of it. "I hope I don't look too out of place here," she said softly.

Michael flashed a smile. "I think it's a little late for that."

"Well, whatever do you mean?" she teased.

He took the bait. "C'mon, when was the last time you saw an Amish girl with such a fancy dress or her hair all down, without a head covering?"

She'd almost forgotten they'd just met. Amelia poked his arm like she would a mischievous big brother. "Oh, you!" she said, all too convinced in that moment that Michael Hostetler was anything but a brother figure.

Chapter 11

The sweeping spread of land that was the Kurtz dairy farm reminded Amelia of movies she'd seen set in fertile, lush river valleys. She didn't recall the actual movie titles, though, and assumed Michael wouldn't know them anyway. Besides, it really didn't matter. She was enjoying the day immensely.

Walking farther down Hickory Lane, she spotted three teenage girls in matching green dresses and aprons, coming this way. They were clasping hands, talking in *Deitsch*—Pennsylvania Dutch—and smiling so cheerfully, Amelia was unable to take her eyes off them.

"Hullo!" Michael called to them. *"Wie bischt?"*

Two of the girls smiled, but they didn't reply, and one of the girls ducked her head as if she was too shy to meet an Englisher.

When they were out of earshot, Amelia asked, "Are they sisters?"

"No." Michael explained that young women well into their twenties often held hands when walking. "Of course sisters do, but also cousins and close friends."

Amelia was touched by such open affection.

"You'll see that sort of fondness amongst most all the women. We're close-knit here in Hickory Hollow. Might seem a little old-fashioned to you." He laughed a little. "Those girls are more like ya than you'd think. They all have iPods—and so do their brothers who haven't joined church yet."

"Really?"

He nodded. "Cell phones, too . . . some even have Facebook accounts. The bishops aren't happy about it. The whole thing's caused a ruckus, 'specially because most parents aren't at all informed about social networking."

"So do teens keep in touch with other Amish Facebook users, then?"

"Supposedly." He paused and shrugged. "It's not something I've gotten into just yet."

She could hardly imagine this happening with the Ohio Amish teenagers up the road from her grandparents' former farmhouse, but no doubt Michael knew more about it.

He motioned for her to follow him down the long lane that led to the big white clapboard farmhouse where the Kurtz family lived. "You'll enjoy meeting Joanna Kurtz—she's an Amish girl who toes the line. But very friendly to Englischers—you'll see. She's one of two daughters who still live at home."

Amelia wondered if Michael had ever dated Joanna; he seemed so fond of her and her family. But then, he had a kindhearted way of speaking about nearly everyone.

"Joanna and her mother, Rhoda, take great pains to plan the flower beds each and every year."

"With plenty of color and varieties, I see." Amelia admired the pristine lawn and flower gardens with a profusion of purple and pink asters. There were yellow daisies, too, as well as white and pink ground cover, and roses scaled up a trellis along one whole side of the whitewashed front porch. The beds were so thick with color, she wished she could stand still and soak in the beauty.

"Some of the womenfolk boast that gardening is their way of being creative," Michael said.

Creative yet controlled, Amelia thought.

"That and quilting are a good way for the womenfolk to show off a little."

Amelia noticed two gray cats scampering across the yard. "Oh, look at that, they must be twins!"

"I'm afraid Nate isn't fond of cats. I won't tell you what he does to control his feline population."

Amelia grimaced. "Um . . . thanks for sparing me."

"You have no idea how many dozens of them reside in our barns."

"Couldn't they be put up for adoption?"

Michael raised his hand in a wave to a middle-aged man wearing black trousers and a blue short-sleeved shirt, with tan suspenders and a straw hat identical to Michael's. "There's Nate now," he said.

So much for the cats. Amelia matched Michael's pace as they rounded the house and followed the dirt lane all the way back to the barn.

"Is Joanna inside?" Michael pointed to the white two-story structure.

Nate nodded quickly and muttered something about getting back to the team of field mules.

"All right, then." Michael handed the boots back to Amelia

and suggested she put them on. "It could be, well, a bit messy in the barn, ya know."

"Good idea, thanks!" she replied and quickly slipped on the boots.

"Joanna might have a pair of old work boots for you to wear, if you'd prefer," he said, shoving open the barn door. Once they were inside, he took a moment to slide it shut again.

"Oh, I'm fine this way." Yet again she was taken with the fact that he always seemed to be thinking ahead on her behalf.

"Nate's got two new calves. You'll see 'em—cute little critters," he said, seemingly eager to give her a tour of his neighbors' barn.

She wondered why Nate hadn't stopped to greet them or shake hands like Michael seemed to enjoy doing.

Then, as if sensing the direction of her thoughts, Michael explained that Joanna's father hardly talked. "Just so you know."

So I won't think he's rude, Amelia mused.

He mentioned that some area Amishmen were known to say very little. "Some scarcely ever crack a smile, either," he went on. "They pass on their knowledge of farming and whatnot by simply doing. Even so, whether your father's quiet or outspoken, there's never any doubt about what to do or how to do it," Michael added. "That's true whether it's farming or blacksmithing, welding or carpentry."

Amelia wondered if he wished his own father were less blunt. She was thankful that her dad, for as much as he had pushed her in her career, had always had a patient, reassuring temperament.

They strolled past a double row of milking stanchions, and Michael paused to show her the new calves in their own small pen. Like twin babies, they slept nose to nose on a soft bed of hay.

"Oh, they *are* cute . . . and look how pretty their coats are." She leaned down for a better look.

Michael crouched close to Amelia. His arm brushed against hers momentarily as he moved his hand slowly toward the calf nearest them. "Wouldn't ya just love to have a pet like one of these?" he said, his eyes soft.

"Oh, would I ever. But I'm not sure where I'd keep a calf in my townhouse."

"Ya mean, there's no attached garage?"

She realized she was giggling but didn't stop herself. When had she laughed like this?

One of the calves opened its enormous milky eyes and blinked at them.

"Hey, look at that," he whispered. "God's handiwork in front of our very noses."

Amelia wondered if she'd signaled that she wanted to touch the calf, too, because before she realized what Michael was doing, he reached for her hand and placed it gently on the calf's side, holding his own strong hand on top of hers for longer than necessary.

She hardly knew what to think, but she didn't pull away. When she finally found her voice, she told him more about her grandparents' farm. "I waited all year for summers, eager to visit them. Working alongside Papa and Grammy in their barn was a little slice of heaven on earth."

Michael gave her an understanding smile. "Too bad your parents didn't live nearby or right in the big farmhouse there, so you could all be together. Like we Amish tend to do."

She nodded and choked back the lump in her throat.

Michael sensitively changed the subject. "I think you'll find

Joanna a delightful person. She's closer in age to you than her younger sister, Cora Jane. Joanna used to attend the youth Singings, back when I was going, too. Her pretty soprano voice could be heard high above the others'."

"I would like to meet her," said Amelia, still recovering from Michael's hand on hers.

"Follow me, then," he said, leading her through the stable.

"And . . . if you don't mind, when you introduce me, please tell her my name is Amelia Devries." She paused, suddenly feeling self-conscious. "Okay?"

He frowned. "Not . . . Amy Lee?"

"That's just the name I use for country music circles."

"Oh." He scratched his head. "So . . . is there anything *else* you'd like me to know?"

She laughed, releasing the tension. "That's it for now."

"So there *is* more." Now he was smiling, actually flirting. "Well, what would you like to know?"

They walked a few more paces. "Since you asked . . ." Michael stopped walking and looked at her more earnestly. "How serious are you with your boyfriend back home?"

Wow, she hadn't seen that coming! "Byron and I are nearly engaged," Amelia said. After all, it was true.

"I see."

"We've been dating for three years." For some inexplicable reason, she wanted to reinforce that fact, although she knew it wasn't necessary. Because as intriguing as Michael Hostetler was, there was no way he'd fall for a violinist with two very different lives. Even if she was interested in him.

Chapter 12

Michael found Joanna Kurtz in the far corner of the barn, filling the water troughs. Her blue eyes lit up immediately when she spotted him with Amelia.

"*Willkumm!*" Joanna called cheerily, her willowy form nearly as tall as Michael's own. Her wheat-colored hair was neatly pulled back, and she was wearing a plum-colored dress and matching apron with black work boots.

"I'd like you to meet someone," Michael said, smiling. "Joanna, this is Amelia Devries . . . a new friend of mine."

"*Wie geht's*—ach, I meant to say, how are you?" Joanna wiped both hands on her apron and put out her hand.

"Just fine," replied Amelia, shaking her hand and smiling. "Nice to meet you."

Joanna looked at Michael, then back at Amelia. "Goodness, but you remind me of someone."

Michael nodded. "Doesn't she, though?"

"Well, I hope that's a good thing," Amelia said, still smiling.

"It's your dark hair, for sure," Joanna said. She then turned to look at Michael. "She kinda looks like your niece."

He agreed, not wanting to embarrass Amelia further. "Would ya like to show Amelia round the farm for a little while?"

"I'd love to!" Joanna brushed her brow with the back of her hand. "*Kumme*, Amelia—and what a perty name, by the way! I can show ya a-plenty, if you'd like." Joanna peered over her shoulder at Michael and seemed to indicate he could scram. Such mischief she was!

"All right, then." He shook his head and gave her a grin. "I know when to take a hint."

Amelia looked his way, and what he saw in her face both delighted him and put dread into his soul. "I'll return for you in a bit, how's that?" He said it to Amelia, but it was Joanna who answered, saying that it was just fine if Amelia stayed around for as long as she wanted to.

Making his way out to the road, Michael glanced back at the barnyard and saw Joanna and Amelia there with a few of the new goats. And just then, Amelia raised her head and smiled, then waved to him.

It was a simple gesture, for certain, yet . . . to think an English girl like Amelia could make his heart pound nearly out of its rib cage.

What the world?

Amelia liked Joanna immediately. She liked the way Joanna smiled and kept drawing her in, eager to share the four corners of her farming life.

"Honestly, our baby goats tend to shy away from most folk," Joanna said, a glint of sweetness in her blue eyes. "But they sure aren't skittish round you."

"Well, I did pet one of the calves earlier," Amelia admitted. "Maybe the goats picked up the farm scent. Could that be?"

"Maybe so. But it's a rare thing for 'em to take so to a stranger. You must be an animal lover, jah?"

"I grew up with a couple adorable cats—both golden tabbies."

"Ah, then . . . see?"

"But goats? I've never spent much time around them."

Joanna studied her. "I take it this is your first visit to an Amish farm."

"Actually *any* farm in years," Amelia replied.

"Well, I daresay you're doin' fine."

"Thanks." Amelia smiled to herself as Joanna led her next to a hen house, where they had to stoop to go inside.

"Cozy little place, jah?"

Amelia looked at the two rows of nests stacked on top of each other. "Just big enough for chickens, right?"

"You'd think so, but my Kurtz great-great-grandparents lived here with their first wee babe . . . came down from New York."

"Really?"

"Jah, while they finished building the main farmhouse." Joanna motioned toward the spacious farmhouse across the yard. "That was many years ago."

"How long did they stick it out?" asked Amelia. " I mean . . ." she began again, suddenly chagrined.

"No, no, that's all right." Joanna perused the area. "I agree it's awful close in here. But they stayed six weeks, till they could move into part of the new house."

Amelia was doubtful that such tight quarters could offer enough space for a couple, let alone a family with a baby.

"I was so startled by Mamma's tellin', first time I heard it, I sat right down and wrote a story called 'The Chicken Shed *Haus.*' " Joanna's eyes grew wide and the pink in her cheeks turned distinctly red. "I mean . . . ya didn't hear none of that from me, all right?"

Amelia nodded and wondered why Joanna was anxious to cover up what she'd said. "So you're a writer?"

Joanna's eyes bored into her, and Amelia was taken aback by the peculiar, almost horrified look on the young woman's pretty face. "Ach, I don't know what got into me," Joanna said, looking over her shoulder nervously. "I never should've—"

"Aren't you allowed to write stories?"

Joanna shook her head forlornly. "You won't tell, will ya? You're friends with Michael, ain't?"

Amelia considered the strange way she and Michael had met and realized they had secrets of their own. "Your secret's safe with me."

Joanna broke into a relieved smile. "I felt sure you were trustworthy by your eyes," she said.

Amelia blushed. And the more minutes that ticked by, the more she felt a curious kinship with Joanna. Their worlds couldn't be more different. Yet she felt as if she and Joanna were on equal footing.

A short time later they strolled across the backyard and into the large farmhouse. The smell of freshly baked bread filled the kitchen as Joanna introduced Amelia to her middle-aged mother, Rhoda, and a neighbor, Rachel Stoltzfus. The plump, blue-eyed women were dressed nearly exactly like Joanna, only in gray dresses and black aprons as they sat and peeled potatoes for the noon meal. They were polite yet reserved, and Amelia hoped they weren't concerned about the worldly girl standing in the safe haven of Rhoda Kurtz's kitchen.

"It's nice to meet both of you," Amelia said.

The women smiled shyly, but neither offered her hand, soiled as they were from the chore.

Meanwhile, Joanna reached for a piece of fruit from the bowl in the middle of the table mounded with fleshy red and green grapes. Amelia had never seen such a large bowl. Joanna urged her to take some, too, as did Rhoda, who nodded when she looked up from her work. Amelia thanked them and plucked off only a few, noticing that the neighbor woman seemed ill at ease.

Because of me? Amelia wondered.

Thankfully, Joanna led the way upstairs to her room. There, she explained that her mother and Rachel rarely interacted with English folk. "They've been sheltered more than many of the women in Hickory Hollow. Others work outside the house at quilting shops over in Intercourse Village and at Central Market in downtown Lancaster."

"Well, I'm grateful to them for letting me visit you," Amelia said as she took in the room—a double bed with a headboard and footboard, as well as a small square bedside table and a large multicolored braided rug between the bed and the dresser. There was a cane-back chair under each of the two tall windows, and a hope chest at the foot of the bed. Amelia went to peer more closely at the lovely quilt on the bed. "This is so beautiful," she said.

"Quilted and hemmed in a single day," Joanna said.

Amelia admired the tiny hand stitches. "How many quilters does it require to do it so fast?"

"Oh, ten to twelve."

"Impressive."

"We work as a group—like very close friends."

Friends . . . Amelia sighed, wishing for more time to develop closer relationships with her own existing acquaintances. *What would that be like?*

A large rag doll on one of the cane-backed chairs caught her eye. The faceless doll was dressed in a blue dress with a white see-through apron and white head covering. "What a cute doll," she said, going over to look at it.

"She's my little bride doll," Joanna was quick to explain.

"How can you tell she's a bride?" Amelia asked curiously.

"Ah, well, Amish brides typically dress this way on their wedding day." Joanna motioned toward the chairs. "Please take a seat, Amelia. You can move the doll if ya like."

"Thanks," Amelia said, feeling as comfortable with Joanna as she had with Michael. "What is it about the Amish?" she blurted before realizing what she'd said.

"What do ya mean?"

"I feel so content here."

"Ya know, now that you mention it, I know other Englischers who say that." Joanna knelt on the floor beside the hope chest. *So it's not just me. . . .*

Amelia thought of Michael again and was relieved Joanna had mentioned this, because it seemed to explain the strange attraction Amelia had initially had to him. And here she'd thought she might actually be a little infatuated with an Amishman. How absurd! *We haven't even known each other a full day.*

Joanna opened the lid to her cedar hope chest and removed an assortment of embroidered pieces that had been arranged and folded neatly inside. "These are just waiting for the day when I'll set up housekeeping," she whispered, then blushed as she caught herself. "You think I'm *bapplich*, ain't so?"

"You're not too talkative at all." Amelia grinned.

Joanna leaned her head back. "Talkative I am—if not a blabbermouth." Then, as if just registering what Amelia had said, Joanna asked, "Wait a minute, do you know Deitsch?"

"A tiny bit." Amelia told her quickly about her summers in Ohio Amish country with her grandparents.

"You must miss going there. Do ya?"

"Yes . . . very much." Amelia nodded. "And I miss my grandparents, too."

They talked awhile about Joanna's own two sets of *Grosseldre.* "Mamma's parents live in the *Dawdi Haus* next door, and *Dat's* live neighbors to Abe and Rachel Stoltzfus . . . but within walkin' distance. We look after them, ya know."

"I wish mine had lived closer to us all those years," Amelia said.

Joanna agreed. "Jah, 'tis a joy, for sure."

Amelia nodded, knowing she'd missed a lot by living so far from her mother's parents. Thankfully, her paternal grandparents were still alive, though she had never been as close to them. *Why not?* Amelia wondered, wishing to remedy that.

She'd only just arrived, yet visiting Hickory Hollow was already beginning to stir up a myriad of memories.

"Well, what's this?" Lillianne Hostetler's hand flew to her mouth. She was out weeding her flower beds when she spotted Michael walking up the road, coming this way. She tensed up immediately, swallowing hard. Just yesterday he'd taken a week's worth of food to wherever he'd rushed off to. Was her son returning already?

Oh goodness, she surely hoped so. With all of her heart she did. And she promised herself she would not question what had caused Michael to come back this soon. Watching him walk toward the house now, with such confidence, threw her off beam.

She ought to look for Paul to alert him. "Glory be!" she said as she left the hand trowel on the ground and got up.

She dashed around the side of the house, past the old well pump and the clotheslines. She found Paul in the stable, grooming one of the driving horses. His light brown hair was oily from the heat and humidity, and there was a piece of a cornstalk stuck to the back of his shirt. "Paul . . . Paul," she said, quite out of breath. "Remember what the bishop said to do if Michael returned?"

He frowned and paused, brush in his hand. "What's all your fluster for, Lily?"

"Our boy's a-comin'—just saw Michael walking up the lane," she told him. "We must welcome him back." She caught her breath and waved her hankie to cool herself.

By the look of consternation on her husband's face, Lillianne could tell the bishop's recent admonition was still fresh in his mind.

Paul gave her a practiced frown and turned back to his work. "I'll do my best."

Without delay, she began to pray silently as she made her way toward the house. O Gott, *help my husband give it his all.* Then, realizing what she'd prayed, Lillianne changed her mind. *No, I mean help Paul soften his tongue, dear Lord.* . . .

Feeling altogether anxious yet at the same time joyful, she intended to see this through, come what may, and not just for the sake of the bishop. Her skirt flapped against her legs as she hurried around to the front of the house in time to see Michael marching her way.

Lillianne stared, quite befuddled. *What does it mean?*

Chapter 13

Michael's heart went out to his mother, whose face was alight as she spotted him. He simply could not let her think he was returning for good . . . wouldn't be fair. His gut wrenched. "I'm just comin' to talk to Daed awhile," he explained.

"Oh." Her dear face turned sad. "He's out yonder . . . in the stable."

Michael gave his head an abrupt nod. "Why don't ya come along, too?"

"Are ya sure?"

" 'Course I am, Mamma."

"All right, then."

He noticed her stiffen, and the worry lines on her forehead were suddenly visible. *One way or the other, I have to do this. O Lord,* he prayed, *have mercy on all of us.*

The humid stable air smelled like a mixture of sweet hay and feed. Daed stroked the horse's side, working the currying brush as dots of perspiration stood out on his neck and face. His middle hung slightly over the waistband of his dark work pants.

Mamm busied herself in the next stall, then went to water

their younger horse. Michael hung back at first, observing Daed's caring way with old Cricket. *He's so gentle with the animals. . . .*

Drawing in a slow breath, he made his feet move forward. It was time to go through with it. *Long overdue.*

Thoughts of their many quarrels came rushing back. In reality, they were all about differences of opinion—molehills made into mountains. Michael knew that now. Even a short time away from this familiar setting had brought a measure of perspective. As had Amelia . . .

His father glanced over at Michael, spotting him there. The horse neighed loudly, and Daed looked back at the animal, still moving his grooming brush. *Demanding soul, Cricket . . .*

"Daed, I'd like to talk to you for a minute."

"What's on your mind?"

Pausing, Michael wondered whether to blurt out his decision and just be done with it. Just get the *hatt*—difficult—task over right quick. Wouldn't it be less painful for both of them that way?

Turning again slightly, Daed ran a callused hand through his thick, dark beard. "Listen, Michael, I've thought 'bout what I said yesterday. Frankly, I was out of order." His voice was quiet, unruffled.

"I'm not here for an apology, Daed. I've provoked your anger unnecessarily, and all too often."

"But I lost my temper—a sin and a shame," his father rebutted. "Never should've talked that way."

"Daed, I—"

"If ya don't mind, let your old man finish, won't ya?"

Nodding but feeling frustrated, Michael waited. "Jah . . . sorry."

Daed scratched the horse behind his ears. "Your Mamma and I are hopin' you'll stay on here as long as need be . . . till you join church. We mean this, son." Daed extended his hand. "Making your life vow's a mighty serious thing."

Even though astounded by his father's tone and offer, Michael accepted his handshake—a stronger grip he'd never felt. "Tellin' the truth, I never expected this," he said, uncomfortable now.

"And, son, there's something else."

"Jah?"

"I don't want ya parkin' your car over yonder at your uncle Jerry's. I ain't blind, Michael; I know you thought you were hidin' it there." Daed's brawny shoulders rose and fell. "From now on, keep it here, parked in the lane." He pointed at the window across the stable.

"I wouldn't think of disgracing you thataway," Michael replied.

"Bishop John insists . . . and so do I."

The bishop? Michael was stunned, yet he knew better than to question.

Daed's eyes were moist in the corners.

No . . . no, Michael thought, *don't go soft on me!*

Nearly an hour passed, and Amelia wondered what was keeping Michael—hopefully things were going well with his visit home. She mentally stopped herself. Was it possible she cared too much about the outcome, having identified so readily with Michael's woes?

Joanna was presently talking about several sewing projects, some of which she sold at Bird-in-Hand Farmers' Market on Route 340, she said.

"Do you have many encounters with Englishers?" Amelia asked.

"Not much other than at market." Joanna shook her head

quickly. "My cousin Marissa was the closest English friend I had . . . 'cept Mennonites aren't really considered fancy folk so much anymore. Her family is pretty conservative."

"Marissa? Is that the same girl who was engaged to Michael?" Amelia stared at the hope chest within feet of where she sat, determined not to meet Joanna's eyes—like Michael, she seemed to read her far too easily.

Joanna told her that Cousin Marissa was indeed one and the same. "You know 'bout her?" Her tone revealed her surprise. She might as well have said, "*I think you know Michael better than you're letting on. . . .*"

"She must be a very special girl," Amelia said.

"Oh, is she ever."

Amelia wasn't sure she should ask the question but did anyway. "Where is your cousin now?"

Rising, Joanna went to the window and looked out. "She's training to go overseas, as a missionary."

"Don't mean to be nosy," Amelia said.

"Not to fret."

"I'd guess you find it somewhat awkward talking to an outsider. Especially about family."

Joanna shook her head. "With you, not at all." Then her face broke into a pleasant smile. "*Gut* friends—the way I feel with Marissa."

Do I remind her of Michael's former fiancée? Amelia cringed.

Then, as if reading her thoughts, Joanna pulled the other chair over next to hers and sat down. "I'm not comparing you to her, mind you. It's more of a feeling, I guess. But like I said earlier, you *do* resemble someone from just up the road." Pausing, Joanna gazed into her face. "Michael's only niece is slender and tall, too, and has dark hair like yours." Joanna frowned momentarily, looking away suddenly. "I guess Michael didn't tell you?"

"Tell me what?"

"That Lizzie's been a-yearnin' for the English world. Got her first taste of it when she begged Michael to let her drive his car some time back." Joanna shook her head sadly. "'Tis just a shame—such a *gut* girl she used to be. To think she's bringing heartache to her parents."

"Has she left Hickory Hollow?"

"Jah, she wanted to get her education, like Michael's doin'. Enrolled in the spring quarter at a college in Harrisburg is what I heard."

Suddenly Amelia felt somehow party to Michael's rebellion, knowing he was speaking to his father even now about his intention to leave home.

They sat there, neither adding more to the conversation. Finally Joanna revealed how "awful anxious" everyone had been about Michael the past few years, hoping he might become a church member . . . someday.

Amelia did not have the heart to tell her how close he was to "going fancy." Instead she shared something of her own father's aspirations for her.

One thing led to another, and eventually Amelia told Joanna about the storm that blew in last night and led her to Michael.

"Michael's an upstanding fella, I'll say," Joanna said.

Amelia agreed, careful to hold her smile in check.

Lillianne shooed flies with the hem of her long black apron. She had nothing at all to hide, despite the fact she'd overheard everything her husband and son had said to each other. And oh, if she wasn't ever so pleased with Paul's kindly way. *This time . . . thank the dear Lord.*

Yesterday, their strict bishop had stopped by and declared that Paul must use a gentler hand—and words—with Michael from here on out. *"Heap coals of fire,"* Bishop John had encouraged them. He was adamant that they retain Michael for God and the church, no matter what it took. Obviously, what they had been doing was not working one iota.

Lillianne had never known Bishop John to be so sympathetic, and she couldn't help but wonder if he felt sorry about past harsh demands on some of the young folk. *"You must learn to rein in your temper—show kindness and be longsuffering,"* the bishop had told Paul, who had nodded, clearly wretched after Michael had fled the house.

"O Lord, show our Michael the way," Lillianne whispered as she headed down to the springhouse. She glanced out toward the road, hoping Michael might take his father's invitation to heart.

Their son had looked mighty ferhoodled when he came out of the stable. *He must've come back to say he was leaving.*

He had surprised her, though, by telling Paul he would consider staying on at the house for a bit longer. And, oh, if her heart hadn't leapt at that!

Just maybe Paul's words will burrow down into Michael's heart. Lillianne trusted so.

Amelia was happy to wait as Joanna went to a nearby room to get the piecework to show her. Moving to stand at the open window, Amelia looked out at the patchwork field patterns that stretched as far as her eyes could see. Enjoying the tranquility all around her, she remembered Michael's request and lifted her eyes to the blue of the sky, spotted with clouds like cotton puffs. *Please help my new friend, Lord,* she prayed briefly.

Yet Michael was counting on a heartfelt prayer, not merely doing lip service. Lowering herself onto the cane chair again, Amelia bowed her head and folded her hands reverently as she pictured Michael sitting at the table in his Amish mother's kitchen. She prayed more earnestly now, trusting God that all would go well for Michael and his family.

A *clip-clop*ping from outside led her to glance toward the window—a horse-drawn buggy was coming down the road. She rose and watched curiously. The speed of the trotting horse brought the carriage closer more quickly than she had anticipated. Now she was peering down at a young Amish couple with a babe in arms and four small children sitting in back. Two little girls leaned their chubby arms out, looking very happy on this laid-back day.

Imagine traveling together all bunched up like that. The girls looked nearly identical—were they twins? She recalled several sets of twins in one family up the road from her grandparents' old farmhouse. Grammy had once told her that she'd known seven sets of twins from that area, which had made a big impression on young Amelia.

She watched the boxlike buggy go up Hickory Lane, feeling a bit strange about spying from her high perch. The sun cast its radiance over the carriage, causing the gray to look nearly silver.

She wiggled her bare toes against the hand-braided rug on the wooden floor. The homey scent of a chocolate cake baking

Chapter 14

J oanna's eyes twinkled when she returned with a stack of colorful piecework for a quilt she planned to make with the women of her family. "We're passing on the art of quilting to the young girls in the Hollow," she said as Amelia ran her fingers over some of the more intricate designs. "My school-age nieces have already learned to make simple knotted coverlets for their dollies."

"Did you teach your nieces?" Amelia was taken by Joanna's obvious devotion to them and to her nephews. Surely she would have many children someday, like most Amish.

Joanna happily nodded. "I'd rather quilt than do most anything." Then she stopped. "Well, not more than write stories."

Amelia asked more about her stories, but it was quickly apparent when Joanna changed the subject back to quilting that she did not wish to share more about her writing. So Amelia listened as Joanna told about the upcoming quilting bees.

Then, later, when there was a break in the conversation, Amelia asked, "Should we watch for Michael to return?" She didn't want to sound in a hurry to leave, nor did she wish to be rude, but she also didn't want to wear out her welcome. The truth was, she enjoyed Joanna's company.

"Ach, he'll throw a pebble up at the window . . . if he doesn't see us outdoors," Joanna assured her.

Glancing at the open window, Amelia guessed he might also hear them talking. "It's been wonderful getting to know you, Joanna," she said, "but I don't want to keep you from your work."

"*Puh!* I'll catch up—I always do." Joanna began to lay out the squares on her bed. "Here, would ya like to arrange them, just for fun?"

For fun . . . There it was again. Amelia so rarely took time to relax—really she should be rehearsing her newest pieces even now. "Sure, let's do it." And she began to move the squares around, creating a design that pleased her.

When she finished, Joanna went to get a disposable camera and snapped a picture of the design. "We don't take pictures of each other, but it does help to have some of the quilt patterns." She smiled.

"Great idea." Amelia stood back and eyed her pattern. "I think I could get used to creating such lovely quilts."

"Well, it'd be nice if you came to visit in the wintertime, then. There are lots of work frolics goin' on when the soil's resting."

"I'd like that," Amelia said before even thinking.

"Well, you could stay now, too, if you'd like. At least for the weekend." Joanna's eyes danced with the idea. "I'd love to have you—and with Cora Jane gone, there's a nice, quiet bedroom right across the hall from me. What do ya say?"

Joanna's unexpected invitation tugged at her heart. "Really? Would you mind?"

"Mind? I'd love it!" Joanna reminded Amelia of a youngster at a birthday party, not sure which present to open first. "Will you stay, then?"

Amelia had told Byron she was taking a little detour, but she hadn't intended to make a weekend of it. "How would your family feel?"

"My sister wouldn't mind at all—she's away in Strasburg bein' a mother's helper. And Mamma, well . . . we've never had an Englischer stay with us before, so she might want to dress you up Amish," Joanna joked. "But really, she'll be fine with it, especially when she sees how happy it makes me."

"You must miss your brothers and sisters."

"Jah, something awful. But I do see them quite often. It's just not the same, though, with most of them not livin' here in the house anymore."

Amelia considered what seemed like a genuine invitation. As was typical, she'd overpacked for her trip to Philly, and she had the dress she'd worn last night, as well as several flowing skirts and blouses in a similar retro vein. She even had a pair of sandals along, something to soothe her sore feet. *Ideal for spending time with Joanna.*

"All right, I accept," she said, thrilled at this rare opportunity. "But I hope you were kidding about my wearing Plain clothes."

"Oh, I was." Joanna rushed over and gave her a hug. "This is wunnerbaar-*gut!*"

"I do have one small favor to ask," Amelia said tentatively.

"Sure." Joanna's face shone happiness.

"I'll need time to practice my fiddle—several hours a day, at least."

Just that quick, Joanna's face fell. "You play?"

"Is that a problem?"

"I guess not, since you aren't Amish." Joanna paused and glanced out the window. "Sure, it should be fine."

"Well, what if I played somewhere other than in the house?" *Out of respect*, she thought.

"Jah, I believe that would be best."

"I can easily drive somewhere . . . practice in a meadow, under a nice shade tree."

"Where's your car now?"

"Parked at Michael's uncle's house."

"Jerry Landis's?"

Amelia wondered if she'd blown Michael's cover. "Um . . . not sure you're supposed to know that."

"Oh, all the young folk know about Michael's car, so don't think anything of it." Joanna lowered her voice to a whisper. "And if ya do play your fiddle outdoors, maybe take me along."

"I need to retrieve it—and my bag—from the car. Usually I try not to leave it there long, especially on a warm day like this one."

"Well, we rarely get to hear instruments here in Hickory Hollow—that kind of music is forbidden," Joanna said. "Though word has it that Ol' Mathias Byler up on Grasshopper Level used to play the mouth organ while he sat on his front porch come twilight . . . serenading the courtin' couples as they rode by. But he's passed on. The night he flew to Jesus, Ol' Mathias was thought to have seen his lovely Mattie, long since dead, come to take him to heaven with her."

Amelia was struck by the account. "That is the dearest story," she said. "But how would anyone know what he experienced as he was dying?"

"Well, according to the account in *The Budget*, his daughter found him slumped down in his hickory rocker, his harmonica lying on the porch . . . and all around was the sweet scent of lily of the valley—his wife's favorite fragrance."

Amelia blinked back a tear. "But can you explain why music is forbidden?"

"Unaccompanied music is okay, especially if it's from the Ausbund—our hymnal."

"But many types of music offer hope," Amelia insisted.

"Maybe so, but you'll do best to hide your music makin' here, like one of our girls did some time back."

"Someone related to you?"

"Well, I s'pose Katie Lapp *is* kin but by adoption—we perty much all are related one way or another, ya know."

"What instrument did she play?"

"Guitar—and oh, did it ever sound perty."

"You heard her play?" Amelia was surprised.

"Only once. I came upon her just a-strummin' and crying her eyes out, over near the crick one afternoon."

"Did she know you were listening?"

"She never did." Joanna shook her head solemnly. "And she eventually got caught."

"What happened?" asked Amelia, curious to know more.

"It's a real sad story. Katie's under the Bann for the rest of her life. But Mamma knows for truth that Katie's adopted mother sometimes slips away to the convenience store in Bird-in-Hand to call and talk to Katie—others have some fellowship with her now and then, too. The bishop lifted the shunning a bit is all I know."

At Joanna's forlorn expression, Amelia let the subject drop, thinking that if Joanna wanted to share more, she would without further probing.

Joanna turned now to talk about the people who lived neighbors to her on Hickory Lane, including the revered bishop, John Beiler, who had once been a rather young widower with a houseful of children. "When he remarried, it was to a girl twenty years younger—Katie's best friend, Mary," said Joanna, a faraway look in her eyes. "Each and every one of these folk has an interesting life story, ya know?"

"Don't we all," Amelia whispered.

Joanna nodded her head. "What's *yours*, Amelia?"

She laughed quietly. "I can only tell you if you promise not to put me in one of your stories."

"Ach, I can easily promise that." Joanna blinked repeatedly. "Goodness, we *both* have promises to keep, jah?"

"We certainly do." Amelia had every confidence that she could trust a young woman like Joanna Kurtz with any secret, even her fiddling life. *Without a shadow of doubt.*

Chapter 15

Joanna excused herself to help her mother make the noon meal. And while Amelia had also offered, Joanna insisted she relax. "You can help make breakfast tomorrow, jah?"

So Amelia went outside to sit beneath the soaring shade tree in the backyard to wait for Michael, assuming he would return any minute. Now that she'd agreed to stay, she was looking forward to seeing more of life on an Amish dairy farm, although she'd definitely keep her shoes on when exploring!

She recalled all too well the time she'd stepped in a cow pie in Papa's barn—the squishy, smelly manure was still vivid in her mind. She'd smelled it for days afterward, even though she took long bubble baths each night to wash away the stench. *Fun times*, she thought, smiling to herself.

Amelia was still under the tree when Michael appeared, hurrying across the back lawn, his straw hat pushed back slightly on his head.

"How'd it go?" she asked, eager to know.

"Just terrible."

She stared up at him.

"I couldn't go through with it." He crouched beside her.

"What happened?"

"Daed took great pains to apologize. I don't know when he's been so appeasing." His voice trailed away, and he sat near her in the soft grass. "Guess I won't be moving out this week."

"You've changed your mind?"

"Daed changed it for me, and so it goes." Michael forced air into his cheeks, puffing them momentarily. "Things are mighty complicated, Amy . . . Amelia, I mean."

She felt for him. Even though she had never tried to talk openly to her own father about her hesitations, she couldn't imagine things turning out much different than they were for Michael right now. For all the gumption he'd exhibited earlier, Michael surely felt fenced in. *More spunk than I could muster*, she thought, not blaming him for caving. With his father's compassionate welcome, how could he do otherwise?

Three birds flew overhead and Michael glanced up, watching for the longest time, seemingly deep in thought. Then, looking back at Amelia, he said, "Daed wants me to park my car in his driveway."

"Really?"

"I don't understand any of this." Michael picked at a few blades of grass. "Offering the right hand of fellowship . . . a very peculiar tactic, I daresay."

"Will you take him up on it?"

"Well, it would be more convenient." Michael nodded slowly. "I just can't get over this."

Amelia wondered what Michael might think of her agreeing to stay with Joanna and her family. Would he be pleased, or would it further complicate things for him with his parents?

"So tell me about your morning," he said. "Did you get acquainted with Joanna?"

"Oh, wait until you hear this." She filled him in quickly—the barn tour, meeting Joanna's mother and neighbor, laying out a quilt design, the entire delightful visit. Except for Joanna's secret. "She's even invited me to stay for the weekend."

Michael looked shocked, then brightened. "Did you accept?"

She almost thought he was holding his breath for her answer. "Yes, I said I would."

He beamed. "*Des gut!*" He stood right up and reached down, offering his hand to help her up. "This'll give ya plenty of time to meet Ella Mae."

"Who's that?" she asked.

"The Wise Woman."

"Oh, I hope so. I could use some wisdom about now."

He laughed a little. "Couldn't we all?" They walked across the yard, pausing at the back porch, where Michael waited while she went to tell Joanna she would return later with her car.

"Why don't ya come back for dinner, if you'd like?" Joanna asked, standing barefoot in her mother's kitchen.

Since Amelia didn't know what Michael had planned, she declined but said she would another time. "If that's all right."

"Well, I hope you'll stay long enough to see all of Hickory Hollow—ev'ry nook and cranny."

"Thanks, Joanna."

"You're ever so welcome." Joanna walked her to the back screen porch and looked curiously outside. "Hullo again," she said, waving to Michael.

"I'll take good care of Amelia," he joked and glanced at Amelia, then back at Joanna. "Don't ya worry."

"No doubt in my mind." Joanna stood to the side as Amelia made her way down the back steps. "Well, have a nice walk, you two." Joanna shot a knowing look in their direction.

"Denki again for showin' Amelia round the farm. She should be all ready now to get up at four-thirty to help with milkin'," Michael said over his shoulder.

"Oh, no . . . that's awful early!" Joanna replied with a chuckle.

"Sure, I'll help," Amelia volunteered, game for anything. But her intuition told her Joanna was more preoccupied with Michael's attentiveness toward an Englisher than with what time Amelia would get up tomorrow.

To be honest, Amelia was very curious about that herself. While she knew enough about modern men like Byron to understand what made them tick, she had no frame of reference for an Amish guy.

She fell into step with Michael, finding it interesting that he seemed so happy she'd decided to stay over.

Michael knew it was imperative to show his father that he appreciated his unusual invitation. As he and Amelia walked back to their cars, Michael tried to explain that being asked to park his vehicle in Daed's driveway was an enormously benevolent gesture. "You have no idea."

"Sounds like your dad might be trying to win you back."

"It does seem that way," Michael agreed. "I wonder what Mamm makes of this." He looked at Amelia. "Don't be surprised if she peeks out the window at us when we arrive. Might even ask us to stay for the noon meal." He suspected she and Daed were in goodwill mode, pulling out all the stops.

Amelia was astonished. "Will I alarm them in my fancy getup?"

"I don't think so. Besides, I've thought it over, and I'd like you to meet my parents after all." Though he did hope they wouldn't jump to any conclusions.

Michael gave her a smile. Of course, Amelia was a guest of Joanna Kurtz's—he could mention that if necessary, although he would not deceive his parents. *Her presence might shake things up a bit,* he thought. But then again, Amelia might just be the distraction they all needed right now.

⋯ ➤ ➤ ⋯

"Ach, Paul, look there . . . out the window!" Lillianne called to him across the kitchen.

Her husband was washing up at the sink and splattering dirty water. "What is it, Lily?" He was grumpy now, making up for being so accommodating to Michael before, just maybe. Still, she loved him all the same.

"Michael's returned with his car . . . and there's a young woman with him." She pointed, speechless for a moment. "She's got herself a car, too!"

Paul moved to the window and peeked out. "Well, she sure ain't Plain, is she?"

Lillianne squelched a little laugh as together they watched the two young folk meander up the driveway, the young woman's car parked behind Michael's. "Now, Paul, we've already welcomed our son back, so we must welcome her, too." *Whoever she is.*

He nodded and harrumphed, then moseyed to his chair at the head of the table. "They're just in time for the table blessin', ain't so?" Paul observed as the knock came at the back screen door.

"Food's on the table, son," her husband called over his shoulder. "Come on in and have dinner with us."

"Puh!" Lillianne said, scurrying to the back porch and opening the door. "You never have to knock, Michael . . . you know that." She got a closer look at the pretty dark-haired girl with him, which shook her up but good. *Well, if she doesn't look nearly like our Elizabeth!*

"Mamm, this is Amelia Devries," Michael introduced her. "She's visiting the area . . . stayin' over at Kurtzes' place."

"Well, bless your heart," Lillianne said, gathering her wits. Rhoda hadn't mentioned anything like this!

"We didn't mean to barge in. Just wanted you to know Amelia's goin' to be around for a few days." Michael seemed to go out of his way to explain.

"Won't ya come in and eat with us—both of yous?" She held out her hand and was met by the softest, most petite handshake in all her born days. "Ever so nice to meet you, Amelia."

"Likewise," the young woman said, looking for all the world like she'd stepped out of a dress shop somewhere at the Prime Outlet Mall over on Route 30.

Lillianne followed them into the kitchen, standing back as Michael reintroduced Amelia. Paul was not nearly as cordial as Lillianne had hoped he might be. Was he also struggling with the close resemblance to their missing granddaughter? *Run clean off to the world and the devil, too.*

She waited to take her place at the table till both Michael and the young woman were seated—Michael in his usual spot, and Amelia next to him on the bench. Any other day in the past few years, Michael would have rejected their mealtime invitation if he was with one of his many Mennonite buddies.

Though he'd never brought the girl home to meet them, Lillianne nevertheless knew more than she let on about his former fiancée.

But now, this one?

"Let's return thanks," Paul said with a look at Michael; then he bowed his head.

Her husband's silent prayer lasted longer than was customary. She guessed he was making up for lost time, since Michael had missed two meals here since storming out.

At last Paul coughed slightly and raised his head to indicate the silent prayer was done. Then he reached for the cooled-off beef gravy and mashed potatoes. Lillianne felt sure all was well—or would be by the time the men had their stomachs filled. Neither her husband nor Michael uttered a word for the next few minutes, leaving her to wonder what on earth to say to Amelia, with those big blue-gray eyes that twinkled a smile, like she was trying hard to make nice.

Oh goodness. Lillianne wondered if this pretty young woman had romantic thoughts toward Michael. But if so, why would he announce that she was staying over at Nate and Rhoda's? Michael didn't flaunt his sweetheart-girls. Never had.

"Pass the salt and pepper," Paul said, reaching before the polite young lady even had a chance to hand them to Michael to give to Paul.

Lillianne held her breath, waiting, but there was no thanking either of them. If she didn't quit caring so much about what transpired at her table, she'd be a nervous wreck by the time it was time to serve the orange nut bread with real whipped cream for dessert. What must the beautiful outsider be thinking?

Truly, Lillianne could hardly wait to dish up dessert. Anything to get up and move about—keep her hands busy so her mind had a chance to calm down some.

"Amelia's from Ohio," Michael was telling his father. "She knew quite a lot of Amish there, back when she was a girl."

Paul's ears perked up. "Beachys, maybe?" he asked.

But Amelia didn't seem to know specifics about the Plain folk there, just that they were neighbors to her deceased grandparents. "I do remember that their prayer caps were cup shaped with many little pleats," Amelia said. "Does that help any?"

"Ah, like Cousin Mandie's in Walnut Creek, ain't so?" Lillianne said, looking at both Michael and Paul.

"If you don't mind my asking, why are there different head coverings?" asked Amelia.

"Different styles of Kapps identify the church group," Lillianne replied.

"Kapps and many other things related to the ordinances," Michael quickly added.

"Ordnung," said Paul, eyeing Amelia now.

Lillianne wished someone might change the subject. "Amelia, you'll enjoy stayin' with Joanna Kurtz," she piped up. "She's one fine Amish girl—joined church years ago now." She said the latter for Michael's benefit, but by the expression on her son's tanned face, her remark must have come off as scheming.

"Amelia spent part of the morning over there," Michael said.

"I loved getting acquainted with the baby goats." Amelia exchanged a smile with Michael.

Jah, definitely a spark between 'em, thought Lillianne. *Might spoil everything Paul and I have set out to do!*

Feeling downright jittery, she rose and went to slice her freshly baked orange nut bread.

Chapter 16

While Michael unloaded the cooler of food he'd taken to the cabin and got resettled at his father's house, Amelia drove the short distance to Joanna's, then inched the car into the lane. She wished she'd thought to ask Michael about the advisability of parking on the Kurtzes' property. *Will it cause problems?* She intended to ask Joanna first thing.

She slipped her overnight bag over her shoulder and retrieved her fiddle case, then headed for the back porch. Joanna's family seemed to prefer using the back door that led through the screened-in porch and utility room to the kitchen.

Standing on the steps, looking in, Amelia knocked lightly. Inside, she could hear the laughter of small children and the chatter of Pennsylvania Dutch. "It's Amelia," she called when she saw Joanna coming through the kitchen.

"Nice seein' ya again," Joanna said.

"I parked my car, um . . . in your driveway. If that's a problem, I'll move it."

Joanna shook her head quickly. " 'Tis just fine where I saw

ya park it. Kumme . . . I want ya to meet my little nieces and nephew visitin' from Bird-in-Hand, just up the way a piece."

Relieved about her car, Amelia followed her, setting her fiddle and luggage down in the kitchen before making her way into the large front room. The door was standing wide and all of the windows were open, too, letting in a sultry breeze. The cute Amish children sat on the floor, giggling and building with blocks. The girls looked like miniatures of Joanna and Rhoda, and the boy was around the age Amelia had been when her father first placed a tiny violin in her little hands.

Joanna went over to them and bent low, patting each child's head as she said their names: "Stephen, Sylvia, and Susan. Our three S's—my older sister Salina's little ones."

"So four S's," Amelia said, squatting to greet them. "Hey, kiddos. Looks like you're having fun." Then looking at Joanna, she said, "They're absolutely darling."

"Salina dropped them off for a few hours while she cooks up a feast to take to an ailing relative."

Amelia studied the children. "They look so close in age," she said, eyes glued especially to the handsome little boy.

Joanna said the oldest and youngest were but two years apart. "Nearly like triplets, ain't?"

Amelia couldn't imagine having three in a row so close together. She could hardly pull herself away from them as she admired the girls' tiny dresses and aprons. They looked nearly like dolls with their golden blond hair pulled back tightly in a knot.

Little Stephen followed her into the kitchen when she went to retrieve her things. "*Vas?*" He pointed to her bag.

"Just some clothes, sweetie." She stopped and smiled at herself. "Do you speak English?" she asked softly.

Towheaded Stephen just cocked his head and looked at her with round eyes.

Soon, Joanna came to rescue her, talking in Deitsch and motioning toward Amelia and the staircase, perhaps explaining that Amelia was going to go upstairs and unpack. Turning to Amelia, she said, "Cora Jane's room is all ready for ya. Or if you'd like mine, we can switch."

"Oh, I wouldn't do that." Amelia was taken aback by Joanna's generosity. *So very thoughtful!* "But thanks so much."

After she found her bedroom, just across the hall from Joanna's, Amelia went straight to the window and looked out. *Ah, perfect!* The view overlooked a meadow where the grass was lush and green. She couldn't imagine a more inviting place to practice her music.

More than anything, she wished for a pair of shorts, but she was actually glad she had packed the feminine clothing she typically relied on for fiddling shows. That way she wasn't tempted to wear something Joanna—or her mother—might think immodest. Shorts would certainly be that.

She gave her clothes a slight shake, then hung them on hangers on the wooden pegs. The humidity would take care of any wrinkles.

Walking to the oak dresser, Amelia admired the handmade doilies, the pretty hand mirror, and a dainty white china pin holder with a tiny top. There was also a small candleholder with a votive inside, and a German prayer book. Like Joanna's room, the wide plank floor was adorned with a single oval hand-braided rug. The walls were an interesting shade of gray-blue that worked nicely with the blues and greens in the bed quilt.

"*Simple things are best,*" Grammy had told her years before. In that moment, Amelia believed she was right—she didn't want to contemplate the European tour any longer. In fact, she wished time might stand still.

Amelia hummed the beginning strains of Mendelssohn's "Sweet Remembrance" while strolling through Joanna's backyard and toward the row of poplars along the west side of the house. Young Stephen and one of his younger sisters had come out to the screened-in porch and babbled at her. She turned and smiled and waved at them, hoping they might still be visiting when she returned.

Stepping past the poplar windbreak, Amelia rambled through the open field profuse with black-eyed Susans and other summertime wildflowers, making her way with her violin to a mighty oak, where she claimed her spot.

Amelia left the case open under the leafy tree and took up her fiddle. She tightened the A string to its correct tone—though she had never bragged about having perfect pitch, the sound resided in her head. Just as quickly, she tuned the remaining strings to the A string.

Then Amelia leaned into her fiddle, transforming the instrument to her present needs as, slowly, she walked back and forth. She played through the Galamian acceleration scales using the metronome in her head, striving for perfect intonation, orderly shifting, and complete bow control.

After an hour of warm-ups—her daily regimen of etudes, scales, arpeggios, and octaves—she began to play the first of her encore pieces, one she particularly loved because of the pathos in the first section before the more buoyant—even optimistic—second section.

The blue of the sky increased in intensity, and the brilliance of the sun became even more pronounced as she fell into the music. She could hear the delicate piano accompaniment in her mind as she played the exquisite solo part.

Her mind wandered as it often did while practicing—her fingers knew where to press the strings. *"Muscle memory,"* her father described it. And while Amelia missed her more expensive violin, her father's fiddle would do her well for as long as she was here.

Next she played "Vocalise" by Rachmaninov, a piece she'd played as a child. The haunting melody poured over her, and tears dimmed her eyes as she thought of Byron. True, their commitment had never been formalized, but there were so many expectations. She was unable to see herself undoing the past in order to create a new and different outcome. Surely she'd cared for Byron at some point, but . . . The thought hit her with a jolt: How long ago had their relationship fizzled?

Amelia forced her mind back to her music and continued to work through her entire selection of concert pieces, imagining thousands of smiling faces in the U.K., Netherlands, and Germany, and the eventual applause that would follow. For this moment, though, she felt peaceful, there beneath the shadow of the sheltering tree. How she'd needed this reprieve from the weight she had carried for so long within her heart.

Chapter 17

Never before had Michael heard such lofty-sounding music. The piece was nothing like the country fiddling he sometimes enjoyed listening to.

He followed the haunting melody down Hickory Lane, certain that what he was hearing must be Amelia. Except that this music was completely unlike the fiddle tunes she'd played at the cabin.

Looking in the direction of the music, he saw not a soul in the wide field where Nate Kurtz turned out his colts in springtime. In fact, not a single grazing animal could he see. Maybe, because of the heat, they'd wandered back to the stable for water and feed.

He bent low to slip under the fence, pulled toward the splendid sounds coming from the far end of the meadow. The sun beat down on him, and Michael was glad for his straw hat, pushing it back on his head to shield his vulnerable neck. The skin there burnt crisp red every summer, then peeled even after he put the cool sap-gel from an aloe vera plant on it.

Eventually, he found Amelia beneath an enormous oak tree, her rich brown hair moving in the breeze as she swayed. He decided to remain out of sight, merely an observer soaking up the beauty—of the music and the musician. She wasn't just talented; she was brilliant, playing without a speck of music to look at. For the next half hour or more, he sat listening several trees away.

Then Amelia paused in her playing and sat down in the grass, her violin tucked under her arm. As in the cabin, he felt incredibly drawn to her. The depth of emotion in her performance, even while practicing alone here, signaled some sort of inner conflict. But what? Did it have to do with her father? He longed to know.

After a time, she surprised him and raised the instrument and began again, now sitting against the tree trunk. This tune was slower and richer, two strings played simultaneously—the way she'd played her fiddle tunes.

Interested to know the name of the sorrow-filled piece, he rose and walked toward her, circling out a bit so as not to startle her. But her eyes were closed as she drew her bow across the strings, and if he wasn't mistaken, her cheeks glistened with tears.

What's wrong?

Michael was startled. Certainly, he should not interrupt her reverie. And just as he was about to turn back out of respect for her solitude, Amelia opened her eyes. She continued her song, her face breaking into a slow smile. She was smiling at him!

He nodded and removed his hat, although it seemed a foolish thing to do under the excruciating sun. Quickly, he put it on again, now grinning at her.

He pointed to the ground, silently asking permission to invade her space. She nodded, all the while still playing the pretty tune. Although he liked it, the music baffled him.

When the final note came, she sustained it for the longest time, so long in fact he wondered if she might run out of bow. Then, raising the bow ever so gracefully, Amelia lifted her eyes to him again. "You found me," she said softly with that amazing smile.

"Hope ya don't mind."

She shook her head. "It is a little lonely out here."

"That was mighty perty—your playin'," Michael said, not daring to say anything else. She just looked so angelic sitting there, the sun-dappled light falling around her.

" 'Humoresque' by Alexander de Taeye. Ever hear it?"

"Not till now."

"By an obscure composer from Brussels, Belgium." She placed her fiddle in the case, as well as the bow. "I happen to think it's one of the most incredible violin pieces ever written."

"I can see why."

She smiled as she closed the case and snapped the lid. "I love it." She pushed her glossy waves of hair back over her shoulder. "There's something serene about that melody."

"Please . . . don't stop on account of me."

She leaned back on her arms, her feet pointing toward him. "I'm surprised you enjoy this type of music . . . since you also liked my fiddling."

"Well, it sounded like something straight from heaven."

"I think so, too." Amelia sighed and wiped her face—her tears had dried. "I thought you might actually prefer the fiddling."

"I wouldn't want to choose," he said honestly. Then he asked, "You always play without music?"

"I read the notes until I memorize the melody lines and chords. My father—and my formal instructor—taught me never to rely on repetitious practice for my classical performances . . . but to analyze the musical form, too." Her eyes clouded; she must've realized then she'd said something she hadn't planned to tell. Revealed something she preferred he not know?

"Performances?" he asked. "You mean . . ."

She bowed her head. "I should think before I speak."

He waited, aware of her inner struggle. What was she hiding?

A long, awkward moment passed when the only sounds were the buzzing of insects in the grazing grass, and the occasional bleating of a far-off goat.

"I have two names, Michael, for a reason." She raised her head to look at him. "Because I have two lives of sorts."

"I don't understand." He removed his straw hat and scratched his head. Women were truly a riddle.

"You know me as Amy Lee, a fiddler. But I'm also Amelia Devries, a concert violinist."

He studied her. "And is Amelia your *real* name?"

Nodding, she offered a fragile smile. "It's the name my parents gave me at birth."

"But why does this make you so sad?"

"It's a very long story. One no one really knows . . ."

He glanced back at the barn in the distance. "Well, as you can see, it's just me, myself, and I out here." He shifted his legs, resting his chin on his knees, mighty curious. Yet he wasn't certain she was going to open up. Despite her apparent candidness toward him last night, she seemed resistant to letting him in on her secret.

"My parents don't know I'm a country fiddler, Michael. And they've never heard my country stage name, Amy Lee."

"Listen, Amelia . . . or whoever you'd like to be," he said. "You can trust me."

Her eyes searched his face.

"I'm sayin' you can count on me . . . all right?"

Tears filled her eyes, and she looked away. Then, after gathering herself, she slowly began to tell him about her other life. "The fiddling came out of necessity," she said, grimacing. "I had to do something to make it all more bearable."

He listened intently to her unusual story—the gift that had appeared at such an early age, and the years of touring the country as a child prodigy. And the enormous expectation that she continue to perform and travel. Sprinkled in were occasional comments about her boyfriend—a trumpeter named Byron. And the more she revealed about her life, the more Michael sensed her frustration and disillusionment. Michael found it peculiar that she seemed to talk about this Byron as if she felt she ought to . . . not out of a sense of love, but out of obligation.

Up till now, Michael had seen Amelia as a very confident young woman, musically and otherwise. So what was keeping her in the apparently less than satisfying relationship?

Just then, he heard the distinct sound of a dinner bell clanging in the distance. In Hickory Hollow such signals were used at mealtime and for emergencies. Michael strained his ears, trying to decipher if this was his own father's dinner bell. *Clang, clang . . .* pause. Then came the repeat—the agreed-upon pattern.

"Something's happened," he said to Amelia, leaping to his feet. "I must get right home."

"What is it?" She rose quickly, as well, and brushed the grass off her long skirt.

"The bell serves as a warning when it's rung that way. My father needs my help." Michael felt terrible running off and leaving her, but something was definitely wrong. *I have no choice.* He took off toward home, not looking back to see if Amelia was still standing there looking bewildered and concerned.

Chapter 18

The bell continued its disquieting call even after Michael was out of sight. Amelia wondered what could be happening in this small community populated with mostly Amish farmers and their families.

Whispering a prayer of concern, she resumed her practice of Tchaikovsky's Violin Concerto in D, playing several measures of the opening movement, the most technically difficult section—*the pyrotechnics*, she liked to think of it. The popular piece was the ultimate romantic concerto by any standard. How she loved its torrent of sinuous melody, extravagant harmonies, the fast runs, and the musical tricks. And oh, the spirited finale! There were times when she felt as if she were falling in love all over again—with music, at least—when she performed the very challenging piece.

Repetition had always helped her to iron out any rough spots. The speedy fingering in the *allegro moderato* first movement was sheer bliss when played perfectly. But going for a day without practicing was devastating to any violinist. To Amelia it was much more than keeping up with fingering or bowing techniques: It was about her well-being. Like the legendary violinist Sir Yehudi Menuhin once said, *"Music is a life-support system."* The violin was such a part of Amelia's daily existence, she felt lethargic, even ill, if she did not practice.

Glad for the chance to play outdoors under the canopy of clouds and sky, she stayed put, not wanting to get in the way of whatever had triggered the alarm. Yet Michael had turned so white just before hurrying away. The remembrance made her even more anxious.

Should I have gone with him?

Lillianne was ever so relieved to see her older son Joseph and his wife, Lena, arrive on foot after she'd tugged on the warning bell. From her vantage point in the downstairs bedroom, she could see them hurrying up the walkway.

The back door *clack*ed shut as they came into the kitchen. Immediately Joseph called to her, inquiring about his father as he made his way into the bedroom, where Paul lay stretched out and pale as anything, not uttering a sound.

"What happened?" Joseph asked, still wearing his old straw hat that had the beginnings of a hole on the crown.

Dark-haired Lena crept into the room behind him, hanging back some, her big brown eyes wide. "Is he out cold?"

Quickly, Lillianne explained that Paul had somehow managed to slip through one of the hay holes in the barn, turning his ankle when he landed below. "He's conscious . . . but might need to rest some."

"Well, I'll call a doctor," Joseph said, indicating the very swollen ankle. "Sure looks broken."

Lillianne knew better than to say too much. Paul didn't want to be made over, and Joseph and Lena were doing just that. "It would be a *gut* idea for a doctor to have a look-see, for sure."

Paul's eyes flickered open just then. He moaned and closed them quickly when he saw all of them hovering near. His bangs were stuck to his forehead from perspiration. Eyes still shut, he flailed his hand, motioning for them to leave him be.

Lillianne led the way, doing his bidding, and Joseph and Lena did the same, making their way to the kitchen. Lillianne leaned on the counter and shook her head. "No sense even sayin' what oughta be done," she whispered to them.

"Jah, no doubt. Daed's got his own mind." Joseph removed his straw hat and ran his hands through his brown hair. "Sure hope Michael will stick around to help out now that Daed's laid up."

"Hope so, too," Lillianne agreed.

"I wouldn't think he'd run off again—" Joseph paused and glanced at Lena—"like our Elizabeth did."

"Could be they're two peas in a pod," Lena said. She pushed her Kapp strings back over her slender shoulders.

Lillianne hated to think this. If only Michael hadn't been bit by the education bug!

If only a lot of things hadn't happened round here . . .

··· ➤ ❮ ···

Another forty-five minutes passed, and while Amelia was accustomed to practicing four to five hours at a time, she decided to pack up and head back to Joanna's. The way Michael had rushed off after hearing the alarm bell still nagged at her. *What could be wrong?*

High clouds made the heat more tolerable as she walked through the meadow toward the house. When she reached the backyard, she heard someone calling. She looked up and saw a little Amishwoman in a blue dress and black apron sitting out on the small square porch of one of the attached houses on the main house's east side. Amelia was taken off guard when the woman waved, smiling. "Yes?" Amelia called back.

A delicate voice asked, "Are you Amelia?"

"Yes."

"Kumme sit with me, won't ya?"

Glancing back at Joanna's house, Amelia observed how quiet the place seemed—no one in sight. *Have they all gone to the Hostetlers'?*

She walked up the narrow sidewalk, dotted to the right with red and white petunias. The petite house pushed out from the larger white clapboard farmhouse, an attached trellis adorned by many red climbing roses. A tall four-sided birdhouse stood halfway across the yard from the smaller house—a Dawdi Haus, Amelia had learned in Ohio.

The elderly woman introduced herself as Mrs. Zook and said she had been visiting with Joanna's *Mammi*—grandmother. "She's takin' her afternoon nap." Without Amelia's asking, the pretty little woman explained that everyone had gone over to Paul Hostetler's to help out.

"I wondered about that." And when Amelia inquired as to what had happened, she was told that Paul had fallen from the upper level of the barn.

She wondered why she hadn't heard any sirens. "Is he badly hurt?"

"Well, knowin' how stubborn Paul is—*Glotzkopp!*—I doubt he'd think of goin' to a hospital or doctor for even a broken limb. He'll just wrap it up and hobble round."

"But wouldn't the pain be too difficult to manage?" She'd never heard of not seeking medical help for something like that.

The older woman shook her head. "Ach, ya don't know the man!"

Amelia was horrified as she contemplated the possibility of leaving such an injury untreated. "I heard the bell earlier."

"Jah, 'tis the farmers' way of callin' for help round here." Mrs. Zook explained that there'd be plenty of folk over there doing Paul's chores in the barn and out in the field, too. "Ev'ryone pitches in—shares the load."

This tugged at Amelia's heart. "Like one big happy family, as the saying goes."

The woman pushed back in her rocker, her wrinkled hands gripping the chair arms. "There are times when things are far from happy, believe me. Just like with any family, I 'spect."

Amelia found it interesting that the woman would be so forthright. "Did Joanna ask you to watch for me? Is that how you knew my name?"

Mrs. Zook smiled. "Jah. She told me to listen till the music stopped . . . an' you'd be a-comin'. And then, there ya were, just like Joanna said."

"You heard me playing all the way over here?"

"Why, sure. Ain't deaf yet!"

Amelia was mortified. "No . . . no, I didn't mean to imply . . ."

The woman reached over and tapped Amelia's knee. "Now, honey-girl, I was just pullin' your leg. All right?" She leaned back then, holding on to the chair once again. Sighing, she closed her eyes for a moment. "Can ya hear Gott's music on the breeze?" she asked, her eyes still shut.

"Sometimes."

"That same gentle wind carried your music right here to me." Mrs. Zook's blue eyes fluttered open. "Heard ev'ry note." Then, turning her head, she fixed her gaze on Amelia. "You sure can make a fiddle talk."

"Thank you."

"And I don't mean just talk, mind ya, but sing and dance and carry on like there's no tomorrow." The woman's hands were suddenly in the air, flapping about in a dance of their own. "I sure hope you ain't just sittin' under a *tree* playin' such perty notes every day, now, are ya?" She looked at Amelia. "Such music's meant to be shared. Just as any blessing is."

Mrs. Zook's candor again caught Amelia off guard, yet she sensed the woman was harmless as a dove. "No, I rarely practice in a cow pasture. In fact, that was the first time ever."

"Well, why not play right here on the porch or in the house somewhere? Ain't because someone's said folks would object, is it?"

"Actually, I—"

"Puh! I guessed as much!" Mrs. Zook leaned nearly out of her rocking chair. "Listen to me, dearie. You have a wunnerbaar-*gut* gift. Don't ya hide your light under a bushel on account of someone's warning." She ran her hand across her high forehead. "You'll hear all kinds of peculiar things if ya stay round here long enough."

"Oh, I'm just visiting a short time."

"We'll see 'bout that," she said. "Hickory Hollow tends to be a bit addictive to some folk. You ain't the first Englischer to stumble across these parts and decide to hang your hat for a spell."

The woman had arrested Amelia's attention from her first

word, and Amelia was even more inquisitive now. "Were those outsiders you just mentioned very well accepted? I mean, were they frowned upon for not dressing Plain?" Amelia worried she might offend especially Joanna's parents with her modern attire, since they were hosting her. And rather hesitantly at that.

"Frowned on for bein' fancy—for who they are?" The woman tittered. "Well, if they aren't Amish, they'd better *not* be dressin' like us!"

"Makes sense." Amelia leaned back, more content now in Mrs. Zook's presence. The woman sat straight and tall for her advanced age, and although she was a bit prickly, Amelia found her confident manner irresistible.

Mrs. Zook eyed the fiddle case. "You didn't just start playin' that fiddle yesterday, now, did ya?"

Amelia caught the flash of mischief in her watery blue eyes. "And not last week, either," Amelia teased right back.

"S'posin' you were a wee one when ya first took it up."

"My father said I was only three and a half when I first showed interest in *his* violin," Amelia said, remembering it like it was just last week. "He was a very accomplished touring violinist and could play like no one else I've ever known." She quickly explained that, back in the day, her father's remarkable tone and easy style were touted by many as similar to a young Isaac Stern. "The way he immersed himself in the music allowed audiences to detect the genius of the actual composer, more than my father's own interpretation. Dad had an uncanny way of making the music spring to life."

Mrs. Zook seemed interested, her face alight.

"He liked to say that music has a way of perfecting the performer, and not the other way around." Pausing, Amelia suddenly missed him. "But that all changed . . . when Dad became very ill."

"Aw, now . . . say." Mrs. Zook pursed her lips, the wrinkles around them like so many gathers in a skirt. "Is he still living, your father?"

"Thankfully, yes." Amelia nodded. "I actually got the idea from him to play fiddle tunes, but he doesn't know it. You see, my dad, like Isaac Stern, called himself 'a fiddle player.' " She contemplated whether or not she was revealing too much.

"Go on," Mrs. Zook prompted her. "*Sei so gut!*—Please!"

Amelia couldn't help but be taken by her enthusiasm. "My father doesn't know anything about my country fiddling and would be very displeased if he did."

An endearing smile appeared. "Is the fiddlin' you mention different from what I just heard ya playin' in the meadow?"

"Very different in some ways and quite similar in others, depending on the piece."

"I see." Mrs. Zook paused and glanced at her curiously. "I'm thinkin' I'd like to hear a fiddle tune, yuscht to hear the contrast, ya know."

"Sure, I'll play for you sometime before I leave. I would be happy to."

They talked easily, like old friends. *Three Amish friends in less than twenty-four hours*, thought Amelia, more delighted than ever that she'd opted to stay awhile.

Mrs. Zook was particularly interested in Amelia's upbringing as a "wee fiddler."

"My father was my first encourager. He believed that a child's playing is filled with honesty—unlike adult performers, whose feelings can be curbed, even suppressed, over time. "

"Who better to understand than a parent? The People know

that, for sure and for certain, as we pass down the simple gifts to the next generation."

The simple gifts . . .

"Michael mentioned that to me, too."

Silently, the woman nodded.

Uneasy because of her own sudden mention of Michael, Amelia changed the subject. "How long do you expect Joanna and her parents to be gone?"

"Oh, they'll be back for afternoon milkin' at four-thirty. The cows can't wait."

They sat a bit longer, enjoying the sun and the birds and rocking away their cares in the hickory rockers, the two chairs swaying in the same rhythm.

"You sure do give yourself up to your music, Miss Amelia."

"It's been nearly my whole life . . . our house was constantly filled with music. It was my dad's great love."

"Well, and you must enjoy it, too."

Amelia pondered that. She *did* love music, but she wanted to avoid talking about her life, the fame and stardom eagerly sought by the top musicians. *Not with this humble woman.* "Yes, I'm passionate about what I do." She paused for a moment, feeling strangely compelled to tell what had been buried in her soul for too long. "It's just that . . ."

The dear woman's eyes held Amelia's own, as if looking deep into her open heart. And in that awkward moment, Amelia realized Mrs. Zook must be the Wise Woman that Michael had talked so glowingly about.

"Are you . . . Ella Mae?" she asked.

"Why, they call me all sorts of things, but jah, Ella Mae's what my Mamma called me first."

Michael was right. She has a way about her. . . .

"You all right, child?"

If only Ella Mae hadn't asked! The woman was much too sweet and sympathizing. Amelia pulled herself together. "When I play for crowds of people on the concert stage . . . as I tour all over the country," she blurted out, "I sometimes wonder if I perform in hopes of somehow finding my way . . . my purpose."

"Oh, now, honey-girl."

Amelia looked away. "It must sound strange to you."

"Not a'tall."

"But even if I wanted to stop my touring now and pursue marriage and a family, my father would never hear of it," she added, giving in to tears. "I feel stuck."

Ella Mae's eyes probed again. "Well, then, can ya remember what I'm 'bout to say, Miss Amelia?"

She listened, her heart swelling with tenderness again.

"There's only one person ya need to think about ever pleasin'," Ella Mae said quietly. "Only one."

Amelia recalled the many nights she and Grammy had talked about such things while they sat outdoors eating strawberry ice cream and watching fireflies flicker in the pastureland.

Ella Mae stopped rocking and turned in her chair slightly, and a thoughtful expression played across her crinkly face. "You're a mighty talented young woman—perty, too. If ya ask me, your maiden days are numbered."

Amelia felt her cheeks blush.

Ella Mae smiled. "You have tender emotions; I heard it in your playin' . . . mighty deep ones, I s'pect. But there's no sense playin' music unless you're called to it, jah?"

Amelia listened.

"Do ya ever think that you play to please the Lord God above?"

It had been a long time since Amelia had considered pleasing the Almighty within the equation of her career.

Ella Mae continued. "I believe you want to make a difference in this ol' world, ain't so?"

She reached for Ella Mae's thin, freckled hand. "Your fame certainly precedes you," Amelia said, smiling through her tears.

Inching out of her chair, Ella Mae reached for her cane propped on the white porch banister. "S'pose ya haven't had time to hear 'bout my peppermint tea just yet." She moseyed past Amelia, glancing down at her. "Drop by and have some over yonder at my little house 'fore ya up and leave the Hollow, won't ya?"

"Thanks, I'd like that."

They exchanged smiles, and although Ella Mae was moving toward the door, Amelia actually yearned for her to stay and chat longer.

"Well, I best be lookin' in on Joanna's grandmother, lest I talk your ear off."

"I enjoyed visiting with you," Amelia said. *More than you know.* She rose quickly and stood near the little woman, concerned she was too frail to move about, even gingerly.

"Remember, now: Play your fiddle for the Good Lord above." Ella Mae raised her pointer finger skyward. "He's the master musician . . . and the closest, dearest friend you'll ever know—closer than even a brother, the Good Book says." With that, Ella Mae Zook stepped inside, closing the screen door.

Amelia promised herself she would not leave for home until she played one of her best fiddle tunes for the dear Wise Woman. *I have to see her again!*

Chapter 19

As Amelia walked back to Joanna's parents' house, she continued to be surprised at herself for having shared so deeply with Ella Mae Zook. It was all so surreal, similar to last night at the cabin with Michael. And to think he had not only enjoyed her fiddling there but also seemed transfixed by the classical music she'd played in the meadow, too. For a country boy raised in such a cloistered setting, Michael certainly seemed to appreciate the classics!

Back inside the house, Amelia saw a short note on the kitchen table, near a large platter of sliced sweet bread covered with clear wrap. *Dear Amelia, please help yourself. There's ice-cold homemade meadow tea in the fridge, if you like. We'll return soon—Joanna.*

Amelia took the note and her fiddle case with her and hurried to her haven of a guest room, closing the door. She sat on the bed, contemplating the encounter with the Wise Woman and the effect the sweet little woman had had on her. She thought then of her mother, recalling again the early days of her father's diagnosis. Almost immediately Mom had begun to throw herself into her writing—making a snug but lovely studio in the basement. There, she'd typed out her heartache, or so Amelia presumed.

Did her father know what had caused her mother to start writing? Surely it had been his tenuous future—his inability to maintain his shining and lucrative career—that had sent Mom into an emotional tailspin. *She needed an escape, of sorts.*

Amelia shook off the thoughts and reminded herself of this tranquil location. There was abundant sunshine here in Hickory Hollow—inside and outside. Was it the Amish way, or the beautiful things Ella Mae had said about the heavenly Father that showered light and truth into Amelia's heart?

She decided to finish working on several more passages from the Tchaikovsky concerto, since the house was empty and would likely be until milking time rolled around. In her tenderhearted state, Amelia knew she could pour the angst of her life into the music . . . just as her father had taught her to do.

Michael's mother lifted one eyebrow as she took stock of Daed's injury. "He'll shuffle round like that till his foot heals eventually," Mamm told Michael. "No doctor's going to touch that ankle of his. Ain't so, Paul?"

Not wanting to side with either parent, Michael rose from his spot at the table and followed his father, who was limping—and wincing, surely!—back to the barn. "Daed!" he called after him, knowing there was not much that could slow down such an adamant, mulish man.

"I'll be fine—*allrecht*, ya hear?" Daed stated a bit too loudly, not even turning his head. "Work's a-waitin'!"

Four more farmers had come to assist after hearing the tolling bell. Michael, too, was able and ready to work, wanting to be a support to his father, as well as his mother. But not even Mamm could keep Daed off his feet for long. No, Daed had insisted she wrap his foot and ankle up real tight in an Ace bandage, then push the foot into his old bedroom slipper, of all things. That done, he asked for his walking stick to help him shamble out to the porch for a time. And there he'd sat for the last hour, shooing everyone away who had anything to suggest—*because they cared*, thought Michael. But his father mistook it for folk telling him what to do. And he'd have none of that!

Concerned, Michael trailed after him to the harness shop in the barn, aware of his father's grunts of pain, cringing every time Daed placed his wounded foot in front of the other.

While Michael hauled harness parts to the counter to be repaired or oiled, he thought of Amelia and her violin playing in Nate's pasture. Goodness, but her music had seeped clear down into his soul. Sitting out there on the soft, grassy ground and watching her, her music—and her remarkable beauty—had touched him. And for just a moment, he wished Amelia might stay around in Hickory Hollow for longer than a weekend.

A brown barn swallow swooped down and startled him, almost knocking his straw hat off his head. "Jah, that woke me up—all for the better," he whispered, not sure what on earth had gotten into him. "*Lecherich*—ridiculous!"

"You talkin' to yourself again, son?"

"Guess I was, jah." Michael picked up yet another harness, giving the strap a harder tug than was necessary.

If Daed only knew!

Amelia concentrated on the most demanding section of the concerto as she walked back and forth in the upstairs hallway. She lost herself in the music, still playing as she headed down the steps. Outdoors, she walked toward the quaint potting shed, enjoying the arrangement of color in Rhoda Kurtz's flower beds even as she continued to play. An interesting rock garden filled nicely with sedum and thyme and the vibrant purple blooms of asters caught her attention near the narrow cobblestone walkway leading around the side of the house to the front lawn. The picturesque path led to an old wooden bench, where clay pots of varying sizes displayed velvety green mosses—one looked exactly like a large pincushion. She stopped playing, taking in the beauty.

Quite unexpectedly, Amelia heard voices on the opposite side of the house. *Joanna and her parents . . . home so soon?*

She held her breath as the voices, especially Rhoda's, grew louder. Then, if she wasn't mistaken, Joanna was talking now, more calmly.

"It won't matter none, honest it won't," Joanna was insisting.

"You didn't think 'bout what could happen, now, did ya?" Rhoda said, her voice fading as she headed inside the house.

What won't matter? Amelia crept farther down the cobblestone walkway, her violin tucked under her arm. She stared at the weather-worn bench, once again admiring the artful collection of pots set there.

Suddenly, from overhead, Joanna called to her. "Psst. Amelia!" It was a whisper at first, then slightly louder. "Amelia . . . up here!"

She raised her head and saw Joanna standing at the window, her white head covering shaped like a heart. "Hullo," Joanna said softly. "Can you come upstairs for a bit?"

"What's going on?"

Joanna leaned closer to the screen. "Mamma's a little upset." She turned her head briefly before glancing back. "She heard you playin'."

"I guess I lost track of time." Amelia explained that she had been watching for them to return and was sorry. "It's my fault for causing this trouble."

I've already blown it, she thought. *Should I just pack up and leave?*

"Mamma will be all right if she doesn't hear any more playin'," Joanna tried to reassure her.

"Well, I really do have to practice," Amelia replied.

Joanna nodded. "Just not so near the house, jah?"

Amelia felt bad for her friend, who was stuck in the middle. "Maybe I'll go into town for a while and check my email—get in touch with a few people," she told her. "Or will my driving create more problems?"

"No. That's all right. I'll see you later, when you return."

Joanna hadn't invited her to stay for supper.

"I'm really very sorry. I thought—"

"No need to fret," Joanna said quickly, but Amelia wasn't so sure she meant it.

She really did need to get online—simply renting time on a computer in town was easy enough. But as Amelia drove leisurely up Hickory Lane, she considered asking Michael to borrow his laptop instead.

When Amelia pulled off the road at the entrance to the Hostetlers' farm, there were a number of gray carriages parked in the side yard, lined up in straight rows. *Did all of these people show up to help?*

The community response impressed her. She switched off the ignition and made her way up the driveway in search of Michael, not wanting to call attention to herself. But how could she not, dressed as she was?

Near an old well pump, she noticed a man who looked several years older than Michael. She quickly explained that she was a friend of Michael's and wondered where she might find him.

The man introduced himself as Michael's oldest brother, Roy. "I s'pect he's in the barn somewheres," he said with a motion of his head in that direction.

For a split second, Amelia almost said *Denki*. The impulse made her smile, then cringe. Was she so enamored with the Plain life that she actually wanted to fit in here?

Do I crave a place to belong?

Lillianne saw Amelia standing out in the lane, looking quite befuddled . . . even lost. Not giving it a second thought, she picked up her long skirt and hurried outdoors. "Did ya hear the bell earlier?" she asked.

"I did," Amelia replied, looking worried. "Is there anything I can do . . . this late?"

"Ach no. The crisis is past, so not to worry, jah?" Lillianne smiled down into her pretty face. "And if it's Michael you're after, he's workin' in the harness shop with his father." She mentioned how busy Paul was with orders this week, a pained expression on her face. "And then of all things, if this accident didn't happen."

"How bad is it?"

"Oh, you know, plenty-a folk have fallen through a hay hole. A dangerous thing, to be sure. We can be thankful his injury wasn't worse. Paul must've had something on his mind and just wasn't lookin'." Lillianne could see that Amelia was sincere in wanting to help—and in her kindly inquiry, too. She wasn't just making small talk, like some fancy folk who stopped to purchase her homemade root beer or strawberry jam, hoping to snoop. "Paul's had mishaps out in the field and whatnot more times than I can count. Some say he's accident-prone."

"Well, I don't want to bother Michael if he's busy."

"I'm sure he can step away for a minute," Lillianne said. "He's s'posed to be on vacation. But maybe you know that already, ain't?"

Amelia gave her a cordial smile. Apparently she *did* know.

Oh, for the life of her, Lillianne would like to know how her son had gotten acquainted with this worldly Englischer—all that eye makeup and the artificial blush on her cheeks. At the same time, there was something ever so sweet about her, though. *Put a cape dress and apron on her, and how would that be?*

Shaking away such folly, Lillianne offered Amelia something cold to drink.

"You know what—I'll take a rain check. I need to run an errand in town," Amelia declined politely.

Lillianne hardly knew how to act around her. "I'll tell Michael you stopped by," she said right quick.

"Thanks very much."

She glanced at Amelia's car parked near the mailbox. "Do ya know how to get where you're goin'?"

"I think so" was the reply.

"All right, then. Be careful out on the highway, jah?"

Amelia's face lit up. Perhaps she appreciated that Lillianne was trying to meet her halfway. Yet whatever Michael's fancy friend was thinking, she waved gracefully before heading up Hickory Lane.

Chapter 20

Amelia went around the car to get in, still having mixed emotions about Rhoda's negative response to overhearing her practice. Nevertheless, Amelia knew she only had herself to blame. After all, Joanna had made it clear where she could and could not play. Regardless, Amelia felt perplexed at being locked in by an antiquated set of rules. *Rules that squelch creativity and individuality.* "Unbelievable," she muttered. "What would I do without music of all kinds?"

She turned the key in the ignition and checked her blind spot. Then, slowly, she moved onto Hickory Lane.

"*Schtoppe*—halt!" Michael leaped out in front of the car, his arms held high, his hat in his hand.

She slammed on the brakes, a rush of blood pounding in her head.

Michael grinned and hurried around the car to her. "Hope I didn't frighten you."

"You appeared out of nowhere!"

His eyes softened. "Sorry, I hoped you weren't leavin' without saying good-bye." He leaned his tan arms on her open window, still holding his hat. "You aren't, are ya?"

"I just stopped by to see if I could borrow your laptop, but your mother said you were busy. I didn't want to bother you."

"No bother at all," he said, smiling into her eyes. "Wait right here." With that, he ran back up the lane to the house.

She really hadn't wanted to put him out. Sitting there waiting, she contemplated Michael's sticky situation. With his father's injury, he was needed more than ever, wasn't he? Wouldn't Michael say so—and wouldn't his father, too? It seemed that one thing kept leading to the next for Michael, propelling him deeper into the very life he had been trying to leave behind. She shivered at the thought—and yet what did her own future look like?

At least he tried to leave. . . .

Up ahead, Amelia watched an Amish farmer hauling hay down the middle of the road, his wide wagon weaving and creaking as it came this way. She was glad she'd pulled so far off the road.

Then she saw the youthful farmer nod his head at her, his straw hat firmly planted on his head. Like Michael and many Amish here, he was quite blond and blue-eyed. *No mistaking his Swiss heritage.*

Surveying the copious cornfields around her, Amelia realized that this time yesterday, she had been tuning her fiddle backstage at the Mann Center for the Performing Arts . . . waiting for her gig to start. And with the same instrument Joanna's mother had reviled a short while ago.

How could a fiddle be so wonderfully appealing to English audiences and yet completely objectionable to the people of Hickory Hollow? *Except for Michael and the Wise Woman,* she thought. She recalled the day her father had offered her the beloved instrument.

The atypical gesture and his rather protective comments were nearly like a christening over the transfer. She'd known at the time that it wasn't his best violin, but it had been his favorite—the violin he had played in college and during his first professional performances. Reverentially, she had taken it up in her hands, propped it beneath her chin, and in honor of her father's beautiful gift, played her arpeggios and scales up and down the taut strings, faster that day and with more clarity than any day before.

Her father's deep-set eyes had shone with joy. And the two of them stood smiling at each other, alone there in the music studio. *"There are no shortcuts to any place worth going,"* he'd emphasized, quoting one of his favorite Beverly Sills lines.

Only eleven at the time, Amelia had fought back tears. She'd loved that glimpse into his more sentimental side.

How I wish he'd open up again, just like that, she thought wistfully.

Amelia took her time driving through the Village of Intercourse, past the quaint strip of historic buildings on the south side of the street, and the massive, modern Kitchen Kettle Village on the north.

She quickly headed west toward Bird-in-Hand and located a coffee shop. There, she ordered an iced white chocolate mocha while she waited for the computer to boot up.

Funny, she thought, *I've scarcely missed my cell phone.*

She waited a few minutes before taking the first sip. So much was hanging in the balance back home that she hated even to think of checking her email or other online accounts. Before she did, though, she perused the reviews for Tim McGraw's concert, curious to see if either she or the Bittersweet Band had been given a mention in the *Philadelphia Inquirer*. Sure enough: *Move over, national fiddle champion . . . Amy Lee hits the Philly stage!*

Amelia winced at the disparaging line—she was not in favor of putting down someone else, no matter the context. She closed the site and went to check her email, then blinked, shocked, when she saw her packed inbox. There were multiple emails from her agent, as well as from Byron.

She opened the first one from Stoney, which proved to be an attachment showing a fabulous mock-up for a promotional poster for her European tour. Just seeing it, even without a comment from her shrewd agent, put more pressure on her. Marketing bucks were already being thrown at something she hadn't formally agreed to as of yet. Everyone was operating on the premise that things were on the same track as last year and the year before that. Amelia had not taken her musical passion to Europe, however, and Stoney and her father believed it was long overdue.

There were other emails from Stoney, as well, but she couldn't bring herself to open them. *I need your signature, Amelia!* read one subject line.

The old tension returned, more fiercely than before. She was actually grinding her teeth as she scrolled up to click instead on Byron's first email, sent earlier this morning, before they'd talked. *I hoped you would give me a call once you were home, Amelia. I'm still trying to understand everything you told me yesterday—it's going to take a while. Wish we could have been together on our anniversary. With love, Byron.*

"Love?" she whispered.

Amelia leaned back in the comfortable booth, letting her

eyes roam the coffee shop. She was somewhat amused by the many patrons hunched over their laptops. Several slurped on iced coffee or chai lattes, and one man moved his lips as his fingers flew over a keyboard. ,

She experienced a sudden surge within, a need to control this one minuscule part of her life. Amelia turned off the laptop and reached for her icy drink. Stoney and Byron could wait.

Lillianne had witnessed Michael run out to wave down his friend. *He could've gotten himself run over*, she stewed. *Why's he chasing after an outsider?*

Shaking her head, she went to feed the chickens, scattering corn feed in the open pen. While they scurried about, eating and pecking at each other, Lillianne entered the warm, dark little hen house, going around to collect the eggs from the nests and place them in her wire basket. Once, years ago, she'd encountered their oldest son, Roy, out here smooching the girl he ended up marrying.

Oh, thought Lillianne, *if only Michael might fall for one of our church girls*. But Michael was clearly carrying a torch for the young woman right now driving her car to town. Not even Marissa could hold a candle to this here Englischer, it seemed.

Lillianne took great care with the egg basket and its precious contents, not wanting to drop a single egg. Not like she'd done yesterday, while Michael and his father were exchanging heated words. Today she'd use some of these very eggs to make a welcome home cake for their youngest son, who would surely never think of kissing a girl out in the hen house, of all places!

At least, she hoped not.

Chapter 21

Saturday morning very early, Lillianne found Michael sitting alone in the kitchen. He turned ashen when he saw her, his hands dropping quickly to his lap.

"Michael, I *know* you have a cell phone. No need to hide it."

His eyes were ever so serious.

"Well, you don't much care for it, Mamm."

She ignored that. "You look awful worried."

He hesitated. "It's a text from Elizabeth. She must've sent it last night," he muttered. "Didn't check messages till just now."

"Everything all right?" Lillianne asked.

He shrugged, suddenly acting casual. "Well, you know, it's hard to tell 'bout her."

Lillianne stared at the cell phone in his hands, her heart racing. How she longed to know where their dear granddaughter was after all these months. "When was the last you heard something?"

"A few weeks, maybe." Michael's voice was quiet, like he could barely get enough breath to speak. He pressed a button, which caused the screen to blacken. "I just texted back. I'm sure we'll hear more soon."

"Tell her that *Dawdi* and I pray for her every day, won't ya?" Lillianne wouldn't ask more, although she could hardly stand not knowing what was going on. And something was, too, just from the look on Michael's fretful face.

He glanced anxiously toward the door. "I should get back to the barn. Daed will wonder what's become of me."

She nodded, worried sick as she watched him trudge out to the harness shop. *He knows more than he's letting on!*

Michael was in the stable feeding the mules when Amelia arrived. His pulse quickened as she stepped into view; then he chided himself. Her being in Hickory Hollow was only temporary, after all.

"I put your laptop on the kitchen table," she told him. "Thanks for letting me borrow it yesterday."

"Just let me know if ya need it again."

"Something wrong?" she asked. For pity's sake, if she didn't see right into him!

"Actually, there is," he admitted.

"Can I help?" She reached out as though to touch his arm, then seemed to think better of it.

"I'm not sure anything can be done," he said in a low voice. Michael continued to pour feed into the trough. "Lizzie, my niece, is in a bad way."

Amelia's eyes filled with worry. "Where is she?"

"Harrisburg . . . in the hospital." He explained about the rough crowd she'd fallen in with and asked Amelia not to say anything to Joanna or anyone else. " 'Specially not to my parents."

"Oh, I hope and pray she's okay."

"She says it's nothing. But scrapes and scratches and scratches don't land anyone in the hospital. So something's not quite right." He shook his head. "She's not answering her phone. I tried texting, too."

"Maybe you should just go to her."

He bowed his head. "She and I have been through this before. Lizzie doesn't want me to interfere—she can be as stubborn as a mule sometimes."

"But *she* contacted you, right?"

Michael nodded.

"Maybe that's her way of asking for help."

"Well, I can't just leave here . . . not with Daed like he is. Besides, you're my guest," he replied.

"Don't worry about me . . . it's Joanna I'm staying with. You should go, Michael. Wouldn't your father want you to?"

Feeling awkward at what he'd implied, Michael finished up his chore before continuing the conversation. What did Amelia know about any of this? Yet she seemed to care. "You're probably right," he said suddenly. "You know what? You're English. Maybe you could help make sense of all this—with Elizabeth, I mean."

Amelia's expression grew doubtful. "You two are obviously close, Michael. She's asking for *you*. I'm just another English stranger."

"But, seriously, would ya mind?" He was at a loss to know how to handle his niece, especially with this latest news. *Look what good I've been to her. . . .*

"Are you sure?" she asked.

He straightened, fixing his eyes on her. "It sure would mean a lot."

"Okay, then," she relented. "When do you want to go?"

Michael's shoulders dropped with relief. "As soon as I wash my hands and put on trousers that don't have manure stickin' to the hems."

"I'll be ready," she said with a slight smile, which Michael would have returned had he not been so nervous about naïve Elizabeth living outside the Plain community. If anything terrible had happened to her, a big part of the blame would fall at his feet.

··· ✜ ···

Once they were on their way, Michael wanted to level with Amelia. "There's more to what's goin' on with Elizabeth," he confided. "She's in over her head with a worldly fella."

Amelia looked over at him. "Is that why you wanted me to come along?"

He nodded. "I just hope she'll listen to wisdom for a change."

Amelia smiled quickly and folded her hands. "You might want to go easy on her, at least at first."

Michael chuckled under his breath. "I was hopin' you could help with that."

"So, you must want to talk her into coming home with you."

He nodded quickly. "When you meet her, you'll know right away she belongs in Hickory Hollow." He meant it. "If she'll just open up—to both of us—she'll know it, too."

He dreaded the thought of Lizzie dating a man outside the Plain community, someone who might influence her away from God. Unlike him, his niece showed little interest anymore in faith.

"I'll do what I can," Amelia said quietly.

"Well, she has to make the choice to return." He realized how strange this must sound to Amelia, considering his own struggles with the church. "For Elizabeth, it's most definitely the right thing," he added quickly.

"But . . . not for you?"

Amelia had him, and he suspected Lizzie would ask much the same. This was always where things ended up. But it didn't matter now. What mattered was helping his niece. And if that made him seem a hypocrite, then so be it.

After a lull in conversation, Amelia asked, "You know, right now I'm really wondering how the Amish church retains young people. How does Hickory Hollow manage to hold on to someone like Joanna or your siblings?"

"Some think it's a peculiar riddle, but the Rumschpringe years give youth a chance to see what the outside world is like. Not all teens leave the confines of the People, mind you. Only a small percentage dip their toes in the modern world."

"Just a small few, you say." Amelia looked unusually thoughtful.

"Yes, very few," he repeated, wishing he could sit again across a table from her, to focus solely on her.

Amelia seemed to consider this. "Strange as it might sound, I recognize a bit of my own life here in Amish country. In some ways, I've been just as cloistered from the world as the People, though my parents would hate to hear it." She gave him a wry smile. "Maybe this is *my* Rumschpringe, eh?"

Michael wasn't sure what she meant until she told him about the European tour and all the hopes surrounding that.

"I feel like everyone's holding their collective breath, waiting for me to sign on the dotted line. And, well, suddenly I'm not so sure anymore." Amelia sighed and shifted in her seat. "It's a little like you, I guess, with your bishop and your family waiting for you to join the church. There's so much that depends on that decision." She turned away from him, glancing toward the window.

"It's not possible to make a decision like that lightly, is it?" he said, understanding more fully now why they had connected from the very first.

After Michael and Amelia pulled into the hospital parking lot, he hurried around to the passenger side of the car to open her door. She waited, smiling at his attention.

"Wow, thanks . . . it's been ages since I've been around a gentle-man." He tipped his straw hat, and they laughed a little as they made their way toward the Harrisburg hospital. The lighthearted moment felt good after the frank discussion they'd had during the trip here.

In a short time, it was discovered that Elizabeth had been discharged more than an hour earlier. As no other details were forthcoming, Amelia could only imagine what had happened to cause her to be admitted.

Michael pulled out his cell phone, and as they walked back to the car, he texted his niece. Amelia held her breath, hoping the trip had not been in vain. "She must be at her apartment by now," he said with a pensive look.

Amelia was glad she'd accompanied him—how would it have been for him to be alone right now?

"Why not just call her again? She might need to hear your voice."

He nodded, his face solemn as he tried once more to reach young Elizabeth.

At last Michael got through to his niece. "You had me worried, Lizzie," he said when she answered. "I kept texting ya, but heard nothin' back."

"I couldn't use my phone in the hospital—so didn't get your texts right away."

"Well, I was just there and was told you're out now. I want to visit ya . . . see for myself that you're okay."

Elizabeth paused, and Michael could hear voices in the background. *Male* voices. "Ain't such a *gut* time, really," she said, sounding strange.

"I drove here to check on ya." He softened his tone. "You asked me to come, remember?"

"I'm fine now," she said, still resisting. "Really, I am."

"Mamm's awful worried."

Elizabeth gasped. "Grandma Lily knows . . . ?"

"Listen, I was careful what I said. I really want to see you, Elizabeth." He pleaded this time.

"Hold on just a minute." She must've covered the phone because he heard her talking—and someone responding rather loudly—although the words were muffled. In a few seconds, she returned. "Okay, I'm back."

"What's your address?" he asked, hoping she'd comply.

After a long pause, she told him the street name and number. "I'll be right over."

"Don't make a fuss, jah? I'm fine, really!" Was she protesting too much?

"Okay, bye!" Michael clicked off his cell phone.

We'll just see if she's fine.

Chapter 22

E lizabeth's apartment was located in a section of the city where row houses lined the street for blocks on end. Michael didn't tell Amelia what he was thinking as he pulled up to the curb in front of a rather rundown-looking building. *It's a good thing her parents don't know where she's living!*

He asked Amelia to come along, and they stepped out of the car and up the steps. They met Elizabeth coming out the front door, which she closed quickly behind her, a large canvas bag slung over her slight shoulder. One side of her face was badly bruised and bandaged, and her right arm was in a cast and sling. She reeked of cigarette smoke.

Elizabeth raised her blue-gray eyes in surprise at the sight of Amelia, though she did not acknowledge her. His niece looked nothing like the innocent young woman she had been, growing up in Hickory Hollow. She wore her dark hair loose and hanging down her back, and more than half the length of it had been cut off—so unevenly that Michael wondered if she'd lopped it off herself. What little eye makeup she wore had smeared onto her bruised face as if she had been crying.

"Come, let's talk in the car," he suggested, missing terribly her formerly cheerful countenance.

"This is Amelia, a friend of mine, by the way," he told her, hoping Elizabeth might show some manners and say hello.

Elizabeth nodded quickly, then looked back at him as she got into the front seat of the car. "I don't have much time," she stated quickly.

"Why don't I go for a short walk," Amelia said as he hurried around the car to the driver's side.

"Okay," he replied, opening the door. "Thanks."

Michael slipped in behind the steering wheel, uncertain how this would turn out, given how very crumpled Elizabeth looked— not only her battered face and broken arm, but her nearly sullen attitude.

Amelia strolled up the street, taking her time. Most of the brownstone houses were fairly well kept, but farther down, a broken tricycle appeared abandoned near the curb. Besides Elizabeth's building, one house, in particular, was in disrepair, the exterior paint chipping off in places. For all its supposed inhabitants, the neighborhood felt surprisingly devoid of life compared to the countryside around Lancaster County.

How could a sheltered Amish girl be happy here in the city? she wondered, feeling certain from what she'd seen that Michael's dear niece was at risk.

"Don't you get it?" Michael's voice rose out of control. He paused a moment, taking a quick breath, forcing himself to be calm. "This isn't what you had in mind when you left. Can't you see this, Lizzie?"

Elizabeth pouted, her arms folded defiantly.

"You came here to attend school. What happened?"

She shook her head. "You really don't understand, do ya?" Now she started to cry. "I dropped out, all right? I had no choice!" She shouted the words, her face red. "I couldn't keep my grades up. It wasn't enough to go to the one-room Amish schoolhouse . . . I just barely passed my GED test," she explained. "So I'm a failure. I couldn't cut it, and my precious dream's gone for *gut*."

"No . . . no." Michael reached over to touch her head lightly. "Lizzie, you're not a failure."

She stared at him, her eyes pink. "But I am, Uncle Michael. I'm not as smart as you or anyone else in the Hollow."

"Honey . . . no. Listen, you *are* smart—you're very bright."

"I wanted an education, more than anything. I wanted to make my way in the world, not end up married to an Amishman, expected to have a whole houseful of kids . . . with no time to read or study like I've always longed to." She paused to wipe her eyes. "Like you, Uncle Michael."

He couldn't refute that. He was her role model, she'd once said . . . she wanted to follow in his footsteps. But where had it led her?

Elizabeth looked over at the brick house. "Even if I can't make it in college, I still want my freedom." She motioned to the rundown building. "This is my life now. My waitressing job . . . and that apartment there."

"And the girls you share it with?" he asked pointedly. "Are they nice?"

"Sure," she said, looking away. "And the guys, too. They're all nice to me."

He stiffened. "Guys live there, too, Elizabeth?"

"Please don't make me go back to my old boring life," she pleaded. "I'd rather die—"

"Apparently you came awful close last night!"

She sobbed into her hands, leaning forward and rocking back and forth. "I hate bein' told what to do all the time."

"Listen, I really just want to take ya home."

Elizabeth's face darkened. "I'm *not* going back."

This isn't going well. He spotted Amelia slowly walking back and wished she'd stayed. Maybe then this conversation wouldn't have gone so awry.

"You're in trouble, Elizabeth. You asked to see *me*, remember?" He stopped and wished he had a handkerchief to offer her. "I came because I care about you."

"Well, I'm done with this lecture. I'm gettin' out of this car and going back inside . . . and I don't want you to follow me, ya hear?"

He reached to touch her arm and she pushed away. "You're not thinkin' clearly."

"How can ya know that?"

"Well, I'm not blind, Elizabeth." He paused. "Sharing an apartment with men?"

She looked away, then noticed Amelia coming this way. "So, are ya courting *her* now? Guess Marissa didn't mean so much to ya after all."

That stung hard. "You know me better than that."

"Do I?" She reached for the door handle. "It's your fault, ya know. You never should've let me drive your car that day last winter." She threw it right in his face. "You gave me my first taste of freedom . . . and the world."

"Lizzie . . . please."

"I can't believe you came here. I really can't. After all these months . . ." She sighed loudly. "What took ya so long?"

He recalled the hundreds of texts they'd exchanged. "I didn't visit before now because you never wanted me to. You sounded settled . . . and happy."

"Then I fooled ya, like I fooled everyone else back home."

Struggling with her impudence, he looked away. "You don't mean a word of that."

She sniffled and pushed her long hair over her bare shoulders. "I might not look very happy, but I am. I like bein' a waitress and I like the man I'm seein'—a whole lot."

"The one drivin' drunk last night? Isn't that how the accident happened, Lizzie?"

She kept her face forward, not answering.

"You honestly *like* a fella who doesn't care enough 'bout ya to drive sober? You could've been hurt very badly, or even killed."

"It's only the first time it's happened," she said.

"The *first*? If he does it once, he'll likely do it again."

Elizabeth opened the car door. "I'm sick of this! You remind me of Bishop John . . . and Dat, too!"

Michael's heart sank as she got out and slammed the door. *I blew it. I totally blew it!*

Amelia had seen Michael and his niece talking animatedly in the car. Then, unexpectedly, Elizabeth had opened the door and stumbled out of the vehicle. She scowled back at Michael. Whatever he'd said must have made matters worse.

Hurrying over to catch up with the disheveled young woman, Amelia asked her gently, "May I talk to you for a second?"

Elizabeth looked her over, up and down. "What do you care? Who are you, anyway?"

"A friend." She tried to think of something to say to win this girl's trust. "I'm staying with Joanna Kurtz—do you know her?"

Immediately, Elizabeth's face softened. "Jah . . . she's my best friend's older sister."

"I like Joanna," Amelia said. "A lot."

Elizabeth nodded her head. "She's real nice. S'pose I needed a sister like *that*."

"Come walk with me," Amelia invited, pointing up the street in the opposite direction from where she had just been.

"Actually, how's this?" Elizabeth indicated the front steps.

They sat down, not talking for a moment.

Then Elizabeth said, "Uncle Michael's a little intense."

"Well, he's worried." Amelia nodded. "And I would be, too, if you were my niece. I'm talking crazy-out-of-my-head worried, Elizabeth."

Elizabeth rolled her eyes.

"You know your family loves you. They miss you, too." Amelia bobbed her head toward the apartment behind them. "The people who truly care about you are probably not the type who live here with you, are they?"

"I don't know. . . ."

"Well, are your roommates kind to you?"

"Sometimes." Elizabeth stared at her. "But really, how can you know anything about my life?"

"Just guessing." Amelia smiled. "Maybe you could use a break from all of this. You could return later, if you want."

"What're ya sayin'?"

"I'm on a similar break myself, actually."

"From your horrible life?"

Amelia patted Elizabeth's knee. "We all struggle . . . sometimes."

She breathed a short prayer, concerned she might mess things up now that she'd gotten this far. Forging ahead, she asked, "Why don't you come home to Hickory Hollow for a day or so?"

"No one there wants to see me," Elizabeth replied. "No one listens to me."

Amelia paced herself, pausing for a second. "Well, I know of one person who might listen. Michael calls her the Wise Woman."

Elizabeth fell silent and her eyes welled up. "You're right—I do miss Ella Mae."

"And Michael's so fond of you, too. I'd like to get to know you myself."

"Honestly?"

Amelia nodded and offered a smile. "I know he cares about you, Elizabeth." She stopped again and glanced at Michael, still sitting in the car. "I know it for a fact."

Elizabeth stared at the car. "I was hard on him just now," she whispered.

"Oh, he's a guy—he'll manage."

"Yeah . . ."

"So what do you think?" Amelia held her breath. "Want to ride home with us?"

The front door of the apartment house opened, and when Amelia turned around she saw a burly man in a sleeveless red T-shirt. He had to be in his thirties at least.

"Get yourself back inside, Liz," he bellowed.

Elizabeth leaped up, her eyes blinking. She glanced first at Amelia, then back at the man.

Amelia froze, wanting to call to Michael, but thankfully he was already getting out of the car. "Elizabeth?" she said, the name catching in her throat.

"I have to go in." Elizabeth looked pale suddenly.

Michael rushed to Amelia's side. "You don't have to, Lizzie."

Elizabeth looked again at the angry man, then back at Michael and Amelia. "I, uh—"

"It's all right, honey," Amelia heard herself saying, unsure where her courage was coming from. "You really don't have to listen to him." She held out her hand. "Make your own decision."

Elizabeth took a step backward, toward Amelia. "I have nothin' to wear 'cept what I have on . . . if I come with you." Her words were a near whisper.

"We'll go clothes shopping at the outlet mall—I'll get you some cute things."

Elizabeth blinked back tears. "You'd do that . . . for me?"

The man shouted at her again, the door still open. "Don't let them put ideas in your head, now, honey. You say good-bye now and come on back in here."

"Lizzie," Michael said, his voice breaking. "You're safe with us."

Amelia inched closer. Her heart pounded, her hand still outstretched toward the girl. *O Lord, help us!*

The man moved forward, and then Elizabeth reached for her, clasping her hand. She followed Amelia as they hurried across the walkway, toward the car. Michael ran back around to the driver's side and jumped inside, immediately starting the car. Quickly, they sped away.

Chapter 23

With the city in the distance at last, Elizabeth ceased her crying. The headrest blocked Amelia's ability to see, but she could tell Elizabeth was fidgeting and restless.

Amelia's own stomach was still in knots. She kept reliving the threatening encounter. What could a nineteen-year-old girl see in such a man?

Michael was driving more cautiously now on the return trip, staying in the right lane and not passing. He had to be nervous about Elizabeth's accident last night . . . and shaken by what had transpired with the man at the apartment building.

Michael turned on the radio softly, possibly to provide a calming atmosphere. *Such an afternoon!* Most important, Elizabeth had made the decision to come with them. She was, however, presently voicing her concerns again about "staying put" in Hickory Hollow. Amelia couldn't help but hear what she was telling Michael.

"It might be wise to stay at my parents' house tonight," Michael suggested.

"Dawdi Paul's goin' to have my hide—I just know it."

"You might be surprised at how glad he'll be to see ya—and Mammi Lillianne, too."

"But what'll the ministerial brethren say?" Elizabeth's voice sounded thin. "Will they make me repent?"

"Not when you aren't baptized."

"Well, you don't know Dat."

Michael chuckled softly. "Oh, I know my brother, all right. He's worried sick."

She looked at him. "He'll whoop me but *gut*."

"No, Elizabeth."

She bowed her head. "You don't know the half of what I've done."

Michael exchanged glances with Amelia in the rearview mirror.

"I'm awful scared, Uncle Michael."

He offered a reassuring smile. "Trust me, everyone will be thrilled to see ya back."

She turned and gave Amelia the saddest look; then she was quiet for a time. When she spoke again, her voice was soft. "How long are you stayin' in Amish country, Amelia?"

"Probably another day."

"She just arrived in the Hollow yesterday morning," Michael cut in. "Amelia blew into the area with the storm on Thursday night," he said, looking at her again in the rearview mirror. "Want to tell Lizzie what you do, Amelia?"

"Sure," she said, leaning forward. Amelia felt odd, given the circumstances, and she certainly didn't want to boast or make it seem that her career was more special than any other type of work. "I travel around the country playing violin with various orchestras. And sometimes I play in fiddle fests, too."

"No kiddin'?" Elizabeth said, her eyes suddenly bright. "What sort of music?"

"All kinds, but mostly classical and country."

"Country?" Elizabeth seemed thrilled. "God, family, and country, right?"

Michael nodded, glancing back at Amelia. Did he want her to give Elizabeth the whole spiel? She frowned, asking the question with her eyes until he nodded back. Swiftly, she filled Elizabeth in on her recent concert with the Bittersweet Band, as well as a little about her work as a concert violinist. She left off the part about stalling for time in regard to the European tour. *I, too, am a runaway.*

"Is it hard to learn to play the violin?" Elizabeth asked.

"Well, I practice a lot."

"How much?"

"Many hours a day," Amelia said.

Elizabeth pulled her hair back into a ponytail with her left hand and held it there. "I must look a mess, ain't so?"

Amelia wondered if she'd want to try to wash up somewhere before arriving home. "You know what? I'd like to stop off at McDonald's or some other fast-food place and freshen up myself. Maybe get something to eat. Are you hungry?"

"I'm starvin'—and I need to wash my face in the ladies' room."

"Sure," Amelia said.

Michael's face beamed back at her from the mirror.

"But remember," Elizabeth said, looking now at Michael, "I'm only goin' for a short visit." She sounded like she was trying on her confidence once again.

"Yes, you've told me," said Michael. Then he gave her a serious glance. "How's your arm feeling?"

Elizabeth sighed. "S'pose it's time for some more pain meds," she said, unzipping her canvas bag. "It still hurts a lot. Fortunately the hospital sent me home with some."

"Do you have your wallet?" asked Michael.

"Oh jah . . . everything I need's right in here." Elizabeth patted the canvas bag on her lap. "Even the key to the little café where I'm a waitress."

"You got the kitchen sink in there, too?" Michael teased.

"Like I said . . . everything important to me." Elizabeth gave Michael a smirk.

If she has her wallet, she doesn't have to go back. Amelia felt an enormous weight lifting.

While he waited for the girls, Michael ordered a round of burgers with fries and milkshakes for the three of them. He was still in awe of Amelia. There was no question in his mind that Elizabeth would have remained at the apartment if Amelia hadn't come along. He had observed the entire exchange between them, listening through the open window as they sat on the step, amazed at how quickly Amelia had turned things around.

When Elizabeth and Amelia emerged from the restroom and came to sit with him, he noticed a big improvement in his niece's appearance, although the cuts and bruises on her face would still be met with concern on the part of Mamm, he was sure. The mascara smudges and eyeshadow were gone, though, giving his niece a younger, more innocent look.

"You feel better?" he asked as he handed the packaged burgers and ketchup packets around.

"Jah, much better."

Elizabeth started to eat without bowing her head, which startled Michael. "Wait a minute, Lizzie. Let's pray first, okay?"

Elizabeth gave him an *oops* smile. "Oh jah. I forgot."

Michael bowed his head and offered a brief table blessing. Afterward Amelia glanced his way, her eyes gentle but pleading: *Take it slow,* she seemed to say.

He nodded back. *Message received.*

Amelia was encouraged by the gracious welcome Michael's mother gave her granddaughter. Lillianne wrapped her arms around Elizabeth and held her near, talking softly in Deitsch—things Amelia did not understand, although by the endearing looks exchanged, they were definitely affectionate words. Elizabeth said little but soaked up the attention from her grandmother, who clucked over her injuries and then gently took her free hand and led her to the kitchen table, sat her down, and brought over a plate of cold cuts and crackers, and a two-layer chocolate cake. "*Fresse,* now . . . eat *gut,* dear girl!"

When Paul came in the back door, looking tired from the day, his eyes lit up when he saw Elizabeth sitting there with Lillianne, Michael, and Amelia. "Well, what's this—a party?" He removed his straw hat and placed it on a wooden peg high on the wall. "Nobody told me 'bout this!"

Amelia noticed the quiver in his chin as he limped over to his granddaughter, kissed the top of her head, and put both hands on her shoulders. "Mighty *gut* havin' ya home." The light in his eyes went out as he took in the bruises and the bandage . . . and her broken arm. "What on earth happened to ya, Lizzie?"

Elizabeth shrugged and looked away.

"Give her some time," Lillianne urged softly, reaching to touch Elizabeth's good arm.

Amelia held her breath and wondered if Elizabeth would say she was merely visiting. But Elizabeth was quiet as Paul sat at the head of the table and folded his arms across his chest.

"The Lord God brought ya back to us," Paul said, his beard bobbing as he nodded his head. "Many prayers have gone up for ya, Lizzie. Many-a prayer from this here old man, I'll say."

Elizabeth and her grandfather did the nibbling while Lillianne continued to fuss over her "one and only *Grossdochder!*"

There was a knock at the door and they all turned to look. An Amishwoman peeked in, and Elizabeth squealed when she saw her.

"Annie Fisher Lapp!" Elizabeth got off the bench and hurried across the kitchen, pushing the screen door open and giving her a one-armed hug on the porch.

"What a surprise to find you here, Lizzie! Elam will be glad to hear it," said Annie.

The rest of them watched as the two women stood outside jabbering.

"Mighty nice to see Lizzie again," Paul said again.

"I doubt she's back for *gut,*" Michael said quickly.

"Oh now, Michael, we'll see 'bout that," Lillianne scolded.

Michael added that Amelia had been key in convincing Lizzie to come home. "I would've returned empty-handed, for certain."

His mother blinked repeatedly as she looked across the table at Amelia. "Ya know, you could almost pass for Elizabeth's twin," she said, smiling through tears.

"That she could," Paul agreed. He pulled on his beard and looked over his shoulder toward the back door.

Michael smiled broadly, and his eyes twinkled at Amelia.

"Where did ya say you're from?" asked Lillianne.

"Columbus, Ohio," Amelia said, wishing Michael hadn't made so much of her efforts with Elizabeth. It was enough that in one small way she had made a difference in young Elizabeth's life.

Even so, Amelia realized that, without a change of heart, the Hostetlers' granddaughter might end up right back where she and Michael had found her.

Chapter 24

B efore leaving the Hostetlers' early that evening, Amelia asked Elizabeth to let her know when she might want to shop for a few clothes, if she still wanted to. "I'll be around yet tomorrow if you need me," she offered.

Elizabeth thanked her but said now that she was at her grandparents', she didn't dare shop tomorrow. "Not on the Lord's Day."

"Of course! Whatever you think is best," Amelia said, then offered to loan a skirt and blouse, which Elizabeth quickly accepted. "I'll stop by with those later tonight," Amelia promised as she departed for her car.

Amelia returned to the Kurtzes' farmhouse, trying to push the memory of the day's terrifying moments in Harrisburg out of her mind. She went in the back way and found Joanna in the kitchen washing supper dishes by herself. Amelia greeted her and went to stand next to the sink, where she picked up a tea towel. She began to tell what had transpired with Elizabeth.

"Lizzie's back, ya say?" The look of disbelief on Joanna's face was revealing. "Ach, 'tis a miracle."

"It was certainly difficult persuading her," Amelia said, leaving out the nerve-wracking details. "But yes, she's back."

"And Michael asked you to go along?"

Amelia nodded, realizing Joanna's brain was whirring in all sorts of directions. "He thought it might help that I'm an Englisher," she added.

"Oh, such wonderful-*gut* news!" Joanna quickly dried her hands on her apron and excused herself to hurry out to the barn, presumably to let her father know.

Glad Joanna was occupied, Amelia slipped up the stairs to the guest room. *What a couple of days!* She sat on the edge of the bed and relived her first moments in Hickory Hollow yesterday morning . . . meeting delightful Joanna and later, sweet Ella Mae . . . and Michael's parents, as well. And today, poor, dear Elizabeth.

So much has happened since my fiddling performance Thursday night!

Suddenly, the vision of the promo for the European tour sprang to mind. Stoney must be pulling out his last hairs as he awaited her return. Her father must also be wondering what was keeping her from home—was the stress affecting his illness?

Amelia looked about the simple yet comfortable room. *What a restful cocoon I've wandered into.*

Never would anyone back in Ohio imagine she was sequestered away from the modern world . . . soaking up the serenity of an Amish setting. But Joanna's old farmhouse wasn't just any respite, and Hickory Hollow wasn't just any peaceful community. It was a unique and appealing world all its own, and Amelia had never felt so happy.

A while later, Amelia heard Joanna coming up the stairs, calling softly, "Yoo-hoo, are ya up here?"

Amelia must have dozed off. "Yes." She sat up and stretched. "Come in, Joanna."

"Hope I didn't wake ya." Barefoot, Joanna stood in the doorway, wearing a big smile.

"I just feel so relaxed here."

Strands of Joanna's hair had fallen out of the thick bun at the nape of her neck. "I'm all done redding up the kitchen. And I went to give the *gut* news of Elizabeth's homecoming to my parents, too."

"They must be pleased."

"Oh goodness, are they ever!" Joanna's smile lit up her face. "All the People will be grateful to you, I'm sure."

Amelia shook her head. "I can't take the credit. Michael was a big part of it." *And God.* She remembered her frantic prayer on the front steps with Elizabeth.

"No matter how it happened, Lizzie's back."

Amelia agreed.

"Well, if you'd like—if you've had enough rest—we could take a nice long walk together," Joanna suggested, clearly eager for one. "Before sundown."

Amelia was delighted. "Sure, I'd like that." *Very much,* she thought.

The sun was low and red in the sky as they made their way along Hickory Lane. After a time, they turned off onto a side road, and Joanna again brought up Elizabeth's return. "I hope

Lizzie gets a sweet taste of home—something she's surely missed," Joanna said, her long dress blowing gently in the breeze.

"Maybe your sister can help with that."

Joanna's eyebrows flew up. "Lizzie mentioned Cora Jane?"

"Not by name, no."

"Oh." Joanna explained that her younger sister and Elizabeth had been nearly like sisters themselves, but Cora Jane's heart was broken when Lizzie left without a word to her. "Only Michael knew what was goin' on, but he kept mum for the most part." Joanna sighed. "I assume Cora Jane will be hard-pressed to forgive Lizzie, but she will, sooner or later. That's what we're taught to do—what the Lord expects from us."

Amelia considered that as she enjoyed the coolness of the evening. The birds twittered high in the trees lining the old dirt road. "Do you think Michael will forgive Marissa . . . for leaving him?" she asked quietly.

"Oh sure . . . but these things take time. And it's not like she left Hickory Hollow, or wandered from the fold of the Amish church. Marissa was always Mennonite." Joanna paused. "Michael shoulda known better."

"I don't mean to be nosy."

"No, that's all right. I guess ya must know Michael pretty well," Joanna said, swinging her arms. "But if I tell ya what happened 'tween Marissa and Michael, you won't share it with anyone, will ya?"

"You can trust me."

"You have to understand that Marissa adored Michael. She even offered to join the Amish church for him, if he wanted. Leavin' him was the hardest thing she's ever done."

Amelia nodded.

"But in the end, she knew she had to answer God's calling on her life."

"Calling?"

"Missions work. Marissa told Michael that Christ was her first love."

Amelia pondered that. "Why couldn't Michael have joined her church and gone with her?"

"I don't know if she would have asked him. Amish don't evangelize outside the confines of the community like Mennonites and other churches do. We focus on our own children—hoping they'll join the church."

Amelia was surprised. "So, Michael accepts that teaching, but not other aspects of Amish faith?"

"I'm not sure what Michael thinks about everything, honestly, but I know how his parents brought him up. And I don't see how he could've gone with Marissa to study to be a missionary."

An enormous cloud covered the sun as they walked farther from the Kurtz farm, and within minutes a brilliant lining began to shine around the cloud, with bursts of silver rays shooting straight up. "Have you ever seen the sky look like this before?" Amelia remarked. "It reminds me of a painting."

"Ever so beautiful." Joanna stared up for the longest time. Then she said, "Surely that's how it'll look when the Lord comes back."

Amelia was unable to take her eyes off Joanna as she gazed heavenward, her face shining with such expectation, even adoration.

Marissa referred to Christ as her "first love."

Joanna's account of Marissa, coupled with the devout expression on Joanna's face, touched Amelia's heart. *If only my faith were as rich as theirs . . . Does their sense of contentment run so deep because these two women have found their purpose in life?* she wondered.

They walked silently for a few minutes, and Amelia enjoyed the wildflowers, especially the vivid yellow of the many clusters of daisies.

"Just to be clear," Joanna said suddenly, "I hope you don't think Michael was at fault for the breakup with Marissa. Truth is, they just weren't meant for each other." Joanna looked again at the sky. In the space of a few minutes, the radiance had faded.

"Not surprising," Amelia remarked. "Lots of couples discover they don't belong together."

In time . . .

"True." Joanna's expression turned hopeful. "As for me—and my beau—I believe we'll marry . . . one sweet day," she whispered. "Lord willing."

"You have a beau?" Amelia asked.

Joanna blushed and nodded, suddenly seeming shy. "No one knows about him, though."

"A secret love?"

"Jah . . . he's just wonderful-*gut*."

"Well, if he can make you smile like that, I'm sure he is," Amelia replied, hoping Joanna would say more . . . and wondering when she didn't.

Joanna looked at her. "You're interested in us—the People— ain't?"

"How do you mean?"

"Just seems to me you're tenderhearted toward our ways." Joanna smiled.

"I have never experienced such peace . . . anywhere," she admitted.

"Well, stay around if you'd like. There's a canning bee next Tuesday, and if you want a real taste of Amish life, washday is Monday, bright and early."

Amelia laughed. "Speaking of that, Elizabeth wants to borrow one of my outfits, so I'll drive back over there tonight." *I nearly forgot.*

"Oh? Isn't she goin' to wear her old Amish dresses, then?"

Amelia shrugged. She didn't want to speak for Elizabeth. "She might need some time to get reacquainted with Plain ways" was Amelia's best answer.

"I 'spect she will," Joanna replied.

As they turned to head back, Amelia said no more, still curious about Joanna's secret beau.

Chapter 25

In the wee hours that night, Amelia dreamed of an Amish-woman with kind blue eyes and deep laugh lines around her puckered mouth. *"I'm ever so glad you've come, dearie,"* she said, holding out her wrinkled hands. The elderly woman smiled and asked mischievously, *"Will you play your fiddle for me?"*

Sunday morning Amelia awakened before dawn, wondering if Joanna was already up for milking. The room was still very dark, but outside, the robins chirped near the eaves, anticipating the coming sunrise. In the distance, a rooster crowed.

Amelia stretched leisurely. Her body craved more sleep, but she would not give in to it, wanting to be alert to Joanna's rising. She'd overslept and missed milking yesterday—she wasn't about to let that happen again today. Sitting up, she yawned and stretched again, wondering what she could wear to the barn.

Soon she heard Joanna stirring, and Amelia slipped out of

bed to go quietly across the hall. Joanna greeted her warmly but looked surprised to see that she was up. She offered Amelia a man's shirt and a clean pair of trousers. "If ya like, you can put these on under your skirt. It's up to you, but it's all right with us if you just wear the britches, like Dat and the fellas do. The clothes ya brought are much too perty to wear in the barn."

"Thanks." Amelia accepted what she assumed was Joanna's father's or possibly one of her brothers' clothing.

"Oh, and it might be a *gut* idea to borrow a pair of our work boots, too." Joanna eyed Amelia's own boots propped up against the wall in the corner, across the hallway. "Yours are just too nice to get mucked up."

Amelia was grateful. Once again, Joanna had thought of everything.

Downstairs, they worked together to make the lighter of two breakfasts—Joanna explained that the next one would take place following milking. This breakfast was comprised only of some fruit, toast, and cinnamon rolls . . . as well as juice and coffee.

"Did ya sleep well in this ol' house?" Joanna asked while they set the table.

"Very well, thanks. How about you?"

Joanna smiled her answer. "Honestly, I had quite a lot on my mind, though . . . late into the night."

"Perhaps your beau?" Amelia whispered.

Joanna's eyes grew wide, and she shook her head. "Daresn't say."

Amelia carried the butter and jam for the toast to the table, interested to know more about Joanna's boyfriend.

When the table was filled with people, Nate Kurtz bowed his head and silently gave thanks. It didn't take long for everyone to eat the small portions of food—just enough to satisfy any hunger pangs before the larger breakfast later.

After washing her hands, Amelia followed Joanna out to the barn. When the heavy door was slid open, she smelled the aroma of straw and feed, and anticipated plenty of fresh, raw milk from the herd. She recalled what Michael had explained about the diesel-powered milking machines the Amish now used.

Joanna cautioned her to keep her distance. "The cows won't give milk as readily if they sense a stranger near. They're awful tetchy—all thirty-five of 'em."

Amelia recalled her own grandfather's concern on the rare occasion that a visitor was present during milking. Although not a stranger per se, Great Uncle Cleo, her grandfather's oldest brother, sometimes stopped by during the morning milking. Cleo was known to mumble to himself while he carried milk in a bucket to the milk house, where he poured it into the large cooling tank. Amelia remembered her grandmother as being incredibly patient and kind to Cleo, who had served time in World War II and never recovered.

One by one, the cows began to stand up in their stalls, prodded by hunger and their swollen udders, which hung like enormous balloons between their legs.

Joanna pointed out the propane barn lights to Amelia—and the automatic barn cleaner with slats to remove the cow dung. "Is this anything like your grandparents' milking parlor?" she asked.

"Not much." Amelia shook her head. "And my grandparents always had a radio playing during milking. Papa said soft music, especially baroque, soothed the cows and helped them let down their milk."

Joanna chuckled at that. "Maybe you could play a milkin' serenade on your fiddle for the herd . . . jah?"

"You're so funny." She smiled.

Amelia hung back as Joanna crouched in her long dress beside the first cow. She sprayed each udder with a special solution that she said contained one percent iodine, then wiped it down with old newspaper, starting the twice-daily ritual while her married brothers did the same to the next cows.

Joanna's father mixed the feed under one of the silos, glancing over at Amelia with Joanna. He nodded and gave a faint smile when he caught Amelia's eye.

"How can I help?" Amelia asked.

Joanna looked at her father, who was pushing a wheelbarrow of feed their way. "Do ya really want to?"

Amelia nodded. "However you think's best, of course. I don't want to startle the herd."

"Well, it'd be fun for you to give the calves their bottles. How 'bout that?"

"Perfect." Amelia couldn't help smiling. "I'll feel like I'm nine all over again!"

After hanging out in the straw with the calves, Amelia was ready to get cleaned up. First, though, she went with Joanna to the end of the stanchions, where her friend showed her the lever to pull to open the tie rails that kept the cows inside their stalls.

She was glad when Joanna suggested she head in to shower and change clothes. Although Amelia had enjoyed the barn— all the smells and sounds—she was not as enamored with the whole process of milking as she had been as a little girl. That fascination was tucked into the past, along with the days when her grandparents were living.

By the time Joanna arrived inside, Amelia was ready to help start cooking. Evidently it would just be the two of them again, as Joanna's mother had gone over to the Dawdi Haus to help her own mother make a hot breakfast.

Once Joanna had thoroughly scrubbed up, she prepared the batter for blueberry pancakes. Amelia agreed to create the egg mixture for the scrambled eggs, which included onions, ham, and milk.

"Ach, this is such fun," Amelia teased, smiling over at Joanna, who worked across the counter.

"Next thing, you'll be talkin' Deitsch."

"You yuscht never know," Amelia replied.

Joanna giggled. "Do ya make a big breakfast every day back home?"

"Oh, now and then," Amelia replied. "Most of the time, though, I have some fresh fruit and cereal or toast. It's just me, you know."

"You don't stay with your parents?" Her eyes were suddenly wide. "You live . . . on your own?"

"I have for several years."

Joanna frowned a little.

"Why? Do you consider it wrong?"

"Maybe not so much wrong, as . . ." Joanna stared at the large stainless steel bowl in front of her. "It's just that an unmarried woman round here is expected to live with her parents, under her father's roof, ya know."

"The Amish way, no doubt," Amelia said without thinking.

"It's part of God's covering over a single girl," Joanna added, her eyes still fixed on the pancake batter.

So, if you live apart from your parents, God won't look after you? Amelia finished dicing the ham, then dropped it into the eggs. "I hear what you're saying about the way you were raised. But do *you* honestly believe it's wrong for a single woman to live alone?" She was curious, knowing Joanna interacted with Englishers at market and other places.

Joanna didn't answer right away, which seemed to be a clue. "It's not for me to say what you should or shouldn't do, Amelia." She glanced at the ceiling. "I'm not your judge. That position's already taken." She paused. "Hope you're not upset."

Amelia pushed her hair back. This most delightful Sunday morning didn't have to be tarnished by a difference of opinion. There was no way on the planet she and an Amish girl could expect to see eye to eye, even about inconsequential matters. "We come from such different cultures," Amelia said. Yet she appreciated Joanna's willingness to share her opinions. Certainly her views reflected the life stream of Amish tradition.

"No hard feelings, then?" Joanna looked truly worried.

"Not at all."

Relief registered on Joanna's face—even her shoulders relaxed. "Ever so *gut*." Joanna stopped her work and looked at Amelia. "Ya know, this might sound peculiar, but not long ago I prayed, askin' God to send someone along to fill up the emptiness in the upstairs bedroom. Honestly, I did."

"That's amazing—and very nice to know." Amelia meant it with all of her heart.

"I hope you're having a refreshing time here."

"Oh definitely!" Amelia reassured her. "Last night in bed,

hearing the crickets and seeing the moon rise, I actually wished I could stay longer. . . ."

"Well, why not?" Joanna urged.

"Thanks . . . you've been such a wonderful hostess. But I really do need to drive back to Columbus tomorrow."

"Well, I certainly mean it."

Conscious of the sincerity in Joanna's clear eyes, Amelia wondered if her new friend was so readily accepting of other Englishers . . . their foreign ways aside. Was it just Joanna's friendly nature . . . or had Joanna been influenced by Michael?

Chapter 26

Amelia followed Joanna's lead and helped carry a platter of scrambled eggs with crisp bacon along the side, while Joanna brought over the equally large plate of stacked pancakes. Joanna's brothers had returned to their own families for the morning, so it was only Amelia, Joanna, and her parents at the table for the more substantial second breakfast of the day.

After Nate offered the silent prayer, Joanna's mother brought up the neighboring church district, saying they were having their Preaching service today. "The Amish youth from that district will be hosting a barn Singing at dusk," Rhoda added.

Amelia had heard of such gatherings but had never had the opportunity to listen in on the unison voices.

But her first priority was to see Ella Mae Zook again. Something tugged at her heart when she thought about visiting the charming woman, and it was all Amelia could do *not* to tell Joanna what she had planned while they worked to clean up the kitchen.

The minute I'm free, I'll head over to Ella Mae's with my fiddle!

··· ➤ ⋖ ···

Lillianne happily gave her granddaughter the undivided attention she seemed to crave both before and after breakfast. Elizabeth told how very difficult her schoolwork had been and later mentioned her waitressing work and two other girls who shared the rent with her. It was as if the poor thing hadn't had anyone to talk to all these months.

Elizabeth followed Lillianne around like a shadow, sitting smack-dab next to her during morning prayers and Bible reading. Lillianne hoped she would say something about wanting to visit her parents. Truth was, Lillianne worried that if Paul or Michael didn't take her over there soon, Elizabeth's apparent hesitation might cause even more strife in the family. *Jah, for sure and for certain.*

Lillianne's heart also ached for her husband as she observed how hard it was for Paul to get around, although he did not grumble. Each step had to be excruciating, and he'd nearly fallen in the night when he'd gotten up to use the bathroom. She just did not understand such stubbornness or resistance to seeing a doctor. He insisted he was fine with the makeshift crutch he'd created out of wood, with several old towels wrapped at the top for cushioning.

As for having her granddaughter back, Lillianne was mighty thankful after months of beseeching God for protection . . . and divine mercy. But despite her relief, she still could not get over how very strange her granddaughter looked, attired as she was in Amelia's fancy getup. Lillianne feared Lizzie might not stick around for long.

Around midmorning, Michael left the house by way of the back door, heading off to parts unknown. If Lillianne wasn't mistaken—seeing the glint in his eyes—their son was making his way even now over to Nate Kurtz's place. *Where Amelia is staying.*

And for how long? Lillianne mused.

Elizabeth, too, had asked about the slender English girl even before breakfast, while the coffee was brewing. Sure seemed like Amelia's name was buzzing round Hickory Hollow. And since she was ever so grateful Elizabeth was safely home . . . well, Lillianne couldn't fault anyone for that, now, could she?

Michael set off for the Kurtz farm, hoping to visit with Amelia, this being an off-Sunday from church. He didn't even think twice how it might look, his going to see the fiddler. Elizabeth had also hinted, after Amelia stopped by last evening with an outfit for her to wear, that she'd like to see her again. *"Wouldn't you rather spend time with your parents?"* he'd asked her. Incredibly, Elizabeth simply stared back at him. What would he do if she pleaded with him to take her back to Harrisburg?

Best to just let things be, he thought, quickening his pace on Hickory Lane.

When he arrived, Nate was sitting in the porch swing out front. Michael nodded and called, *"Gut* Lord's Day to ya, Nate," and was greeted with a mere nod.

Michael could tell by the driving horse parked outside that Joanna's married sister Salina and her husband and three children were visiting. He didn't have to ask if Amelia was around, since he saw her car parked off to the side of the driveway. And just about the time he was getting cold feet for being there, Rhoda

Kurtz wandered out to the backyard and announced, "Amelia's gone to play some music for Ella Mae."

"Really, now?" he said, quite bemused.

"Jah, and on the Lord's Day, too. Don't that beat all?" Rhoda replied, pulling a slightly disagreeable face.

Amelia's shaking things up, Michael thought, thanking Rhoda. He walked across the north meadow, heading away from the treed area where he'd heard Amelia play Friday afternoon. As he strolled through Nate's cornfield, he thanked God for help in bringing his confused niece this far. He prayed further, asking for divine guidance.

Pausing, he thought he heard the wind whistling through the cornstalks. But then, listening again, he realized the sound was a melody—the strains of a gospel song he'd heard as a boy. But it was not the slow, faltering rendition of "This Little Light of Mine" like he'd first heard it sung. No, this was a real foot-stomper.

Michael approached Ella Mae's and saw Amelia playing her fiddle there on the back porch. The Wise Woman sat in the old rocking chair, her eyes closed, head back, enjoying herself like a cat napping in a sunbeam.

Once again, Michael was moved by Amelia's playing. *Ella Mae's not heeding the bishop's wishes*, he thought, not too surprised. After all, the woman had lived life in recent years her way, although *"under the covering of God,"* as she liked to say. It was as if the church ordinance and what Bishop John Beiler felt strongly about mattered less to her than what the Lord God impressed upon her heart. Michael understood where she was coming from, but he found it interesting that the elderly woman got by with such things. Were the brethren lenient because she wasn't long for this world?

Michael chuckled, seeing Ella Mae's head bob a little, then pop up, eyes bright as the music wound down to the final note. Amelia ended with a big flourish, raising her bow clear over her head, and Ella Mae clapped her hands, all smiles.

Next thing, the elderly woman was herding Amelia inside the small house, which meant Michael should find something better to do than lurk there in the trees. Not knowing how long they'd be, he headed back toward the main road, surprised at how disappointed he was at not having the chance to talk to Amelia again—feeling left out, somehow.

Amelia stepped across the threshold into Ella Mae's small, sun-drenched kitchen. The delightful woman promptly went to her gas-powered refrigerator and poured iced peppermint tea for both of them, then placed the cold tumblers on her table. Amelia looked about her, taking in the old coal stove in the cozy sitting area just off the kitchen, and the modern-looking ceiling fan above. The Kurtzes had one like it, and Joanna had explained it was powered by see-through tubes that carried air from an air compressor. A red, blue, and yellow afghan was folded over one arm of the overstuffed chair in the corner, and there was a large Bible in the nearby magazine rack.

Ella Mae placed a clear glass plate of chocolate-covered strawberries on the table. "Alas, one of my weaknesses," Ella Mae whispered, her lips parting in a gentle smile. "As far as food goes, that is." Her eyes sparkled as she pulled out a chair and slowly lowered herself to a sitting position, across from Amelia.

Ella Mae turned to point out her peach and pear trees through the window, as well as the rows of vegetables in a long strip of a garden in the sunniest part of the backyard. "My daughter

Mattie, who lives next door with her husband, does most of the weeding and hoeing."

"My grandma took her knee pad nearly everywhere she went," said Amelia. "She often joked that she liked to edit things, particularly her gardens."

"Oh, I know that feeling. The least little weed and it's plucked right out!" Ella Mae smiled again as she looked at Amelia over her glasses, which had slipped down halfway to the end of her petite nose. "The way the Lord God prunes us at times."

Amelia's grandmother had also talked about spiritual pruning. *"Does your life magnify or minimize Christ?"* Her grandmother had asked it so often Amelia sometimes wondered if that was her favorite question.

"Weeds are easy to grow," Ella Mae said, holding a chocolate strawberry and looking at it fondly. "But, ah, the fruit . . . now, that's the best part, ain't?"

"My grandmother used to say that it takes good seed to grow good fruit."

"'Such as the tree, so is the fruit.'" Ella Mae nodded, the strings from her prayer cap draped down over her slight shoulders. "And *my* grandmamma used to say, ever so long ago: 'Now, Ella Mae, is today the day you will repent of the sins you've committed against the Lord?' I would just look at her, frown, and duck my head. Of course, she was mighty *schmaert*, knowin' I was battling God's call to holy baptism an' all."

"Other than my parents, no one I know talks like this anymore," Amelia said between sips of the delicious tea.

"Might be that it's not an easy truth for folks to get comfortable with. But weeds have a way of coming up on their own. If allowed to grow, they'll choke out the healthy *gut* growth . . . and, well, there goes any hope of fruit."

"I think you and my grammy would've liked each other."

"What a nice thing to say, Amelia. I daresay there's quite a lot of your grandmother in you."

Ella Mae was as tender a person as she'd ever met. "I think I'm going to miss being around here . . . visiting with you," Amelia said, bowing her head. "And yet we've just met."

"So you're thinkin' of leaving already?"

"I'd love to stay longer, believe me, but everything's on the line back home. . . . I have some big decisions ahead of me."

Ella Mae eyed her thoughtfully, working her jaw. "Aw, Amelia, you seem stressed about whatever's goin' through your mind just now."

"You don't know the half."

Ella Mae reached across the table, her hands open. "Well, we've got today yet, don't we?" She looked out the window, then turned back to Amelia, smiling. "Bishop John admonishes us to visit each other on Sundays when there's no Preachin' services. Sounds to me like we're doin' his bidding." She glanced heavenward with a sigh. "And the dear Lord's, too."

No matter what Ella Mae said, her words were like honey— appealing and sweet. "I believe you're right," Amelia responded before settling back in the chair and drinking some more of her tea.

"What's a-troublin' you?" Ella Mae's eyes looked deep into her.

Amelia hesitated, though she longed to release the floodgates and tell Ella Mae everything she kept bottled up inside.

"Or we can just sit here and breathe the fresh air . . . whatever suits ya." Ella Mae leaned toward the open window, her Kapp strings rippling in the breeze. Beneath the white organdy of the head covering, Amelia could see the tight, low bun at the back of her head.

Amelia hoped she wasn't about to go too far out on a limb. "Have you ever thought you had absolutely no choice—or say—in a particular matter?"

Ella Mae's little eyes widened . . . such piercing, knowing eyes. "Well now, I wouldn't be human if I hadn't felt that way at one time or 'nother."

Amelia considered that.

"Why do *you* feel trapped?" Ella Mae asked softly.

"When it comes to sharing my heart with my father, I always clam up—I spare him my feelings and opinions because he's not well."

Ella Mae blinked her eyes solicitously, not saying anything.

"It's really frustrating, because I have no trouble helping my friends see their way out of situations similar to my own." Amelia paused and thought of her counsel to Michael. "But when it comes to my own issues, do you think I can follow any of that same advice myself?" Her words fell to a whisper. "I really want to change the course of my life, Ella Mae . . . at least my immediate future."

Ella Mae folded her hands. "And just what would that take, Amelia?"

She forged ahead. "What I'd really like to do could actually turn out to be the best thing—or the worst, depending on whose perspective we're talking about." Her stomach churned as she thought of her parents and of Stoney . . . and last, of Byron. Their order of importance.

"What we care most about in life determines what we end up doin', ain't so?" asked Ella Mae.

"But where does nerve come in? That's my problem—I've lost any gumption."

"The gumption, my dear, comes when you believe in your decision so much you simply have to follow your heart, come what may." Ella Mae leaned forward on the table, her eyes fixed on Amelia. "And like I said when we talked Friday . . . if ya believe God's nudging you in a certain direction, you best follow that, no ifs, ands, or buts."

"Even though I want to respect my father's wishes?"

This brought a long pause. "Well now, honoring our parents is expected, too."

"Which puts me right back where I began." Amelia forced a smile, laughing under her breath. "My thoughts travel in complete circles, and it's making me dizzy."

"I see what ya mean—'tis a knotty problem." Ella Mae turned in her chair and pointed at the wall hanging on the other side of the room, a cross-stitched Zook family tree. "See the name at the very top there? That's my husband's great-grandfather, Jesse Zook. He passed down a mighty powerful proverb—wholeheartedly believed its meaning." She stopped to catch her breath. "More than two hundred of his offspring all know the saying to this day."

Amelia was curious about which favorite adage could ring true for an entire family for so long.

"'Courage is fear on its knees,'" quoted Ella Mae, looking again at Amelia. "And that, my dear, might just be the answer to the pickle you're in."

The truth of the saying resonated so strongly, her eyes welled up. "I'll remember this always," Amelia managed to say. "Thank you, Ella Mae."

Later, when she had taken her leave of the Wise Woman, Amelia wondered if God would indeed pave the way for her to talk openly with her father about her future, whatever she might decide. *Will He give me the courage, if I ask?*

Chapter 27

Amelia knew she should pack up her few things and bid farewell to Joanna and her parents . . . and to Michael. But following her morning visit to Ella Mae, she was once again pleasantly pulled into Joanna's engaging company when she returned to find Joanna sitting in the pretty white gazebo in the side yard. She wore a beige scarf tied beneath her chin and was waving to Amelia, calling, "Come and join me, won't ya?"

Settling into the little haven, the sound of birds all around, Amelia listened as Joanna told a couple of stories, one quaint and comical, the other more riveting. When Amelia asked if she'd written them down, Joanna opened a notebook and, very shyly, let her read one.

My own mother has never let me read her writings, thought Amelia. The realization struck her as she read, immediately captivated by Joanna's compelling story.

"You write very convincingly about love," Amelia complimented her when she'd finished. The story had made her feel almost wistful and even a bit envious of the depth of emotion and connection the characters so naturally displayed. "Does it come from firsthand experience?"

Joanna's cheeks turned rosy as she reached for the notebook. "Not everything in a story comes from a writer's life, ya know." She gave Amelia a look. "And anyway, haven't ya ever been in love yourself? You have a beau of your own, right?"

Amelia gave a nod. "I do . . . although both of us are so busy with our careers, we don't see each other that often. But we have talked about a future together. He's a musician, too," she added.

Joanna eyed her curiously. "If ya don't mind me sayin' so, you don't seem very happy 'bout that."

"Guess you're right," Amelia admitted after a moment's pause. "It's complicated—I'm not sure I really understand why myself. Maybe it's just that I'm feeling a lot of career pressure from him right now. It seems to be coming from every corner."

Joanna's fingers traced the edges of her notebook. "So do ya love him?"

"Maybe. I mean, I thought so, but lately I've been less certain." She gave a nervous laugh. "Yet really, who would want to marry someone they didn't love?"

"Well, I know plenty who marry 'cause it's the right thing— the young couple work well together, or the parents are pleased about the union."

"What about love—where's that in the equation?"

"If it's not present at the start, it might just come in due time—or so the womenfolk sometimes say."

Amelia shifted on the white wooden bench. She had a hard time imagining this. "But . . . what if love doesn't show up? What then?" She thought of Byron again and struggled to catch her breath.

"We can trust God to lead us in all things, including the choice of a mate. He is sovereign and does all things well." Joanna's eyes glistened.

Amelia's own parents had often said as much. As for herself, though, she had never really consulted God where Byron was concerned. She sat there, her fiddle case lying on the latticed floor, and let Joanna's words sink in slowly—along with the truth of what they could mean for herself . . . and for Byron.

When it came time for the noon meal, Amelia politely asked if she could pack a small sack lunch. She needed to practice longer today than yesterday. Rhoda quickly volunteered to make a tuna salad sandwich and sent an apple and a thermos of lemonade to go along with it. Grateful for their thoughtful hospitality—and flexibility, too—Amelia drove down Hickory Lane with her lunch and her father's fiddle.

Today she hoped to find a spot farther removed from Joanna and her family to give them a break. A shady clump of trees near what looked like an empty corncrib and an Amish phone shanty seemed the ideal spot. So she pulled onto the wide shoulder and removed her fiddle from its case, tuned up, and began to practice, starting with the first major scale, and then the corresponding relative minor.

She played through her warm-ups, then moved on to a concerto. And as she played, she wept. Was Ella Mae's beautiful, heartfelt advice meant for her? She *had* swerved off the path from her calling, listening instead to the direction of others. Did her life really have a purpose beyond that, and could it include marriage and even children someday?

Hours later, when she had worked up a sweat, thanks to the

high temperature and humidity, Amelia returned to the Kurtz farm and showered for the second time. She then gathered up her clothes, intending to wash them by hand. Joanna, however, quickly suggested she wait until washday tomorrow.

Amelia didn't want to cause a fuss on the Lord's Day, but she wanted to have something clean to wear for her trip home in the morning. Quietly, she gathered her few items of laundry and headed to her car, fiddle in hand in case she found another opportunity to practice while away. She felt caught up in a maze of do's and don'ts. *The riddles of the Amish life*, she thought, a little frustrated. But at the same time, she couldn't deny being incredibly intrigued by their life-style.

Lillianne sat on the back porch, longing for some relief from the oppressive afternoon heat while reading seven chapters from first the old German Biewel and then the same number of chapters in the King James Bible. Toward the end of her reading, she began to doze off. Oh, what she wouldn't give for a nice long nap in her own bed, but it was much too hot upstairs.

She looked out at the grazing land to the east and noticed the cows clustered under a grove of trees. The barnyard was still, as well. She listened for Paul inside but didn't hear his snoring—her poor husband had been extra tired since the accident. An injury like that took a lot out of a body. Of course, he might very well be out on the front porch reading the Bible, too.

Earlier, she'd heard Michael asking permission to take the family carriage. Paul had been in the kitchen then and said it was all right, as long as Michael was back before suppertime.

And now here was Michael, returning to pick up Elizabeth, who still looked surprisingly fancy in Amelia's skirt and blouse. Michael smiled gaily and waved at her from the buggy, with Elizabeth now sitting to his left. Surely they were heading to Elizabeth's parents'.

"Oh," Lillianne said aloud, suddenly grasping the reason for her son's cheerfulness. Then and there, she was mighty sure he'd spent time with Amelia! *That's what!*

··· ➤ ◄ ···

"Do ya think someone who's sinned many times can ever find forgiveness?" Elizabeth asked as Michael hurried the horse along Hickory Lane.

"From God or the People?" Michael replied.

"Well, both."

Holding the reins, Michael considered his niece's state. There she was, sitting in an Amish buggy and wearing the prettiest English outfit, going visiting with someone who was every bit as on the fence about the Amish church. "I guess it depends if that person's truly remorseful and ready to quit sinning." He glanced at her, assuming she was talking about herself and trying not to let on. "Remember, God sees the heart. He knows when a person is genuinely sorry and ready to walk the straight and narrow."

Elizabeth hung her head.

"The Good Book says that if God calls and we answer, we belong to Him—we're His children from then on. Sure, we may sin from time to time, but if we love Him, we no longer care 'bout going our own way." He paused. "We no longer continue in our sin."

Elizabeth seemed to mull that over, then gave him a sidelong glance. "Do you think it's a sin not to join church, uncle?"

"The Bible doesn't address becoming a member of a physical church. It does talk about the fellowship of believers, though—it's actually a command not to forsake gathering with other Christians. I wouldn't think of saying anything against that."

"So are *you* goin' to join church this fall?" asked Elizabeth.

The questions had started out seemingly innocent enough, but now she'd put him in a corner.

"You're not answering," she pressed him.

"I can't." Michael wasn't ready to discuss this now, as they approached the Kurtz farm on the way to Elizabeth's parents' house. Not when Amelia's car was missing from Nate's driveway! In fact, Elizabeth's words were getting lost somewhere between hearing and comprehension as he worried that Amelia Devries might have quietly exited Hickory Hollow when he wasn't looking.

Would she do that?

Chapter 28

Not wanting to ruffle more feathers, Amelia had slipped on her last clean outfit before excusing herself from the house in search of a laundromat. She drove south to Route 30, where there were plenty of fast-food options, as well. A grilled chicken sandwich sounded good, so she ordered that and ate it once her small load of laundry was in the wash cycle. *Joanna must think I'm a heathen, doing my wash on Sunday.*

Amelia wondered how Elizabeth was doing today, hoping no one at the Hostetlers'—including Michael himself—was rankled over the fancy outfit. It was hard to think of Elizabeth returning for very long to Hickory Hollow . . . not after living in the fast-paced modern world. *Unless she wants to slow down after experiencing the other side of the fence.*

Once Amelia's clothes were dried and folded, she drove contentedly around the back roads south of Strasburg, exploring Amish farmland. She enjoyed the drive along White Oak Road, where barefoot Amish children played in the yards, some jumping on a trampoline. There were teenagers—mostly courting-age girls—talking and laughing softly, strolling in groups of threes along the road. Some held hands, like Amelia had seen Friday while she walked with Michael.

Eventually she circled over to the periphery of Gap, again on the back roads. It was then that she remembered there was to be a barn Singing in a neighboring church district that evening. She drove back northwest toward Bird-in-Hand again, wondering if she could possibly locate the youth gathering. She was definitely interested in witnessing this Amish social event, even if from afar.

As a girl, she had seen open buggies heading to one barn or another on certain Sunday evenings, usually at dusk. Even back then, the idea of leaving the house at twilight to meet the boy you loved or to visit with other young people of like faith was appealing to her.

Her mind returned again to her conversation with Joanna earlier that day about faith and its role in courtship. And as she drove, Amelia rehearsed the facts of her relationship with Byron, knowing what she must do. *First thing, when I get home . . .*

Joseph and Lena Hostetler were clearly shocked when they saw their daughter's bruised and bandaged face, and broken arm . . . as Michael and Elizabeth walked into their kitchen. Michael knew his brother well enough to know that Joseph's expression was one of great concern. He must be wondering what his only daughter had gotten herself into by being so rebellious. Her worldly garb didn't help things, either, and Joseph, always outspoken, even went so far as to point this out.

Poor Elizabeth tried to explain that she had been wearing

English clothes all during the months she was living in Harrisburg. "So this is really nothin' new for me," she argued.

"But you're home now." Joseph cast a frown at his wife.

Lena intervened. "Go ahead and get settled back in your room, dear."

"Just so ya know, Mamma, I'm not stayin' for long. I'm only here for a short visit." Elizabeth looked warily at Michael.

"Well, say!" hissed Joseph, glowering at his daughter. "So you're goin' back to the world, then?"

Elizabeth bowed her head and then headed for the back door.

Michael went mum, feeling mighty awkward, too. Little good it would do to speak up in Lizzie's defense. *And with this sort of welcome, she'll never want to stay.*

It took a good half hour or longer to track down the setting of the Amish Singing—on Harvest Drive, southwest of Hickory Hollow. Amelia was sure it was the correct spot when she saw the black open buggies parked in rows along the side yard. They were all shined up and waiting for the couples to settle in for a nice long ride. How fun would it be to be an Amish girl on a night like this, riding in a convertible, of sorts, with your boyfriend.

Amelia smiled to herself as she parked off the road and sat in her car with the windows down to listen, far enough away so as not to draw attention. Or so she hoped.

The Amish teenagers milled around outside the barn, dressed as though attending church. The girls wore green, royal blue, or plum-colored dresses with full aprons, and the young men wore black trousers and white shirts with beige suspenders and straw hats. Because they were all around the same age, they looked like multiples of each other . . . triplets and quadruplets.

Amelia was actually glad she had no camera and couldn't be tempted to take pictures of the memorable scene . . . like something out of a movie.

At a signal unheard by Amelia, all the youth headed for the barn. Within minutes, she heard unison singing—the lower voices mingling with the clear sopranos. Amelia listened, wondering if she might recognize any of the songs.

Her mind wandered back to all the times she'd sat out on the front porch with her grandparents, hearing them recount their own childhood, so long ago, and the days when Papa was courting Grammy, taking her to tent revival meetings or out for ice cream at the old-timey drive-in where the root-beer floats were enormous no matter what size you ordered. Grammy's eyes would light with tenderness as she spoke about the rush of excitement she'd felt when Papa first reached for her hand.

Amelia had never experienced such joy and longing with Byron or any of the young men she'd known in her circle of "serious music" friends and dates. Her own mother, being a private person, had never talked much about her dating years. Yet Amelia knew her mother truly loved her father—she'd been such a support to him since his diagnosis.

"Love bends with time," Mom had once said, though Amelia had not understood then.

Darkness began to settle, and she thought she saw a young doe standing on this side of the two-level barn. She slapped her neck, killing a mosquito, and wondered how many others she'd missed. The heat of the day faded as the songs rang out of the barn on the slight breeze.

And then she heard it, the first song she recognized: "Work, for the Night Is Coming." Listening, she felt like joining in with her fiddle. What would it hurt?

Amelia got out on the driver's side and removed the violin from its case in the backseat. Then she leaned against the car, playing a descant . . . enjoying herself as the moon appeared over the horizon. All around her, the sweet sounds of night joined in with the strains of the fiddle.

She lost herself in the music as the Amish young people sang through the verses. Playing louder now, Amelia closed her eyes as she moved back and forth, playing a harmony to each verse the teenagers sang in the barn.

The next song, "In the Sweet By and By," brought tears to her eyes as she played along, thinking of all the years she had been blessed to know and love her darling Papa and Grammy. And she played for Byron, too, although he could not hear it—just as he'd never heard her heart. A melodious farewell to a plan that would never be realized.

When she opened her eyes at last, she was startled to see three young Amishmen standing near. When had they crept up? She stuttered and offered an apology for intruding.

"Oh no—you play so *gut*, we just wanted to hear ya better," one said.

"Jah," agreed another. "Why don't you come join us at the Singing? Kumme . . . *schpiele*."

Surprised, Amelia finally acquiesced, following them into the barn. She felt a little reluctant as she stood on the sidelines, glad there was no center stage here.

Someone blew into a pitch pipe, and the large group sitting at the tables began to sing "Shall We Gather at the River." Then the same boys who'd wandered out to her car nodded for her to join in playing where she stood.

The rest of the evening was an absolute joy, with each gospel song sung faster and with more enthusiasm—even fervency. And at the end of each song the delightful teenagers clapped, apparently for her, although Amelia felt more like one of them than a soloist.

Soon, she was adding licks and runs at the end of phrases and pauses, cutting loose. Her lead-ins were as upbeat as when she fiddled with the Bittersweet Band. Oh, she felt as if she could play like this all night, bringing happiness to the fun-loving, smiling Amish young people around her.

Abruptly, the singing ceased. A stout Amishman in his forties appeared at the barn door, his arms at his side. *"Des Gesang es fix!"* Then, looking at Amelia, he said in English, "The Singing is finished . . . 'tis best you be goin' on your way."

Suddenly feeling disoriented, Amelia sheepishly looked at the group of singers that had encouraged her and wished she might acknowledge them with more than a mere glance. She opened her mouth to speak but felt the barrier of clashing culture. The shared music that had been their bond for those few songs was at an end.

She turned and saw that the man who'd called a halt to her mischief making, as he undoubtedly viewed her fiddle playing, had vacated the barn. With a final fond look back at the now silent young people, focused once more on one another, Amelia turned slowly and left the barn.

Chapter 29

Michael at last had a chance to sit down and tell his mother what had transpired over at Joseph's that evening. He knew his brother and sister-in-law were quite justified in thinking he was responsible for Elizabeth's waywardness, at least initially. Yet, try as he might to right the situation now, there was little Michael could do without Elizabeth's help.

And if all that wasn't enough, Bishop John's wife, Mary Stoltzfus Beiler, dropped in to see Michael's mother around eight-thirty that night, saying one of the preachers down yonder had caught a young Englischer playing a fiddle at a barn Singing, turning it into a hoedown. "Can ya just imagine?" Mary said.

Michael clenched his jaw, hoping it wasn't Amelia. But who else played the fiddle round here?

The more Mary went on about it, the more he feared Amelia was about to be labeled *der Zwieschpalt*—the troublemaker—unbeknownst to her.

Michael waited till the bishop's wife left before hitching up the horse and carriage yet again, hurrying down to see if Amelia's car was parked at Joanna's or not.

As he steered the horse into the driveway, he saw Amelia getting out of her car, fiddle case in hand. "Amelia," he called. "It's Michael." He leaped out of the buggy and hurried to catch up with her.

"I thought you might be with Elizabeth." She seemed surprised to see him.

"I was . . . took her to see her parents a bit ago." He didn't say he'd hoped to see Amelia, too.

She looked down at her fiddle case. "I'm afraid I may have caused a big problem."

"I heard about the fiddling."

She stared at him, aghast. "You *heard.* Already?"

Michael laughed. "It's nothing, Amelia. It's just—"

"I've embarrassed you. I'm so sorry."

He frowned. "Embarrass me? I'm not even baptized. If you think they're upset with you, how do you think they feel about me?"

She looked at him for a moment. "Yeah, I see what you mean, but still . . ."

"Hey, have you ever wanted to know what it's like to ride in an Amish buggy?" He chuckled with nerves. "Why don't ya come riding with me?"

"I probably shouldn't, Michael." She looked back at his horse and enclosed carriage. "I was asked to leave by one of the preachers."

"Who said that?"

"I was shown the door . . . by one of the ministers, I'm sure of it."

"Well, it's not like you were going to stay forever, Amelia. That preacher will get over it. And the ministerial brethren here in Hickory Hollow can't be any more frustrated with me than they already are."

Then he motioned toward the buggy, and she followed him, still carrying her fiddle case.

He helped her up, waiting till she was seated before going around to the driver's side on the right. She propped up the case against the dashboard and was surprisingly quiet while he turned the horse back onto the road.

Soon, they were heading east on Hickory Lane, in the direction of a very large moon. And at least a trillion stars dotted the dark sky. Michael couldn't have planned a more ideal evening, a perfect night for a spin in the carriage with your sweetheart-girl. Except that Amelia was an Englischer and already seeing someone else.

Michael pushed away the thought. He was very aware of Amelia's presence . . . her cologne, lightly sweet, akin to the scent of honeysuckle and lilac blended. It took some doing to keep his eyes on the road and his hands on the reins.

"I might as well tell you more about what happened tonight," she said at last, breaking the stillness. "I tried to locate the barn Singing, just to listen in . . . and I ended up playing my fiddle out by my car. I was just so caught up in the music!" She shook her head as if with regret. "Anyway, one thing led to another and, at the urging of several Amish guys, I went inside the barn to play along with their songs. They asked me to—I never would have been so bold otherwise."

"You don't have to convince me," he said, looking at her again. "I believe you, Amelia."

He listened to her describe her joy at entering into the young people's music, the interplay between their voices and her own fiddling. He wished he might've heard it for himself.

But then, just as quickly, the joy fell out of her voice. "And then a man appeared at the barn door, out of nowhere, and I heard whispers from the young people—'oh, no, it's the preacher.' He brought a quick end to things." She paused and touched the fiddle case. "It's definitely time I left for home."

"When?"

"Early tomorrow."

He knew it wouldn't be sensible to let on how sorry he was to hear it. "Well, I hope you've had a *gut* time, other than this evening." He didn't want to belabor Amelia's encounter with the minister, though the man was right to stop the fiddling—he had rules to uphold. Even so, Michael could easily imagine the unexpected enjoyment Amelia's playing had given the young people, if only for a short time.

"It's been terrific visiting here," Amelia said. "Thanks for introducing me to your friends and family, as well."

"Elizabeth really wanted to see ya today," he let her know. *If only time might slow down!*

"Please, will you tell her I wish her all the best?"

He nodded, managing a smile. "Sure."

The awkward silence grew long as they rode under the shelter of night. Michael kept thinking he should make these final moments count for something, but what else could he say that he hadn't already? He recalled their idyllic time together in the cabin, the way they'd effortlessly connected despite their very different backgrounds. Had it meant as much to her as it had to him?

"We're heading in the wrong direction, aren't we?" she said at last.

He looked at her now. "You're right, of course." He turned his attention to the road again. "I guess I'd hoped . . ."

"What, Michael?" Her voice sounded eager, but perhaps that was just wishful thinking on his part.

Should he say what was on his mind? Would it put her in an uncomfortable spot? She was leaving tomorrow, for pity's sake! Looking her way again, Michael noticed her hands, so lovely and smooth. "Amelia," he said softly. *She's everything I care about in a girl.* But he didn't dare say that. Instead, he settled on, "I guess I was hoping you'd stay longer."

She was quiet.

"I know you have a music schedule to keep, and there's really no place to practice here."

She touched his arm briefly. "Michael, I would love to stay longer, but that's impossible. Besides, you're right . . . I need to be more focused on my music."

It was all he could do not to reach for her hand. "I'll turn around just up the road, if you're ready to head back."

"I am, thanks." There was a catch in her voice.

There was no point in dragging this good-bye out for either of them, Michael knew. Truth was, Amelia had come to visit Amish country, and now she wanted to return to her English world.

Where she belongs, he thought miserably.

Chapter 30

As they walked up the moonlit driveway, Amelia thanked Michael for inviting her to Hickory Hollow. "And for the buggy ride, too," she said. "It was like something straight out of the history books. Do you take the horse and carriage out much?"

"It's been months, really. I prefer goin' faster than ten miles an hour."

She laughed. "Well, if you did this for me tonight, I enjoyed it." She smiled at him. "It was very thoughtful of you."

He admitted to also having driven the carriage to Elizabeth's parents' earlier today. "But you're welcome . . . anytime."

She wondered if he'd mentioned his niece so she wouldn't think he was singling her out. And it crossed her mind to ask how the visit with his brother and family had gone, but it really wasn't her business. Helping rescue Elizabeth was all she could do. Now it was up to Elizabeth to decide which life she favored. She'd lived on the outside long enough to make that choice for herself.

"Meetin' you has been mighty nice, Amelia," Michael said when they stopped halfway up the driveway, just behind her car.

"I've enjoyed getting to know you, too . . . and your family and friends." She smiled, recalling the many things she'd learned in just a short time. And the secrets she had promised to keep. "I'm glad you talked me into making this little detour."

"Well, you got me thinking about things I'd swept under the rug," he said. "And for that I'm truly thankful." His eyes continued to rest on her as if he wanted to say more, and Amelia had the distinct impression Michael was about to say something that suggested he had the beginnings of feelings for her. But for some reason he pulled back. She hadn't forgotten how he'd seemed to nearly reach for her hand while riding in the buggy. For a moment there, she hoped he might.

"I wish I could have stuck to my original plan . . . to go English." He stopped, still looking intently at her. "But with everything that's happened lately, that just isn't possible . . . at least right now."

She didn't want him to feel he had to say this for her benefit, yet she sensed he wished he could spend more time with her . . . and even regretted that he couldn't.

Michael glanced up at the house, then quickly at her. "Ach, it'd be a wonder if we aren't bein' observed."

"Yes, we should probably call it a night." She turned reluctantly, then waved to him, her fiddle case in hand. "Thanks again . . . or should I say 'Denki'?"

"I hope things work out for you, Amelia—whatever you decide about your career."

They moved slowly toward the house, Amelia willing her feet to keep going forward. "I appreciate that," she said over her shoulder. "And I hope the best for you, too."

"Good-bye, Amelia. *Da Herr sei mit du*—God be with you."

She wanted to say it back. Something . . . anything. But she didn't trust herself. And, besides, what Michael had said about their possibly being watched was unnerving.

She went around the side of the house to the back porch. Pausing there, she waited until Michael's footsteps faded and the horse and carriage moved up the road. The *clip-clop-clip* of the horse's hooves had already become such a welcome and familiar sound. One she would miss.

Inside, Amelia stood near the window as a wave of immense sadness washed over her. *Just like that . . . he's gone*, she thought suddenly. Yet there was nothing she could do to alter things. She'd encountered someone interesting but from a completely different culture. *It's been a lovely moment in time . . . nothing more*, she told herself.

Sighing, she crept through the gas-lit kitchen to the staircase.

Joanna stood at the top of the stairs, a small lantern held high. "I left the gas lamp burnin' for ya."

"Thanks for lighting the way," she said, not wanting to linger in the hallway near Joanna's parents' room.

"Goodness, are you all right?" asked Joanna, studying her. "You look a bit flushed."

"Must be your lantern. I feel fine."

" 'Tis *gut*, then."

She followed Joanna to her room, where the blue notebook lay open on the bed. Several pillows were bunched together at the head. "I hope I didn't interrupt your writing."

"I wanted to wait up for you. Besides, it's not *that* late."

Amelia sat on the bed, eyeing the notebook. "What's this story about?"

"A love story," Joanna said, her eyes sparkling. Then before

Amelia could respond to that, she quickly said, "Michael's awful nice, ain't?"

Amelia smiled, her eyes starting to water. *What's wrong with me?* "Very nice." She blinked hard. "I must be tired."

Joanna watched her closely. "He's a wonderful friend to many, which is where all *gut* relationships begin, Mamma says."

"Well, we're as different as a fiddle tune and the Brahms concerto." She wanted to immediately dispel any romantic notions.

"Oh, of course. I didn't mean to say—" Joanna gave her an almost teasing look. "But people are people, no matter what."

Amelia laughed. "What do you mean by that?"

"I was just thinkin'." Joanna looked away. "Oh, maybe I shouldn't say."

"Michael and I are friends . . . it's okay."

Nodding slowly, Joanna asked, "What if he wasn't Amish—or if you weren't English? What might happen then?"

Amelia laughed softly. "That's purely hypothetical. And I've only known him for, what, a few days?"

Joanna smiled sweetly. "You can know a lot after only a couple hours ridin' in a buggy."

So she was watching!

Amelia welcomed the evening air coming through the open window from where she sat. She was surprised that Joanna would be so direct. Then again, hadn't Amelia walked in with a red face that almost *demanded* a gentle interrogation? "I know you'll never breathe a word of this, so I'll just say that I found Michael to be thoughtful, kind, and fun-loving. Things you already know." She paused, measuring her words. "He's also very insightful and honest."

Joanna's mischievous twinkle returned. "So I take it you're not attracted to him in the least?"

"I didn't say that." Amelia caught herself, noting the speed of her reply. Her cheeks felt warm again, and Joanna was looking at her with that playful expression.

So what *was* she saying? Amelia felt foolish talking about something that could never be. "I'm not putting you off, Joanna."

"All right, then . . . I'll assume that you must be befuddled."

Joanna could be just plain disarming. "Sure, let's go with that. Actually, *ferhoodled* might be even better," Amelia said.

They shared a good laugh, and Amelia hoped Joanna would broach a new topic. Talking about Michael made her head hurt.

"I hope I don't embarrass you further, but I'm goin' to miss talking to you when you go," Joanna said, sighing softly. "Would ya mind too awful much exchanging addresses?"

Amelia was delighted. "You don't have email, do you?"

"No, I prefer writing by hand." Joanna reached for her notebook and tore out a page, then folded it in half and tore again. She jotted down her mailing address, and Amelia did the same. "This way I can keep you informed 'bout Elizabeth, if you'd like."

"Oh, definitely."

"And Michael, too." Joanna grinned.

Amelia kept a poker face, even though she was curious to know what his future held. "I would enjoy hearing about *you* most of all, Joanna. Maybe you can tell me how things progress with your beau."

Joanna nodded, eyes sparkling at the prospect, and reached for her hand. "It's my truest joy to count you as a friend, even though we're different as a tulip and a petunia."

Amelia laughed. "I'm so glad we met."

"Oh, and I am, too!" Joanna offered her a place to stay anytime she was in Lancaster County. "I'd just love to have you come an' visit again."

Amelia thanked her and promised to keep in touch. Then they said good-night.

Joanna slipped downstairs to turn off the gas lamp, then returned to "outen the lantern" before slipping into bed. Amelia did the same across the hall, musing fondly about her new friend. *So sweet . . .*

She rolled to face the window and looked out at the clear moon, thinking back on her first-ever buggy ride. Hopefully, Michael didn't think her in a hurry to say good-bye. *Quite the contrary.* She had curbed her true emotions, like a violinist playing without a stitch of integrity.

Closing her eyes, Amelia sighed deeply. *Tomorrow I must leave all of this happiness behind. . . .*

But it was Joanna's question that lingered as she slipped into sleep: *"What if he wasn't Amish—or if you weren't English?"*

Chapter 31

"Mornin', Rebecca. Would ya like a slice of cold watermelon?" Lillianne asked her longtime friend and neighbor when she showed up at the back door midmorning on Monday washday.

"Sounds delicious."

Lillianne took a plate from the cupboard and cut a thick slice from the watermelon, already halved thanks to Paul, who'd helped her earlier while inside resting his wounded ankle. "I see ya got your washin' all hung out."

Rebecca Lapp nodded as she took a seat on the bench by the table, clearly not interested in talking about washing and who'd gotten theirs out first. "Maybe ya know 'bout the fiddler in our midst. Rhoda Kurtz has her stayin' over yonder, jah?"

"Amelia's her name," Lillianne said right quick, still standing.

"Sounds as fancy as it gets."

Lillianne nodded, guessing what was coming. "But she's gone, is what I've heard."

"Prob'ly a *gut* thing, too, from what's goin' round," Rebecca added.

"Oh?"

"Seems one of the Harvest Road preachers is put out, what with her stirrin' up musical cravings in the youth."

"Well, there's two sides to ev'ry story, remember."

"You can say that again."

Lillianne wondered if Rebecca might bring up her own daughter, Katie's, love for guitar playing.

"Guess that preacher and his wife have been puttin' out fires 'bout last night's hoedown." Rebecca forked a piece of watermelon. "Kinda makes my heart sad." She looked up at Lillianne. "Besides all that, do ya think the Englischer had herself a nice time here?"

"Well, I think so, but Joanna would know better, really."

Shrugging, Rebecca smiled. "Hard to know what goes through young folks' minds anymore."

So true of our Elizabeth . . . But Lillianne didn't mention her, lest they get to fretting over that, too. And from the looks of it, Lillianne felt sure her friend and neighbor might need a respite from gossip. "You just enjoy your treat there, all right?"

"Well, won't ya come over here and sit for a spell?"

"Happy to." She looked out the window and saw Elizabeth feeding the chickens, still dressed English. But instead of saying anything, Lillianne decided the poor thing had been through enough. It was just wonderful-good to know her granddaughter hadn't made any noises about returning to Harrisburg. There'd be plenty of time to wash up the pretty fiddler's clothes she had borrowed and send them back to her. According to Michael, Joanna had asked for Amelia's mailing address. *Of all things.*

Maybe soon, Elizabeth would realize her place was here with

the People. Oh, Lillianne wouldn't dream of giving up hope for that!

··· ➤ ◄ ···

What was I thinking? Michael mused about Amelia while he worked alongside his two older brothers and father in the harness shop that morning. *It would've been pointless.* Still, he deliberated whether he should have revealed his attraction to her.

She has a boyfriend, after all. Despite that, he wished he could go after her, give her an excuse to visit longer. But his father's injury—and Elizabeth's return home—all pulled him back. Daed was in need of all kinds of help now. So much that Michael wondered how he'd even keep up with his draftsman work. He knew he was mighty tied to the People, and he tried not to resent it.

What reason does the Lord have for extending my time here?

··· ➤ ◄ ···

By early evening, Amelia was pulling in to the gated community in Columbus where her parents lived. She stopped at the gatehouse to wave at the familiar attendant.

The pristine landscape reminded her of Rhoda Kurtz's own immaculate yard as Amelia drove onto the stone-paved drive-way leading to the executive-style home. Getting out, she went up the walk to the front entrance, where a water fountain was centered, topiaries nearby. No one she'd met in Hickory Hollow ever entered their home by way of the front door.

Putting the past few days out of her mind, she let herself in with her key and hoped both parents might be home at the same time. When she heard their voices, she followed the sound to one of several decks and balconies overlooking the pool area below. The gardener had recently deadheaded Mom's favorite red geraniums; each cluster of blooms looked perfect. The clay pots stood in a neat row across the length of the lovely balcony where Mom sat on a wooden deck chair next to Dad's.

Amelia hung back a moment, taking in the pleasant sight.

Her father turned, his furrowed brow relaxing as his tanned face burst into a broad smile. His thinning light brown hair had recently been cut. "Amelia . . . you're back in town. Please, come and join us. We have much to talk about."

She held her breath as she made her way outside and pulled up a deck chair.

Her mother smiled with her eyes. "Welcome home, dear."

"Thanks for letting us know you were detained," Dad offered. "Your mother said you called."

"I visited an Amish community in Pennsylvania—Lancaster County, to be exact. It was a bit of a fluke but enjoyable all the same."

"Well, that sounds very nice," Mom said.

"It *was*, actually," Amelia admitted.

Dad nodded. "We wondered what was keeping you." He paused for a moment and looked her way with scrutinizing eyes. "Byron called here . . . filled us in on your little, shall I say, musical adventure?"

Amelia grimaced. So they knew.

"Something about playing with a country band." Her father coughed. "I set him straight, of course . . . let him know he was quite mistaken."

So it didn't matter that Stoney promised not to spill the beans. Byron did it for him!

"No, Dad, Byron was quite right."

Dad frowned. "What do you mean?"

She told them everything: about winning the New England fiddling championship, playing with the Bittersweet Band, and of sneaking around all this time to do so. And she talked glowingly about being one of the warm-up acts for Tim McGraw. The latter mention brought a surprised and elated look from her mother, but it was only fleeting.

"Amelia, my dear girl . . ." Dad glanced at Mom, his eyebrows raised, and Amelia wilted. "The European tour is set to begin in early October. I assume Stoney talked to you?"

"He did. And just so you know, I haven't sacrificed any concerto practice time for the fiddling gigs."

"Well, how can you manage to maintain both musical styles?"

"It's possible, Dad."

"But certainly not well."

She groaned inwardly. Naturally he'd say that.

"When Stoney brings your contract over to sign, I hope you'll show him the greatest respect."

"You taught me well, Dad." Amelia couldn't bear to sit there and hear the same old, same old. Besides, she had been driving all day. "You know what? I'm tired . . . and I really need to check on things at home."

Dad tried to clasp his hands triumphantly, holding them up as they wavered. "Think of the prestige, Amelia . . . and if not that, the money you'll garner for each concert, upward of—"

"Dad, *please* . . . it's never been about any of that." She leaned her head into her hands, willing herself to breathe. "I love the music, remember?" she said.

"Which *is* your career," her father punctuated. "What's gotten into you?"

She rose quickly and retreated inside.

Her mother followed her into the house, where they stood in the expansive family room. "Your father's had another bad night," Mom said: "He's out of sorts."

"I noticed."

"Amelia . . ." Her mom searched her eyes. "He has a dreadful cold. You know he has a tough time with any sort of illness."

"Well, he can relax. Nothing has changed."

"Your father doesn't know how to tell you this. . . ."

"Tell me what?"

"He's not up to traveling with you this fall." Mom bowed her head for a moment, clearly upset. "He won't be accompanying you on the tour."

The news was surprising—Dad lived for touring, said he enjoyed it even more than his own former glory days on the road. Amelia and her mother walked together to the marble-floored entryway and stood there.

Mom continued. "We have a doctor's appointment tomorrow, and we'll see what the doctor thinks—we can't risk his getting pneumonia."

Her father had suffered that several times since the Parkinson's diagnosis years ago. "He does look a bit pale."

Mom agreed, frowning. "He's tired a lot lately, so anything you can do to help alleviate stress would be welcome."

She sensed Mom's protective attitude toward Dad, but the implication was also there for Amelia to be more sensitive, which struck her hard. No matter how she'd felt about the tour, or her musical future—her *life*—while in the tranquil bubble of the Amish community, all of that had just flown out the window. This was reality, and her father's fragile state required that she continue on with the plan, if for no other reason than to honor him.

"Between you and me, Mom, I'd really hoped to have a say in this tour. That's all."

"Well, of course you will."

"No . . . I mean about going at all."

Mom looked puzzled. "Well, honey, why wouldn't you want to?"

Amelia looked away, tears threatening to spill over. Unable to speak, she felt all too aware of her parents' expectations, the walls closing in . . . again.

Her mother inched forward, then stopped. "You'll be well looked after, Amelia. All of your needs taken care of . . . you know that."

She sniffed softly. "I'm thinking of getting off the fast track. I have other goals, too." Amelia shook her head. "No one seems to care what I want."

"But performing is your thing. It's what you do so well."

"Right, but I want some balance in my life. I'm interested in community, in being a part of something. I'd also like to help raise awareness for the arts—for instance, maybe speak at libraries and public schools . . . share my love of music in general."

"Those things are wonderful," her mother said, offering a smile. "Is that everything you long for?"

"I want it all, of course—a good husband, my own family." Amelia hugged herself. "Star status is meaningless without a real life." *I'm losing it,* she thought as the tears rolled down her cheeks.

"Amelia, honey, are you okay?"

She looked at her mother's sweet face and swallowed hard.

"I'm sorry, Mom. It's just that—" Her voice broke, and she left the thought unfinished.

"I didn't know you felt this way, Amelia. It's quite a surprise."

"Well, it hardly matters now. The bookings for Europe are practically set in stone."

Mom nodded. "Your father's counting on you to pull off this tour—brilliantly, as always."

"Most definitely."

"But if you still feel this way after you're home—"

"Well, I have for a few years."

Mom's expression was more serious now. "Then I'll do what I can to lay the groundwork with your father. When you return, we'll sit down and discuss it as a family."

"I'd love that, but what will Dad say?"

"Amelia, he's *convinced* you're excited about touring. So if you haven't told him otherwise, how would he even know?"

Amelia was heartened but wouldn't hold her breath. "I really don't want to hurt or disappoint him."

"I'll figure out something. In the meantime, you enjoy this opportunity in Europe—play from your very heart. Fulfill everything you've worked for, and when you come back, we'll talk."

An enormous burden began to lift. Amelia wiped her eyes again, wishing for a box of tissues.

"Mom?"

"Yes, honey."

"Thanks."

Her mother reached to embrace her. "No worries?"

Amelia shook her head and excused herself, walking back to say good-bye to her father. "I'm sorry about walking away from you earlier, Dad," she said, reaching for his hand. He gave it a gentle squeeze, and she continued. "This is going to be the best tour ever. I'm totally focused on the two concertos I'm planning . . . and there'll be no more fiddling stints in my near future. Okay?"

He suddenly looked frail, his head trembling as he slowly nodded. "Thanks, Amelia."

"We'll talk soon, okay? Take care of yourself." She meant every word.

Amelia returned to the family room, where her mother stood waiting, dark eyes glistening. "Call me if you need anything, Mom," she said.

"We're glad you're home. Come over for dinner sometime, all right?" Mom smiled.

Reaching for the door, Amelia let herself out and strode down the stone walkway to her car, then glanced back to see her mother standing at the living room window. *Please work your magic with Dad!* she thought and waved.

Chapter 32

Instead of going straight home, Amelia headed to the wireless store and purchased a new cell phone. By the time she'd set it up, she was starving. She texted Byron to ask if she could meet him somewhere for a bite to eat. Within seconds, he texted back—he was away at a concert.

When can we talk? she asked.

He waited momentarily, then replied: *I'll give you a call on the drive to the hotel, OK?*

Amelia stopped to pick up a few groceries and headed home to make a quick supper for herself. Tired and very hungry, she was anxious to relax over a nice hot meal . . . and then put in some practice time. After a day of sitting behind the wheel—and the difficult discussion with her parents—the thought of playing her warm-ups and the Tchaikovsky concerto made her feel revitalized.

"Wonderful-*gut*," she said, trying on the words. But they fell flat as Amelia considered her father's delicate health. Even a cold could pose problems for him. She steamed a medley of vegetables and tossed a fresh salad while waiting for salmon to grill out on the deck. Maybe she should have taken the groceries over to her parents' to cook for all of them instead.

But music was her comfort, and she needed to be alone with it tonight. The Wise Woman had counseled her to make music as if it were a divine calling, Amelia remembered suddenly. *"Play your fiddle for the Good Lord above."* And so she did just that.

That night, Byron phoned Amelia as promised. Despite the awkwardness between them last Thursday, their conversation was initially pleasant, filled with casual niceties. But when Amelia suggested their lives were no longer moving in the same direction, he fell silent.

"There's no sense pretending any longer that our 'plan' is even workable," she ventured.

"What's different, Amelia? I haven't changed."

"No, you haven't," she admitted. "It's simply not something I want anymore, Byron."

"Does this have anything to do with your fiddling performance last week?" he asked.

She thought for a moment. "I don't honestly think so. I probably would have reached this point even without the fiddling gigs. I'm just not sure I'm wired for the whole concert diva experience. A quieter, more settled life really appeals to me."

He sighed. "Why haven't you ever told me this? All the times we've talked—you never hinted you weren't happy."

Amelia felt her throat tighten—she was sorry to have misled him in this way, but in truth, she'd been misleading herself, as well. *Too fearful to say what was on my heart . . .* "I'm sorry, Byron," she whispered. "But we haven't connected for a very long time," she added gently. "You know it, and I do, too."

In the end, she was greatly relieved he didn't press for a drawn-out discussion, making things more difficult. Although this surely had been a shock, Byron seemed to accept what she had to say, then politely wished her well. "You're a very talented violinist, Amelia. Don't ever forget that."

"Thanks, Byron . . . you don't have to say—"

"I truly hope we'll remain at least friendly," he said quickly.

She agreed. "I wish you well, too."

The following evening, Amelia met with Stoney to sign the European tour contract over a delicious dinner. Later, when she returned home, she checked her online fan page, scanning through the countless comments since her publicist had last posted. There were numerous questions about her recordings with EMI Classics: Was she going to feature either the Brahms or the Mendelssohn next? Wasn't it time for another U.S. tour? Where was she appearing next?

So many postings, so little time. Amelia clicked off and went to her writing desk, one she rarely used. Who wrote anything longhand anymore? Well, Joanna Kurtz did . . . and if it worked for her Amish friend, then so be it.

Sitting down, Amelia found some stationery in the narrow drawer and began to write a letter.

Dear Joanna,

I've been reminiscing about my visit to beautiful Hickory Hollow. I'm surprised by how much I already miss it!

I am so thankful for the opportunity I had to get to know you, and for your kind hospitality. Please greet your parents for me, and thank them, as well. It was a true joy to share a small part of your life, if only briefly.

> *Your English friend,*
> *Amelia Devries*

P.S. In October, I will begin touring Europe for a little over two months, playing in many different cities. I thought it might be fun if I sent you postcards from my travels. What do you think?
I'll look forward to hearing from you!

Tired and ready to soak, Amelia ran the water for a bubble bath in her jetted tub. The pain in her shoulders and neck was unrelenting tonight, partly from yesterday's long drive, and partly because she had a tendency to internalize stress. Acquiescing to her father's wishes had taken its toll on her. Yet she was also thankful there was an unexpected thread of hope that she might not find herself in this predicament again—not if her mother was able to mentally prepare the way with her dad. *Won't that be a feat!*

While relaxing in the bubble-filled tub, votive candles lit, Amelia let her mind wander, welcoming the quaint image of the lantern in Joanna's hand, just Sunday night. The short interval spent in Hickory Hollow already seemed nearly a world away now that Amelia was home. She didn't want to forget any part of it—Michael in particular. His laughing blue eyes and handsome smile filled her memory. But it wasn't meant to be—just as he'd described his relationship with his former fiancée. Yet Amelia couldn't help feeling sad as she recognized that, wonderful as he was, Michael Hostetler would never be more than a casual friend.

Michael had seen Mamm wrapping up some clothes for mailing earlier this week. She'd acted downright sheepish about it . . . and later, when she headed off to mail it, she looked about her almost furtively, as if she was up to some mischief. For that reason, Michael guessed the package contained the fancy skirt and blouse Amelia had loaned to Elizabeth.

Now Thursday night was closing in around them, and all the while Elizabeth sat outside in her English boyfriend's car. The very man who'd frightened them in Harrisburg was parked right outside in Daed's lane!

Michael was miserably certain Lizzie was not going to stay put in Hickory Hollow. She had not given God anything more than bits and pieces of her life, not her whole self as was required to please Him. Apart from a true miracle, they would lose his dear niece.

Marching to the window, Michael peered out, wishing there were something more he could do. He despised this feeling of helplessness when he wanted to storm out there and demand that Lizzie's boyfriend be gone! But Lizzie must make her own decisions.

He wondered what Amelia would do about Lizzie if she were standing here beside him. Would she be able to make his niece see reason? Michael felt sure she'd have a better chance than he would. He realized anew that he should have made an effort to do something Monday morning. Not just let Amelia leave!

Joanna had let it slip that she was planning to write to Amelia. He'd asked her for Amelia's address, making her promise not to say a word. Oh, the look Joanna had given him!

Michael chuckled at the remembrance. If he could do it over, he would have simply exchanged email addresses prior to Amelia's leaving. How much easier—and more private—that would have been!

After evening Bible reading and prayers with the family, he slipped off to his room to write the first letter he'd written in a good while. Amelia wouldn't think anything of it, of course, once she realized he was writing to update her on what was happening with Elizabeth. The perfect approach to get his foot back in the door.

The days since Amelia's return home had been filled with hours of rehearsing and updates from Stoney and the tour manager. There were meetings with her wardrobe assistant, Dee Walker, too, as they discussed which of her many gowns to take along, as well as shoes and numerous accessories. Amelia's image must be as polished and perfect as her playing.

Apart from the arrival of a package containing the outfit Amelia had loaned to Elizabeth, her visit to Amish country began to seem nearly unbelievable. It was as if Michael and Joanna and the Wise Woman—the whole delightful community of Plain People—were merely a figment of an overactive imagination.

The kind of people who might only exist in Joanna's stories, thought Amelia.

And while real life encompassed her every attention, the tendrils reaching back to Lancaster County tugged on her less with each passing day. Until one afternoon, when an unexpected letter arrived in Amelia's mailbox . . . from Michael.

Chapter 33

Amelia was pleased to receive Michael's letter and found a cozy spot on her favorite chair in the music studio to read it.

> *Dear Amelia,*
>
> *You must be surprised to hear from me! Joanna shared your address with me and promised to keep my request quiet. It would surely cause a stir in the community if word got out I was writing "the fancy fiddler."*
>
> *I really didn't want to share sad news, but Elizabeth has returned to Harrisburg with her friends there, although she says she wants to keep in touch with her family. Between you and me, she surely seems lost in many ways. I can understand the temptations of the world, but I don't know why she's chosen to walk away from God, too. She's giving even her "wayward" uncle cause for concern. Will you keep her in your prayers?*

"Definitely," Amelia whispered, responding aloud to Michael's plea.

She read further and realized much of the letter was regarding his niece's decision to leave the People. Amelia wondered how Michael's family must be coping . . . and Michael, too. *He feels so responsible.*

Despite all of that, she was delighted he had taken time to update her and to make this surprising attempt to continue their friendship.

Amelia's tour launched in early October with a spectacular first night at Carnegie Hall in New York City, followed by an overnight flight to London. She slept soundly, having given every ounce of her energy to the Tchaikovsky masterpiece. Stoney deemed the performance "a sparkling rendition—nothing less than genius."

She awoke over England to bright sunlight, feeling surprisingly well rested and energized about the tour. She relived last night's thrilling concert—the world of the stage, playing her very best for an admiring audience. She'd taken repeated bows before the tuxedoed music director gracefully kissed her hand. Truly, it was nothing like the quiet life she'd known in Hickory Hollow.

Amelia was thankful to both Joanna and Michael for staying in touch with her. Michael's recent promise to fill her in on Elizabeth had meant frequent emails as his niece came and went, apparently still undecided about her future, as was Michael—or so it seemed. He no longer mentioned his hope of going English, and Amelia wondered if Elizabeth's sporadic behavior had made him rethink his own issues.

After landing at London's Heathrow Airport, Amelia phoned her father. This being the first time he hadn't felt well enough to accompany her, she missed him. Then she and her traveling companions checked into the Milestone Hotel Kensington, a five-star boutique hotel overlooking Kensington Palace and Gardens. Though accustomed to doing for herself, Amelia didn't mind the prospect of pampering by the twenty-four-hour butler service. The dreamy sophistication of her well-appointed suite was wonderful, as well.

But her favorite activity of that first day in London was the late-morning tour of Buckingham Palace, where she was honored with a brief private audience with Queen Elizabeth.

Later, the conductor of the London Symphony Orchestra met Amelia and Stoney for an exquisite lunch in an intimate conservatory filled with magnificent foliage and fragrant exotic flowers of every hue.

That evening Amelia performed the Brahms concerto in the Royal Albert Hall to a capacity crowd. And later that week, the Tchaikovsky concerto at the Barbican Centre, the largest performing arts center in all of Europe.

There were also matinee recitals and several evening concerts with the Philharmonia Orchestra at the Royal Festival Hall, located on London's South Bank, where art galleries, upscale restaurants and shops, and even a poetry library caught Amelia's attention during her free daytime hours. She purchased a book of classic poems by Elizabeth Barrett Browning and stocked up on postcards of Buckingham Palace and Tower Bridge to send to Joanna.

Yet delightful as her time in Europe was proving to be, each night when she returned to her quiet suite, Amelia removed the hairpins from her French twist and played country fiddle tunes to relax, holding on to the memory of one incredible evening in a Welsh Mountain cabin, so far away.

Michael worked in the field with his brothers from dawn till the noon meal, digging up the rest of the potatoes for market. He was itching to send another email to Amelia, telling her of Elizabeth's recent decision to return to Hickory Hollow—this time for good. She'd even told him privately that she hoped to join church next year, once she'd taken the required baptismal classes. He, however, had not bowed his knee in baptism this September . . . but he was mighty sure Amelia wouldn't inquire about that.

He recalled her current email where she had shared with him about her father's health, a real concern . . . and about her renewed faith. Even busy as Amelia was with her tour, she seemed enthusiastic about seeking God's plan for her life.

Squinting into the sunlight, Michael made his way across the yard and into the house to wash up, wondering how it was possible to feel so close to someone halfway around the world.

On the seventeenth day of the tour, Amelia flew to Amsterdam, where she was warmly greeted by a handsome escort holding a large bundle of beautifully wrapped tulips. Smiling broadly, he placed the fresh-cut flowers in her arms with a gracious kiss on the cheek. The well-dressed young man talked proudly of the city's cultural arts season, which ran from September to June. "Do you enjoy theatre, dance, or opera?" he asked, smiling as he opened a door for her. "You'll find we have it all here."

She almost expected him to invite her to one of the events, he was that attentive. *Like Michael* . . .

Her luggage arrived in baggage claim, and she was ushered outside to a waiting limousine. The image of a gray, enclosed Amish carriage, a contrast in every way to this limo, flickered across her memory. She smiled as she settled inside, and Stoney gave her a questioning look.

That night when she checked her email, she found a message from Mom, saying that Dad was struggling with a bad case of bronchitis. *But don't worry—he's under good care from our doctor. Remember, this is your moment to shine, Amelia. Your father and I couldn't be more proud of you and your music.*

Are you sure Dad's doing okay? Amelia responded. *I know how tough respiratory infections have been for him in the past. I'm praying!*

But her mom quickly replied that he was expected to make a full recovery.

> *It helps him to hear how well you are being received there— we've been reading the reviews for each concert. He so enjoys your phone calls, dear. Oh, how we both wish we could be there with you!*
>
> *Well, I hope you have a good rest tonight, Amelia. Every night, before your father falls asleep, he says to me, "I hope our daughter knows we love her, and that we're bursting our buttons."*
>
> *One more thing: Your father and I would like to hear you play the evening performance with the Royal Concertgebouw*

Orchestra tomorrow. We'll call Stoney's cell phone and have him hold it up, in the wings. All right with you?

Amelia smiled at the image. *Stoney could video the performance, Mom!* she wrote back. Making a video clip was easy enough. *I'll ask him the best way to do that and let you know what he says. I'd love for you to see the Concertgebouw—it's supposedly one of the greatest concert halls in the world. Some say it's acoustically perfect—lucky for me!*

As she thought ahead to that performance, Amelia realized how few people were able to experience such things. She brushed a tear from her cheek at the thought of all the years her parents had invested to get her to this place . . . to this moment.

Thank you, Mom, she wrote now. *I miss you both. Tell Dad this tour is for him, okay? The culmination of everything we've worked for . . . together. I wish he could be here. And you, too, Mom. It would be really special for me . . . for all of us.*

"For the last time," Amelia said softly.

Later, while dressing for bed, Amelia hoped her father would recover quickly; her mother seemed optimistic he would. Was Mom putting on a brave face so she wouldn't worry?

The next morning, Amelia and her wardrobe assistant, Dee, took a fifteen-minute stroll from the Bilderberg Garden Hotel to the Van Gogh Museum. There, they toured the great post-Impressionist painter's works. Amelia was enthralled by the dramatic colors of each canvas, taken by their emotional impact. The sunflowers, in particular, drew her back once again to the meadow near Joanna's house, where Amelia had practiced for hours amidst the wildflowers—yellow daisies and buttercups. And the painting *Landscape at Twilight* reminded her of the golden sky on her last evening in Hickory Hollow, when later, she'd taken her first ride in an Amish buggy. *With Michael.*

That evening Stoney videotaped Amelia's first encore piece, Caprice no. 1 in E by Paganini, for her parents, capturing the initial roar of applause.

Following the concert, Amelia thrilled to read her mother's long email, sharing her gladness at seeing Amelia's father so jubilant.

Amelia was thankful to be able to include her dear parents in this way. The tour was proving to be not only a triumph musically, but a surprising boost for her soul.

Chapter 34

Amelia's days in Berlin were a pleasant interval, with a bit more time off prior to and after her hectic concert schedule. The charming accents of the Germans reminded her of the Deitsch dialect readily spoken by Joanna Kurtz and Ella Mae. Michael too.

While Amelia enjoyed a delectable brunch on the opulent terrace at the Ritz-Carlton one day with the director of the Berlin Philharmonic, she found herself daydreaming of Ella Mae's quaint little porch, where she'd surprised the dear lady with a creative rendition of "This Little Light of Mine."

How is Ella Mae doing? Amelia thought fondly of the woman who exhibited such determination to remain independent during her twilight years. *Who is the recipient of her wisdom today?*

Later that week, while Amelia and Dee walked the ten-minute stretch to the Brandenburg Gate, part of the infamous Berlin Wall during the time of the Iron Curtain, Amelia felt a renewed interest in history. She reflected on the well-known words spoken by President Reagan as he stood at this very gateway: *"Tear down this wall!"* Amelia found herself dreaming of taking additional graduate classes, especially in history, hoping to branch out from a lifetime of music study.

On their return to the hotel, Dee suggested a shopping trip once they returned to the States. "You'll need some new evening gowns for your next tour."

Amelia didn't have the heart to say this tour might very well be her swan song, at least for touring overseas. She did hope to continue performing stateside and planned to record another CD soon. Most of all, though, she longed to share her love of music with children, and give of her time and energy to less fortunate people—those who needed the healing balm of music but could not afford to pay for concerts and CDs.

Amelia had also been reading through the Old Testament, focusing on Abraham, not a man of seemingly inherent faith like his ancestors Abel, Enoch, and Noah. Yet God chose to use Abraham to bless immeasurable multitudes, and later in the New Testament, his name was the one most often spoken by Christ.

In some small way, Amelia felt a strange kinship with Abram of old—mostly because of Ella Mae, who was responsible for Amelia's growing desire to use her talents to bless others.

Such a wonderful Wise Woman. Amelia wished she might somehow thank her. *Someday, I'll find a way.*

Lillianne welcomed Elizabeth into her kitchen that afternoon. "You're just in time, dear," she said, placing a plate of warm double-chocolate-chip cookies on the table. She hurried to sit at her customary spot, across from her very Amish-looking granddaughter, though still minus the Kapp. That would come once she was baptized, or so Lillianne prayed. "And what brings you by today?" she asked, ever so pleased.

Elizabeth reached for a cookie to go with her cold milk. "Guess I'm tryin' on Amish life again," she said, grinning playfully. "Ya know, I've missed warm cookies and milk, Mammi Lily!"

Lillianne knew she was joking but hoped there were other, more essential reasons for Elizabeth to yearn for Plain ways.

"Seriously, Mammi, I want to catch up on the lost time with you. I've missed out on too much round here." She looked toward the window and sighed. "Tellin' the truth, I've missed my family something terrible."

"Aw, honey-girl, we've missed ya, too." Lillianne choked back the lump in her throat. "More than you know."

Elizabeth took another long drink of milk. "I've been wanting to talk to you 'bout something, Mammi . . . to set the record straight."

"Oh? And what about, dear?"

"Uncle Michael and his Englischer friend."

"You must mean Amelia."

"Jah, my look-alike, as Michael calls her." Elizabeth blushed slightly. Her eyes sparkled this morning, and she seemed so very settled—pretty as could be in her blue cape dress and matching apron. "You have to know I wouldn't be sitting here today if it wasn't for Amelia." Elizabeth paused. "Michael too."

"Really, now?" Lillianne found this interesting. Here all along she'd thought it was Michael who'd influenced Elizabeth *against* the People. "Well, I'll be."

Elizabeth nodded and reached again for her tall glass of milk. " 'Tis ever so true."

"Does Michael know ya think this?"

"Oh jah."

Well now, Lillianne was downright surprised.

"Something else, too—the talk 'bout Amelia's fiddlin' at the barn Singing is all but died down. Seems the fellas who asked her inside the barn owned up to the preacher."

"You don't say?"

"That's right. They said they invited her to play along with their Singin'—and that's all there is to it. 'Twas never her idea."

Lillianne took this all in, beginning to rethink her opinion of Amelia. What else could she do with such news? Maybe the Englischer wasn't such a troublemaker after all.

The final days of Amelia's tour included rehearsals and performances with the *Staatskapelle Dresden* in Germany; then it was on to Munich with the well-known Bavarian Radio Symphony Orchestra.

Dee Walker, who'd become her sidekick on this tour, recommended they spend one afternoon exploring the Hellabrunn Wildlife Park. The zoological park included a complex of animal and conservation exhibits, and Amelia was eager to go, having as a young girl spent time at some of the best zoos in the U.S. with her parents as a way to unwind after big performances. Her memories of such happy times mingled with her worries about her father's health—and how he would react to the news that she was done touring.

While she and Dee walked the parklike setting, enjoying the mild late-fall day, they were entertained by the antics of monkeys running free about the grounds, bringing joy to young families.

Later, while they wandered about the exquisite birdhouse, Amelia realized anew God's great care for even the smallest of creatures. A verse her grandmother often recited came to her mind: *"Consider the lilies of the field, how they grow; they toil not, neither do they spin. . . ."*

"Why do you think we humans worry so much?" she asked Dee.

"Well, not everyone does," Dee said. "There are a few laid-back people, you know." She smiled teasingly. "And then there are all the rest of us."

They shared a laugh, and Amelia urged her on to the historic elephant house, thinking Joanna Kurtz would certainly enjoy this amazing place, as fond of animals as she was.

In beautiful Prague, Amelia played magnificently with the Czech Philharmonic Orchestra, captivated as always by the interplay between orchestra and director. In her off hours, she and Dee enjoyed scenic river views, as well as some much-needed relaxation at a café on the Old Town Square, where she took in the historic buildings and towers surrounding them.

Later that week, she traveled to Austria to play two concerts with the Vienna Philharmonic. In her leisure hours between rehearsals and performances, she took a side trip to Salzburg to tour Mozart's birthplace. Fascinating as she found the artifacts of the musical genius's childhood, Amelia was more in tune with the people around her, particularly a young mother. The woman had to be close to her own age, with a baby and a set of adorable blond twin boys who laughed and jabbered together. Amelia was so drawn to them, she could not keep from watching. But what touched Amelia most was the way they kept looking back affectionately at their mother, whose expression was full of love. And the babe in arms—oh, such a full head of dark, wavy hair! The prettiest baby Amelia thought she'd ever seen.

Amelia found herself transfixed by the sweet Austrian mother and her gentle way with her children. The woman clearly doted on her little ones. And, just before the mother placed her baby in the stroller, she kissed her rosy cheek and cooed down at her.

Will I ever be so blessed?

The night before her flight home, Amelia noticed a post with a faceless profile among the numerous other posts on her fan page. Curious as that was, the name *Mike Hostetler* was enough to capture her attention. "Can it be?" she said, glad she was alone in her suite as she leaned closer to the screen.

I'm praying you are blessing many with your beautiful music! he'd written.

Brief as Michael's comment was, Amelia felt an unexpected thrill that he'd taken the time to post on her very public fan page. The surprising message and his frequent emails made her look forward all the more to tomorrow's return home . . . even though she wondered if she'd ever see Michael Hostetler again.

Chapter 35

B ack in the States, six days before Christmas, Amelia welcomed time at home to rest as she accepted her mother's dinner invitation for the next evening. "Also, we have quite a stack of mail here for you," her mother said, sounding bright and cheerful on the phone. "You certainly have a good friend in Miss Joanna Kurtz."

Amelia thanked her and said she would be happy to come for dinner. "How's Dad feeling?"

Mom paused and Amelia tensed up immediately. "I hope he's not worse."

"Amelia . . . I'm afraid the bronchitis has left him very weak. He is pumped up with medication, however, so he's not contagious." Mom went on to say the doctor was hoping to ward off pneumonia with a rigorous second round of antibiotics.

"I know you're taking good care of him, Mom. I'll look forward to seeing you both."

Amelia sat down to reply to an email, then checked several of her favorite professional sites. She was very surprised to see a notice that the director of the Philadelphia Orchestra was holding auditions beginning in early January—for the coveted position of concertmaster, the first-chair violinist. With a quick prayer for favor, she promptly sent in her initial application and résumé.

"Courage is fear on its knees," the Wise Woman had once said. Ella Mae had lived her long life believing this statement. She had also talked of prayer in such a cherished manner that, since meeting her, Amelia had started opening her heart to God again in daily prayer, just as her grandparents had taught her to do as a child.

Might this be a divine nudge in a new direction? Amelia wondered, waiting for Stoney's arrival. It was time to discuss business. He had been quite resistant about her ideas during the last days of the tour. She could only imagine how he'd respond to her hope of a career change!

On sheer impulse, Michael had hopped in the car and headed for Columbus, Ohio, early that morning. He had been considering surprising Amelia around Christmas, knowing he would be busy with his own family closer to the actual day. Besides, based on her recent emails, he knew Amelia had returned, and he wanted to see if the strong connection they'd experienced last summer, as well as through their months of correspondence, was still evident in person.

It was close to two o'clock when he pulled up to her curb. He studied the address on the townhouse to match it with the address he'd jotted down. Getting out of the car and walking up the driveway, he realized he was not in the least bit tired from the seven-hour drive. In fact, he felt invigorated at the prospect of seeing his friend again. But now that he reflected on it, he wished he'd taken the time and the courtesy to let Amelia know he was coming. Was it a good idea to just show up like this?

Making his way up the sidewalk, Michael took in the neighborhood—the townhomes looked similar in design, but the exteriors featured differing earth tones. He made note of the rather formal colonial accents to windows and the overall architecture, filing it away in his mind for future reference.

As he reached to ring the doorbell, he heard Amelia's violin music coming from somewhere deep in the house. He assumed she was practicing for yet another concert. Or maybe her upcoming recording.

He waited, wishing he might have had the opportunity to hear her in one of the great European concert halls. But that was impossible for an Amishman, especially one helping his father with the harvest. And even if Michael had decided to defy Bishop John and take money out of his savings account to make an airplane trip—absolutely forbidden—he would have had very little time to spend with Amelia, what with her hectic schedule.

No, coming here today was a far better idea. He had so much to tell her . . . face-to-face.

The music continued, and when the door did open, a middle-aged man with light brown hair greeted him with a curious frown. "Hullo," Michael said quickly. "I'm Amelia's friend . . . from Lancaster County."

The man bobbed his head abruptly—he appeared to be studying Michael's attire. "Amish country?"

Smiling yet feeling sheepish, Michael removed his black felt hat. "That's right." He waited for the man to introduce himself, but when none came, he forged ahead. "I'm Michael Hostetler."

"I see. But Miss Amelia's unable to take visitors" came the cold reply. "Was she expecting you?"

Michael hesitated. "No, not exactly . . ."

The man shook his head. "Well, then, I'm very sorry."

Although startled by this turn of events, Michael wasn't ready to simply walk away. "Would you mind tellin' her Michael is here . . . and drove all this way to see her?"

"I'd mind very much, young man." The gruff man suddenly introduced himself as Amelia's agent, Stoney Warren, then stepped outside, closing the door behind him. "I won't have anything—or anyone—jeopardizing my client's musical career."

The effortless sound of Amelia's violin continued in the background. Michael couldn't stand the feeling of being so close to her, yet being denied even a few minutes to speak with her. "I assure ya, I'm not here to make trouble." He paused. "I'm certain she'd want to know I'm here."

Even to his own ears, the words sounded presumptuous. And Stoney ignored his response.

"A talent like Amelia's is rare and should not be cast aside for frivolous things." His expression was stern. "It's my job to help her stay on task." Stoney's forehead knitted into a deep frown. "I simply refuse anyone to see her who might contribute to her reluctance to concertize. She hasn't been the same since her time in Amish country. You wouldn't happen to know anything about that, would you?" He gave Michael a keen look.

"I don't intend to interfere," Michael replied.

"Of course not," Stoney shot back. "And if you're the good

friend you seem to indicate, you'll understand her need to avoid all distractions. . . ."

"Jah," Michael said, momentarily forgetting he was on English turf. He felt very conflicted. As much as he wanted to see Amelia again, to talk with her and reconnect in person, Michael took Stoney's words to heart and realized the older man was probably right. *What did I hope to accomplish here, anyway?* he thought. Someone like Amelia wouldn't be content with a mere draftsman or a farmhand, would she? To keep pursuing her, even by email, might well be interfering with God's calling for Amelia. No, Michael wouldn't think of getting in the way of a "divine appointment," as Ella Mae sometimes referred to God's will for a person!

"I apologize for bothering you . . . and Amelia." He turned to leave, torn between what his heart wanted and what he believed was best for his friend.

"I appreciate your understanding," Stoney said to him. But embedded in Stoney's tone was the unspoken warning: *And stay away!*

Amelia paused in her practice, tired of the intense scale work and eager to dive into the actual music. She carefully placed her violin and bow on a nearby chair and headed for the small refrigerator in the studio bar across the room. Perusing the options of soda, juices, and bottled water, she chose a can of pure apple juice. Not ready to encounter Stoney again this afternoon, she ambled to the window and peered out. A car that looked very much like Michael's was just pulling away from the curb. She leaned closer, second-guessing herself.

Why would an Amish guy come unannounced all the way

from Pennsylvania just to see her? She shrugged off the ridiculous notion and stepped away from the window. Was it wishful thinking, perhaps?

But . . . *what if it was Michael?*

Maybe Amelia had been practicing too long . . . she *was* tired and jet-lagged. Why else would she have such a farfetched notion? Or was it because she secretly longed to see Michael again?

Chapter 36

The next evening, when Amelia arrived at her parents', Mom greeted her warmly, dressed to the nines and wearing her signature pearls. "It's so good to see you, honey." Mom smelled of lavender as she reached for Amelia's hand, and they walked together into the dining room, decorated with garland and tiny white lights placed high across the cornice of the hutch. The very best white table linens and delicate china had been laid, and there were lighted candles on either side of an elegant poinsettia centerpiece. "I decided to have one of your favorite entrées for dinner," Mom said, smiling.

"Let me guess." Amelia felt like she was coming home in more ways than one. "Mustard-marinated Alaskan salmon?" Her mouth watered at the thought.

"How does that sound, dear?"

"Really wonderful." The entrée was one Mom had made often during the years.

"How's Dad feeling today?" asked Amelia, glancing about in search of him.

"He's well enough to brush on the marinade." Mom winked at her. "You know your father—he's a fighter, that man."

Amelia went with her mother to the kitchen and saw Dad sitting at the center island, wearing his red woolen sweater, very deliberately moving the brush over each fillet, his mouth open slightly. "Hi, Dad." She leaned down and gently embraced him. "I missed you."

Despite Amelia's encouraging him to stay put, he insisted on standing to greet her. In the midst of the embrace, she motioned for her mother to join them. "Group hug," she said, relishing the special moment. This time together was like an early Christmas gift, and she recognized this was *not* the night to share her hopes and wishes for her career . . . not the way she felt so completely encircled by her parents' love. She would not for the world alter the course of what promised to be a most delightful evening.

Michael was immediately aware of the smell of oil mixed with leather when he opened the door to his father's harness shop a few days after his Columbus trip. He welcomed the familiar whiff, then within minutes, quickly forgot just how strong the odor really was.

Today, he helped haul the leather to the long measuring table, where he smoothed it out. Lately Michael had been juggling three jobs—the work assisting his father at a busy time of year, a few predawn hours at Nate Kurtz's dairy farm, as well as his own drafting projects in town.

Presently, he and his father laid out the pattern to mark the leather. They would cut it and, eventually, sew up the harnesses.

Bishop John had requested a matched set for his two driving horses, and Daed had taken extra time—far longer than necessary, according to Michael's thinking—to make sure the craftsmanship was exceptional. *"John Beiler being our man of God, and all,"* Daed had said.

Along about midmorning, around the time Daed liked to have Michael run in and get a thermos of freshly brewed hot coffee, Ephraim Yoder, owner of the old General Store, came in the door with a rush order to have one of his older harnesses inspected and restitched. "Just ain't safe to use anymore," Ephraim said, his face smudged with dirt.

"We'll have a look-see." Daed went to his worn wooden desk in the corner to check his calendar. He straightened and pulled on his beard. "You might have to wait a couple of days—can ya manage till then? Michael and I are backed up some."

"Well, I'll do what I can to get by, jah," Ephraim said. "I see your ankle's healed," he added.

"Ach, 'twas nothin'." Daed shrugged.

"Ain't what I heard." Ephraim glanced at Michael. "I daresay you oughta think about markin' those hay holes, Paul."

Michael caught himself nodding in agreement but wouldn't say how severe the pain had been for his father for weeks on end following the accident. Mamm had even wondered, for a time, if Daed might have broken more than his ankle. *"Could be a hairline fracture somewhere,"* she'd kept saying. But Daed would not hear of having X rays or seeking any professional medical input whatsoever, which didn't surprise anyone.

"So you're as *gut* as new, then?" Ephraim smiled shrewdly.

"I'm up and walkin' round, and that's what matters," Daed

replied, shooing him along. "Check back in a couple of days, won't ya?"

"Denki." With that, Ephraim headed for the door, nodding his head at Michael.

Michael followed him out the door to get the hot coffee from the house, hurrying across the backyard, his breath visible in the brisk air. It wouldn't be long before the first snow of the season, and he could hardly wait to get their old sleigh out and running again. Christmas Day was so close now, and he realized he hadn't sent Amelia a card.

Will she wonder why I disappeared from her life? he thought as he made his way into Mamm's warm kitchen.

After several hours of vigorous practice that evening, Amelia curled up on her sofa with her laptop. Eagerly, she checked her email and saw that her webmaster had forwarded quite a few from her web site. And there were a handful from out-of-state relatives, as well. But she scanned the list again and saw nothing at all from Michael.

Nothing in three days . . .

Sighing, she stared out the window and watched the clouds drift slowly across the azure sky as daylight faded. Was it her imagination, or had Michael been pulling away from her in their last email exchange? She pondered it further and knew it was true, feeling saddened. But she had to respect his decision—he must have chosen to salvage his life as an Amishman after all. *I have no claim on him*, Amelia thought, even though the realization hurt.

She recalled Michael's thoughtful post on her fan page during her tour and tried to picture him enjoying a Christmas dinner seated around Lillianne's table with his extended family. It wouldn't be long until Joanna's large family would be doing the same, down Hickory Lane. Ella Mae Zook would most definitely be included with her daughter Mattie and her husband and children and grandchildren. No widow would be left alone on such a day. *The family embraces each person, married or not, young or old,* thought Amelia. *A place of belonging . . .*

"Will I ever hear from Michael again?" she whispered. She picked up her violin and bow. Slowly, Amelia began to play an impromptu medley, a variation on "O Come, All Ye Faithful". . . turning once again to music to ward off her melancholy.

Chapter 37

The day before Christmas Eve, Amelia received an email from Stoney saying that Nicola Hannevold was to be featured on the January cover of *The Strad*. Instead of taking the time to text back, Amelia called him. "Thanks for letting me know, Stoney. I'm happy for Nicola." She smiled into the phone. "She must be recuperating quickly."

"Actually, I have a motive for mentioning this," he said.

"Why am I not surprised?"

"You know me too well, my dear." He paused. "I'd still like South America to be your next big stop on the map, Amelia. I can get you booked *pronto*."

"I thought we had an understanding."

"Right. You want to do some community work, spend time going around to public schools . . . take a history class. Sure, I remember." He paused. "Eight months or so will give you plenty of time for that, as well as keep up your repertoire."

"And I'm recording one more CD, too," she said. "Don't forget."

"Only one? Uh, your entire life lies ahead of you, kiddo. You're still very young."

"Well, time is a precious commodity . . . one just never knows." She was thinking of her father's precarious health.

"You're not sick, are you?"

"I'm fine, Stoney. I'm merely talking about doing other things with my music."

He breathed audibly. "I don't like the sound of this."

She deliberated. Should she tell him about her upcoming audition—the trip to Philadelphia? After all, he hadn't exactly reacted well to the news that she'd sent in her résumé.

"Don't go silent, Amelia . . . makes me nervous."

"I'm thinking," she said.

He laughed. "That's *my* job."

"Seriously, I've decided to take a fork in the road."

Now *he* was silent.

She began to tell him about the Wise Woman, how she'd urged Amelia to pray about her music and about her future.

"Pray all you want—terrific. But how does that figure into your detour?" He sounded tense, and she half expected him to scoff. "Think about it, Amelia. Be logical. Does God care about what musical choices you make?"

She didn't want to get into a theological debate. "I believe He does, yes."

"Have you been hanging around that country band again?"

"Not yet, but I hope to . . . and very soon."

"Oh, so *that's* the fork?"

"Actually, it's something else. And I'll let you know when or if it happens."

He sighed again. "You're going to get the best of me yet."

"Listen," she said. "I don't believe we're chosen to simply *receive* gifts, whether musical talent or something else. The most profound ones come our way so we can extend grace and compassion to others. God's gifts are multiplied when we use them to bless others."

"You didn't get religion in Amish country, did you?"

"Well, it's been coming on gradually, starting way back when I was a little girl, out milking cows with my papa and grammy—learning how to talk to God." She paused a moment. "It has nothing at all to do with religion, Stoney. And everything to do with faith."

Her agent said nothing.

"Maybe you don't understand where I'm going with this."

"That is correct."

She told him straight out that she was ready to start giving away her gift—by encouraging other young violinists, for one thing. "I want to set up music programs in impoverished neighborhoods."

"And where's the money in that?"

She laughed. "My father taught me to be frugal, so I'm fine. I have money to invest in my pet projects. And what I need for myself, I'll earn from my new job . . . if I get it."

Stoney groaned. "You've gone way out on a limb."

"Not as far as you might think. I'm auditioning with the Philadelphia Orchestra right after New Year's."

He groaned loudly. "I hope you're kidding."

"I *really* want this, Stoney."

"But you're a star—a solo violinist . . . a musician's musician. And you have many years of touring ahead."

"No, Stoney. I'm tired of always traveling. I want to belong somewhere . . . I *need* this position for many reasons." Amelia tried to explain the feeling of community she was looking for, something she had so delightfully observed in Hickory Hollow. "I had no idea what I've been missing . . . and for my whole life."

"Oh, Amelia, think about what you're throwing away. None of this makes good career sense."

"You're right, it doesn't."

"Well, your father will—"

"You can't keep threatening me that way in an effort to keep me boxed in." She inhaled slowly. "Look, I'm not trying to be difficult. I'm no longer a child prodigy. . . . I'm all grown up, and I want to contribute to a group—by playing full-time with an orchestra. One of the best in the world, in fact. I'll still do solo work, maybe play in a chamber music setting—you know, start up a new string quartet. Who knows? The sky's the limit."

He was quiet for a moment. "Are you thinking of settling down and getting married, Amelia? Is that what this is all about?" Now his tone was more thoughtful.

"No," she sighed. "I'm not even dating anyone. But marriage to the right guy would be nice someday. Actually, rather wonderful."

"And you want a houseful of kids, too, right?"

"Absolutely."

He stopped grilling her, his voice softer now. "Sounds like you've been thinking about this a lot, kiddo."

"I certainly have."

"Well, I'd rather not be present when you inform your father of your drastic change of plans."

"That's fine," she said respectfully, recalling her mother's promise to pave the way. "I'll manage it myself."

"All right, then. If you think this is the right path."

"I know it is." Amelia wished him a merry Christmas and a happy New Year.

He snuffed a bit. "Same to you, Amelia."

She said good-bye and hung up, hoping her news hadn't been too shocking. It was, after all, the end of an era.

Going to the window, she looked out at the glimmering half-moon as it appeared over the neighbors' rooftops, its light turning the snowy ground silver. Helen Keller had once written that when one door to happiness closes, another opens. But we so often fix our eyes on the closed door that we miss seeing the one opening wide right before us.

Standing there, a strange little seed of a thought popped into her head. And the more Amelia considered it, the more she had a yearning to see the cozy log cabin on Welsh Mountain in this wintry setting. *Why not? I'll just drive by on the way back from my audition in Philly.*

Chapter 38

A melia was delighted to spend a relaxed Christmas Day with her parents. Surrounded by the glistening appeal of seasonal décor, they opened beautifully wrapped presents and, later, enjoyed a four-course brunch. Amelia's father was nicely dressed in his crisp white dress shirt, red tie, and navy blue slacks, but a ragged cough held on, and he looked alarmingly pale and much too thin. His outlook was jovial, nevertheless, and Amelia thought it especially dear when she caught him looking tenderly at her mother during the lovely meal.

After the final course, Amelia offered to play excerpts from the Brahms concerto, her father's favorite. Later, she also played a few Christmas carols, tempted to break into a fiddling style, though she did not. There would be plenty of time to explore more fiddling in the coming year.

Then, when it looked like her father was ready to sit in his chair and snooze awhile, Amelia kissed him on the cheek and went to help carry her mother's finest china and silverware into the kitchen. "You outdid yourself, Mom," she said, lauding her mother's delicious brunch.

Mom smiled as she began to load the dishwasher. "I wanted to make this day extra special for you . . . and . . ." She paused and bit her lip. "For your father, as well."

"I'm so grateful, Mom, and I'm sure Dad is, too."

Her mother nodded thoughtfully, a pensive look on her pretty face.

They continued working together to wash and then dry the china, both aware of their unspoken worry.

Later, while scrubbing a pan, Amelia ventured in a completely different direction. "I've been wondering . . . how's your manuscript coming?"

Mom's eyes sparkled at the question. "Nice of you to ask," she said. "I have to admit, though—writing is an ongoing challenge."

"But you enjoy the process, don't you?"

Mom squinted momentarily. "There are times when it all surprises me and scenes actually flow, yes. Other times, not so much." She laughed nervously.

"So it's a love-hate sort of thing?"

"Most days, yes, definitely."

"Then how do you get started? Do you outline or just write as the ideas come?" She thought suddenly of Joanna, who so dearly loved writing.

"Honey . . ." Her mother grimaced slightly. "Are you really interested in all of this?"

As private as her mother had been about her work, the book hadn't really been a topic of conversation between them, and Amelia understood why her mother found it curious that Amelia should ask so many questions now. "I'm *very* interested, Mom. And always have been . . . just didn't know if I should ask or not." She was heading into deep waters, not sure how far she should go.

"Well, this book is intensely personal, that much I'll say." Mom sighed and looked away. "A family story from more than a generation ago."

"The best kind."

Mom agreed. "Navigating the past is part of the challenge— remembering the way things truly were. And then getting what's in my head onto the page."

Amelia glanced toward the family room, where Dad sat napping to one of the Isaac Stern CDs from his vast classical violin collection. "I've always wondered . . ."

Mom wiped the counters without speaking, her face bright. "Keeping my writing under wraps was the only way I could manage things, I guess. I had very little confidence . . . this being my first attempt at a novel."

Amelia listened, cherishing her mother's unexpected openness.

Mom motioned toward the expansive breakfast nook, where greenery lined the perimeter and a small, colorful Christmas tree stood in the middle of the table. There, they sat down next to each other, and her mother continued to talk about her manuscript, more freely now.

"The book I've been working on all these years is about my grandmother's relationship with her sister and one of their cousins. It's a mystery, of sorts, and it's finally finished. And surprisingly, an agent is interested."

"That's wonderful! Congratulations, Mom."

"Well, it's too soon to celebrate."

"But still, haven't you told Dad?"

"I wanted you to know first, Amelia." Mom smiled.

"Oh, and I'd really like to read it sometime, if you're okay with that."

"Sure . . . someday."

Amelia reached to hug her. "I'm happy for you, Mom. I hope you land a publisher."

"That's up to the Lord now." Mom reached for her hand. "This writing business isn't for the faint of heart."

Amelia considered that as she returned to the family room, where her father stirred from his nap and requested that Amelia play more music. Mom intervened and suggested they sit and look at family albums instead. Together, they journeyed down memory lane. Amelia remarked that this was the dearest Christmas ever, and Dad agreed, tears welling up in his eyes.

Before leaving, she wondered how the news of her upcoming Philadelphia audition would go over with her parents. However, her hopes and dreams could wait for another time. For today, Christmas joy with her family was her sole priority. Amelia watched her father as Mom turned the pages of the large family album, intent on his peaceful, happy expression as the three of them relived their lives. If this was to be her father's last Christmas, Amelia wanted to embrace every precious moment.

After indulging in his mother's delicious feast, Michael agreed to go walking with his niece, Elizabeth, who'd come with her family to spend the day. Both sets of grandparents were settled comfortably in the front room, talking or napping, and the youngest children were cozy playing checkers near the heater stove in the corner.

"Mammi Lily seemed awful glad to have you sittin' at her table," Elizabeth remarked to Michael as they walked along the roadside, their breath turning to wispy columns of white. "She truly did."

"I think you're mistaken, Lizzie. She was happy to see *you* there," he replied, slapping his gloved hands together. "Prob'ly thought they'd lost you to the world."

Lizzie nodded slowly and looked up at him. "Jah . . . but I'm back to stay."

Michael smiled. "A *gut* thing, for sure."

"But you're not stayin' put, are ya?"

Goodness, she knew him too well, which was jarring sometimes. "Mom still wishes I'd catch the eye of a nice Amish girl."

"Well, that's not surprising, is it? Sounds like all the parents round here, jah?"

"You sure got your accent back real quick." He nudged her, and she laughed.

But all the while, Michael was thinking of Amelia, kicking himself now for not sending her so much as a Christmas card— not even a cheerful holiday ecard. It just didn't feel right to let things fade like this. But her agent's pointed words were still lodged in his head, and while Michael certainly wished he'd done things differently prior to going to Columbus, he refused to interfere in Amelia's life any longer. Even so, it didn't make him miss her any less.

"When will ya tell your parents you're goin' fancy?" asked Lizzie out of the blue.

"Well now, how do you even know such a thing?"

" 'Cause I know you, Uncle Michael. It's easy to see how restless you are . . . even at the dinner table back yonder." She turned to look at the house. "And if I didn't know better, I'd say you're lovesick, too."

"Oh, go on with ya!" He kept his face grim, not giving himself away. But he felt sure Lizzie somehow saw through to the truth.

"Just so ya know, I don't blame you for any of my struggles in Harrisburg or back home here. Sure, I was tempted to get higher education because I saw how happy it made you. But in the end, it was all my doin' . . . my own choice." She looked away, toward the flattened cornfields blanketed with snow. "I had lots of reasons why I needed to find things out for myself."

Hearing this made Michael feel some better. "You don't have to say this, really."

"Why, sure I do. 'Tis the truth, and I wanted to say it to your face. Especially if you're leaving home." Lizzie breathed out slowly, pursing her lips. "Or is it just *en Gebrummel*—a rumor?"

The grapevine had Michael doing all sorts of things, now that Daed was nicely healed and Elizabeth was safely home again. The People had him pretty much long gone, especially since he still wasn't talking about church baptism come next year. Now he just needed to wait till Christmas was past to share his plans with Daed and Mamm, tell them he was moving out in a few days. He'd already lined up a room to rent from Uncle Jerry Landis, just up the road.

"It's not a rumor anymore," he told Elizabeth. "I've made my decision."

" 'Cept you're not running away from God, like I was . . . jah?"

"No," he said, absolutely meaning it. "I'd never do that."

"So then we won't lose you at all. You'll be just round the corner."

He reached over and patted her shoulder. "Tellin' the truth, I was never cut out to be Amish," he confessed. "But family ties are mighty strong."

"Thank goodness for that," she said. "And the Good Lord, too."

Michael was glad he could talk so frankly with his niece. But he really wished he might tell Amelia all of this, too. Wouldn't she be surprised?

While putting the final touches on her upcoming audition pieces, Amelia took a short break and checked the mail out front, thrilled to see a letter from Joanna. Always happy to hear anything from Hickory Hollow, Amelia sat near the bay window in her living room, near her beautiful blue spruce Christmas tree, and sipped a cup of peppermint tea with honey.

Joanna described her excitement for all the Christmas fun still to come, sharing that a few of her older relatives on her father's side also observed "Second Christmas" on December twenty-sixth, a day to visit and rest from the daily routine. *Which means we'll enjoy even more feasts and fellowship and spreading cheer, to be sure. Oh, I can hardly wait to go riding again in our big sleigh with all the little nieces and nephews,* she wrote.

Amelia savored the long and newsy letter as she basked in the afternoon sun, wishing for some word of Michael. *I hope he'll be happy as an Amishman. . . .*

She pulled her knees up to her chin, hugging them and admiring her tree decorated with ornaments related to her musical journey—dozens of little gold violins, treble clefs, and miniature orchestral scores with tiny golden bows. Breathing in the pungent scent, Amelia suddenly felt miserable . . . and far removed from Michael.

Chapter 39

Amelia's January violin audition with the maestro of the Philadelphia Orchestra felt very much like playing for an old friend. Twice in the past few years, she had performed as a feature artist under the fine direction of the world-renowned conductor. In many ways, Amelia looked up to the man as a mentor. He was uncommonly hospitable and affirming today, just as she remembered him to be. As a result, there were no stage jitters either while waiting for the violinist right before her or during Amelia's own private audition. She played with great ease and felt confident she performed with clarity and exceptional musicality.

When she was finished, the maestro spoke fondly of her work. "I am very familiar with your solo performances and overall musicianship, Miss Devries, as well as the rave reviews your playing has garnered," he said in his heavy German accent. "Now," he said, leaning closer, "why, may I ask, are you pursuing a position with an orchestra, my dear?"

"I thought you might wonder," she said, eager for the

opportunity to share her new goals, as well as her hope to embrace becoming a part of this wonderful orchestra, as well as the greater Philadelphia community. She didn't go into a lot of detail but assured him of her commitment to the orchestra should she land the position. "I would be honored to be chosen as concertmaster," she said, her heart pounding with hope.

The maestro gave a pleased smile and inquired about her latest tour. Amelia recapped her travels by saying how grateful she was to have stepped into Nicola Hannevold's shoes, at least temporarily.

"Miss Hannevold is a very fine violinist, to be sure—but you, Miss Devries, have real fire. You play with attitude," he said, punching the air with his fist, eyes twinkling. "I like it."

"Thank you, Maestro," she said, enjoying his voice's deep resonance. "I appreciate your assessment very much."

He remarked that Nicola was recovering nicely and was actually in the lineup of featured artists next September, at the start of the concert season. "Which will also be your very first concert with us, my dear," he announced warmly. "Congratulations, Miss Devries, and welcome to our orchestra family."

She was not only delighted at his decision but also very flattered. They shook hands and he walked her out into the hall.

"Perhaps next year we could even talk you into performing the famous O'Connor Fiddle Concerto," the maestro said with a friendly wink. "It certainly takes a skilled classical musician who is *also* a fiddler to pull off such a performance." He paused slightly. "And . . . I expect Miss Amy Lee would do our orchestra proud with such a feat."

Amelia was so shocked, she hardly knew what to say.

"Don't look so surprised, Miss Devries. Why, I know most *everything* that goes on at the Mann."

He had her there, no question about that! She offered a smile, then nodded her head slowly. "Well, it seems I've been found out . . . once again."

The maestro chuckled, offering another handshake. "You will receive the summer rehearsal schedule in a day or so." He mentioned that the contract would be sent to her agent, as well.

Elated, Amelia wasn't sure her feet were still touching the floor as she thanked the maestro again and headed for her car, where she called her parents with the news. She had waited until just yesterday to inform them of the audition, surprised when her father, especially, did not express a negative opinion. Mom had promised to pave the way for the possibility of Amelia's career making a major turn, but Amelia worried his physical weakness had sapped his desire to debate all of that with her. Was it possible he wanted her to remain closer to home now instead of traveling so far away? The relief she'd felt at his quiet acceptance had been tempered by a measure of sadness.

Today, however, her mother sounded animated. "Congratulations, Amelia. We're so happy for you."

"I'm still dumbfounded that this position opened up when it did." She almost said it was providential, but that was the way her Amish friends talked.

"We'll see you when you're home, dear."

"I'm planning to take a short detour," she said, thinking of the little log cabin on Welsh Mountain. *A bit of déjà vu.*

"Be safe—heavy snow is forecast there."

"I'll be careful. Please tell Dad I'm thinking of him."

"He's resting at the moment, but I'll be sure to tell him you called, Amelia."

They said good-bye and hung up.

Amelia pulled out of the parking lot, glad the snow had turned to slush. Perhaps the landscape would still be pristine in the wooded area north of Lancaster County.

Mingled with Amelia's joy at being chosen as concertmaster was also a sense of loss. She longed to recapture the enchanting July evening she'd spent with Michael, in some ways the catalyst that had helped to give her the courage to step out and take a chance as she had. She made the trip to the Morgantown exit, trying to retrace her steps the night of the torrential rainstorm. But to no avail.

It was pointless to stop at the convenience store just off the freeway, as she had done in the storm to get gas, because she didn't remember any of the names on the road signs. She did recall a mobile home park, but she was presently going in circles, and thick snowflakes were beginning to stick to her windshield.

The more Amelia tried to locate the tranquil cabin, the more confused she became on the back roads.

Giving up as she spotted the main highway, she headed in the direction of the on-ramp. Surely she could at least return to Hickory Hollow for part of the afternoon. She wanted to stop in briefly to see Ella Mae Zook and to say happy New Year—and to thank her, as well. Yes, that's what she would do. After all, she was this close, so why not?

With renewed anticipation, Amelia merged onto the highway, this time headed south . . . to the heart of Amish country.

———

Amelia had no trouble finding the Old Philadelphia Pike, nor the back roads leading to Hickory Lane. She was thankful for that, as the snow was coming fast now, and she knew she couldn't stay long.

Ella Mae came to the back door right away when Amelia knocked. She greeted her with a wide smile, eyes big as she realized who was there. "Well, lookee here! Miss Amelia . . . ach, won't ya come right in."

Without more ado, Ella Mae tottered over to her teakettle, which she said was always simmering, "just waiting for tea." Being back in the Wise Woman's cheery kitchen brought back a rush of good memories. And over peppermint tea with honey and some warm cranberry bread and snickerdoodles, Amelia thanked the dear woman for helping her understand what was most important. *Finding one's purpose in life . . . and prayer.*

She also shared with Ella Mae about her exciting new position with the Philadelphia Orchestra. The Wise Woman smiled and bobbed her head. "Do you plan to move closer, just maybe?" she asked, and Amelia said she hadn't gotten that far but would most likely commute and stay over for rehearsals and concerts for the first few months.

"Have you seen much of Elizabeth now that she's home?" Amelia asked.

"Oh yes." Ella Mae's eyes softened. "Our Lizzie finally came to her senses." She reached to give Amelia's hand a pat. "And you, my dear one, are a big reason for that."

"Well . . . I'm sure her family prayed for her, too."

"Oh jah, no doubt. And there's talk that she's hoping to join church next year." Ella Mae drew a quick breath. "I can tell ya there'll be plenty of sniffling when that Sunday rolls round."

"I can just imagine." Amelia guessed Michael would also be among those bowing their knee next September.

"Word has it that Elizabeth is even seein' her former beau—a right nice Amish fella—one of Mary Stoltzfus Beiler's handsome nephews. Don't that beat all?"

"Will she marry him, do you think?" Amelia asked.

Ella Mae chuckled, but she shook her head. "Now, we ain't s'posed to know any of that till the couple's published two weeks before the wedding. 'Tis anyone's guess, for now."

"Well, Elizabeth's still young. She's got plenty of time."

"Round here, seventeen or eighteen isn't too early to marry . . . not when you know you've found the one you're meant for," Ella Mae said.

Looking out at the blowing snow, Amelia thanked her for the tea and wished her a happy New Year. Then she rose and said good-bye, knowing she would miss the dear woman.

"You're always welcome." Ella Mae insisted on getting up and walking with her to the door. Then, peering out at what had become near-blizzard conditions, she said, "For pity's sake! I can't let ya drive in this weather."

"Oh, I'll be okay."

"Well, I didn't say you wouldn't be. But if you ain't in a rush to get home, why not just spend the night here? You can start out fresh in the morning, once the snow's done."

Amelia thanked her but didn't want to infringe on her generosity.

"Oh, I know what you're thinkin' . . . you don't want to be a bother, ain't?"

"You've figured me out," Amelia admitted, feeling so at home here.

"Well, it'd make better sense to just bring in your fiddle and make this old woman mighty happy with some music by the fire. And stay put for the night—safe and sound."

Amelia laughed in agreement. "All right, I'll stay, but only if you'll let me help with supper. It's only fair."

"I'll let ya help if you play music afterward. How's that?"

Amelia couldn't suppress her smile. For all the trouble she'd caused with her fiddling last visit, she hoped word wouldn't get out that she was back serenading one of Hickory Hollow's oldest church members.

Slipping on her jacket and scarf, she hurried out to the car for her violin, feeling incredibly warm inside.

"Such a heavy, wet snow," Lillianne said as she looked at her husband, who'd scooted his rocking chair up close to the heater stove. Paul looked so gloomy today, and she had to make an effort to keep her own voice cheerful. She didn't feel much like making small talk, but Paul seemed to want the company. Christmas had come and gone awful quick, or so it seemed, and now Michael's room was emptied out except for the bed and the oak bureau. The image of him up there packing his clothes and personal possessions was still stamped on her heart, and it was all she could do just now to hold back her tears.

"What's a-matter, Lily?" Paul looked up at her, frowning and pushing his fingers through his beard. "I know you're a-frettin'. Can feel it over here."

"Well now, I'm just missin' our boy."

Paul folded his arms. "I daresay he's better off leaving now—rejecting the church vow—than promising to live Amish all the days of his life and turning his back on it years from now."

Lillianne considered that quietly.

"Just look what happened to another draftsman from round here."

"You're thinkin' of Daniel Fisher." Lillianne put a bunch of potatoes in her apron and carried them over to the table to peel. She sat there working, waiting for her husband to respond, and when he didn't she looked to see him fishing around for his blue kerchief. Oh, how her heart went out to the poor man!

Daniel's under the Bann, along with his Katie, she thought sadly, shuddering to think how that might have been Michael. This way, as long as he had breath, they could hope and pray he'd come back and join church. *Someday, O Lord.*

" 'Least we aren't estranged from Michael," Paul added.

"Maybe he has more to learn out in the world."

"Could be . . . only the Good Lord knows all that," said Paul thoughtfully. "Knows his heart, inside and out. And the day our son falls to his knees in contrition before the brethren will make all this waiting worthwhile."

"We'll just keep prayin' to that end."

Paul got up and went to the sink, where he splashed water on his face. *Hiding his feelings . . .*

Lillianne was glad to make her husband's favorites for supper tonight—Basque potatoes, crunchy chicken, and pickled red beets. And she'd made a cherry pie with whipped cream for dessert, too. Such a fine supper would help boost their spirits some, given it was just the two of them at the table. She wouldn't let herself think about Michael's supper plans just now, no doubt eating over with their English relatives.

Lord bless them. . . .

Chapter 40

Amelia blinked into the glare of sun on the snowy landscape as she waited for Ella Mae to awaken from her nap.
The violin case was open on the table, the temperature of the
small house warming her fiddle. Amelia felt cozy and sheltered in
the welcoming bungalow; she wished some of her musician friends
could see her here. Wouldn't they love to meet Ella Mae, too!

*Such serenity . . . the snow falling against the backdrop of barn
and silos.* Amelia was very glad she'd decided to stay.

When she looked to her right, toward the farmhouse across the
field, she was surprised to see the dark figure of a woman walking
this way, all bundled up in a black woolen shawl over her long
black dress, with a black scarf, mittens, and boots, and a black
bonnet—in a candlesnuffer style—stark against the brilliance.
The woman carried a large basket, head down as she leaned
into the wind.

Going to the door, Amelia peered out, watching as the woman
approached the porch. It was then she caught sight of Joanna's
face. "Hello . . . we meet again!" she said, opening the door, so
happy to see her friend.

Joanna gave the sweetest smile. "Ach, I've missed ya!" Inside, she set down her basket of goodies, then reached to give Amelia a hug.

By then Ella Mae's eyes were fluttering open. The tiny woman had undoubtedly been roused by the sudden commotion. The two young women chattered quietly in the kitchen while Joanna removed her wraps and boots. "I'm ever so glad you're here," Joanna told Amelia. "I kept wonderin' if that was your car parked outside, but with all the snow it was hard to tell, really."

Amelia explained that she was on her way home from Philadelphia, where she'd just auditioned, and she shared the exciting news about her new position there.

Joanna brightened even more, saying she hoped it meant they might see each other more frequently. "Is that a possibility?"

"I'll certainly see to it!"

Ella Mae rose and, using her cane, hobbled over to investigate the basket of goodies from Joanna. She removed the cloth covering and beamed at the sight of the varieties of treats inside. "Well, now, 'tis a *gut* thing the two of you are here visiting, ain't? We'll have us a fine dessert, and there's enough for breakfast tomorrow, too." Then she asked Joanna if she'd like to stay for supper.

Much to Amelia's delight, Joanna agreed. "I'll have to let my parents know, so they won't wonder." Amelia offered to accompany her back home, and they donned their wraps—Amelia's long red coat and Joanna's black one. Then off they went, holding their scarves over their faces. Their eyes peeked out just enough to see where they were going.

··· ➤ ≺ ···

Michael drove slowly on the snow-packed roads, glad for the opportunity for a full day of work on a new blueprint. Then, on the drive back to Hickory Hollow, he had stopped in at his mother's elderly cousin's.

Now, as he made his way down Hickory Lane, coming up on the Kurtz farm, he noticed Joanna and what looked like an English woman in a very red coat coming across the field, huddled against the cold. He saw a car parked in front of Ella Mae's cottage, which was attached to her family's main farmhouse. He slowed his vehicle and did a double take, wondering if it could be Amelia's, though it was impossible to tell under the mounding snow. His heart leaped at the thought. Could it be?

Anxious as he was to know how she was doing, Michael willed himself to remain clearheaded. Her agent wouldn't be at all happy to find out Michael had encountered Amelia here—if he was bold enough to do so.

Pulling onto the shoulder, Michael watched Joanna and the other woman hurry toward the Kurtz house. He sighed and leaned back in the driver's seat.

He glanced in the rearview mirror, still unaccustomed to his modern haircut and clothes, having made the switch from Amish to English at the onset of New Year's.

She probably wouldn't even recognize me. . . .

In that moment, he knew it was best to stay out of Amelia's way—not reopen the already closed door between them. After all, she hadn't emailed him over Christmas, either. So his assumption that she was in total agreement with Stoney's remarks must be correct. In light of this, Michael was almost embarrassed to think of his impulsive drive to Ohio. What if he *had* succeeded in seeing Amelia then?

He signaled back onto the road, even though there was no traffic in sight. Then, staring again at the white that was swiftly covering the strange car, he felt another wave of frustration.

Relax, Michael, it can't be hers. . . .

Turning to focus on the road and the swirling snow, he drove to his new home at the Landis farmhouse on the very outskirts of Hickory Hollow.

··· ➤ ➤ ···

When Amelia arrived inside the warm kitchen with Joanna, Rhoda Kurtz greeted her, her eyebrows rising. Nate Kurtz grunted briefly and nodded his head.

Joanna told her mother why she'd returned, and Rhoda suggested she pack an overnight bag with a change of clothes, in case the snow kept up and she decided to stay overnight at Ella Mae's.

Amelia was secretly overjoyed at the prospect of more time with her friend. *I never thought I'd see both the Wise Woman and Joanna today!*

Upstairs, Joanna closed her bedroom door behind her and hurried to her hope chest to show Amelia a Christmas gift from her beau. It was a small chime clock that played music. "The pertiest clock I've ever seen." Her face shone with not only joy but love. "Thank goodness it arrived when no one was home . . . 'cept me."

"Why is that so important?" Amelia asked. "And why is it hidden away?"

Joanna bowed her head. "Ain't the right time to tell, just yet."

Tell what? Amelia had so many questions, but she knew Joanna was intensely private about her suitor. So instead she said, "Well, whenever that day comes, you'll enjoy it very much." She glanced at Joanna's dresser, wondering if the vacant spot in the middle was the place she was saving for the exquisite gift.

Joanna quickly turned the subject to Amelia's new position, saying timidly that Michael had shown her Amelia's "nice web site" on his laptop not long ago.

Surprised, Amelia wondered exactly how long ago. But not wanting to come across as too curious, she didn't inquire. Nor would she let herself be too pleased at this revelation, although the thought of Michael perusing her web site did make her smile.

No more was said about Michael the rest of the evening—not during the mealtime preparations back at Ella Mae's, nor during the tasty supper of pork chops, rice, and a broccoli-cheese casserole. Afterward they enjoyed the cookies and sweet breads in Joanna's basket. Then the three of them talked fondly between the pieces Amelia played on her violin—everything from classically arranged hymns to excerpts from the grand violin concertos of her recent tour.

It was only much later, when Amelia said good-night to Joanna in the guest room they were sharing, that the subject of Michael arose for a second time. "Not long after you were here last summer, Michael asked me for your address," Joanna confided quietly in the stillness, in the bed across from Amelia.

"Yes, he told me . . . in his first letter."

"So you've been writing to each other, then?" Joanna seemed very interested.

"Only as friends." Amelia didn't reveal that there had been a flood of emails between them, nor how very personal those exchanges had become . . . prior to the sudden and complete absence of all correspondence.

What could've happened? she asked herself yet again.

Joanna stirred in the darkness. "Do ya mind if I say my prayers aloud, in English?"

Amelia welcomed it, getting choked up when Joanna said Amelia's name toward the end of the prayer. "And thank you, our Lord in heaven, for blessing my English friend with guidance and blessing that only come from your loving hand. Keep her ever safe in your loving care, and thank you for showing us the way to eternal life through your dear Son, our Lord Jesus Christ. Let us be found worthy to live in heaven with you some sweet day. Amen."

Amelia felt so thoroughly included in the prayer, she almost believed she had prayed it, too, right along with Joanna. She felt enveloped with compassion, not only because of Joanna's beautiful prayer, but because of the Lord's presence in the quiet room.

Adding a silent P.S.—which included a blessing for Michael's future here in Hickory Hollow—Amelia breathed a deep sigh. For Michael's sake, she hoped he would be very happy.

Chapter 41

Through the bitter winter and into early spring, Amelia spent long hours in her studio, rehearsing for the recording with EMI Classics, scheduled for mid-May. Her father was much too weak to direct her preparations, but rather sat in his recliner listening when not fading in and out of sleep.

She purposely pleased him by practicing the Brahms when he was most alert, knowing his great passion for the composer. A large bronze bust of Johannes Brahms stood on a lovely marble stand not far from Dad's chair, presiding over their hours together.

Letters from Joanna continued to arrive, and Amelia cheerfully wrote back to her friend when she could.

April and May brought warmer, if sometimes volatile, weather, and the threat of tornadoes. When the strongest rainstorms blew in, pounding the roof with their fury, Amelia fondly remembered being lost on Welsh Mountain, wishing she might someday find her way back to the log cabin to see it once more. Really, she hadn't been lost that night at all. That extraordinary hiatus had opened her heart to the good people of Hickory Hollow. And most of all, to her heavenly Father.

EMI's marketing company and Amelia's own publicists blitzed the August launch of her new CD, which debuted high on the classical music charts. The deluge of resulting web traffic and email was heartening not only to Amelia but to Stoney, too.

Also in August began the rehearsals with the Philadelphia Orchestra, and Amelia quickly acclimated to her new role as she became better acquainted with the other musicians, young and old alike. Two attractive male string players her age even showed interest in the idea of forming a string quartet at a future date. As she connected with the other orchestra members, Amelia witnessed firsthand how well they meshed under the direction of the venerated maestro . . . the many blending beautifully into one greater whole.

As often as her schedule permitted, Amelia spent time in Columbus visiting her father, who suffered terribly on his worst days, weakened as he still was from the pneumonia his doctor had been unable to prevent. On his best days, he enjoyed listening to the great violin music he so cherished.

Amelia also went to nearby bookstores with her mother, who tried to practice some degree of patience while waiting for more word from her literary agent. Mom and her agent were quite persistent, however—many now-famous novelists had endured rejection prior to landing a publisher. And Mom was already busy writing another manuscript, once again honing the creative process. She was also occupied with Dad's care, although a home nurse assisted by coming three times each week to track his blood pressure and medications.

During what remained of her free time, Amelia worked with gifted violin students at the prestigious Curtis Institute of Music in Philadelphia. On Saturdays, she offered Suzuki group lessons for impoverished children, supplying the quarter-sized violins free of charge. She taught them plenty of fiddle tunes along with their lessons, which the children loved. She attended several fiddle fests, too, taking great pleasure in the carefree, frolicking melodies. But no longer did she compete, rather focusing on preparing for her upcoming performance of the Fiddle Concerto with the orchestra. It crossed her mind that not many concertmasters could be called upon to play the unusual crossover classical-fiddling composition. In fact, she might be the only one.

In her evening hours, Amelia came to rely on the intimacy and comfort of daily prayer, the precious and life-changing act of opening one's heart to God. And of trusting her life to His will. Ella Mae's words—and gentle influence—proved lasting. So much so that Amelia found herself devouring books on Amish culture, especially *The Amish Way*, by author and Amish spokesman Donald Kraybill and his collaborators.

She also enjoyed Joanna's letters, and while Amelia was curious about Michael Hostetler, she never once asked about him. And since Joanna didn't mention him, either, Amelia did her best to put the handsome and very thoughtful man out of her mind. Short as their time together had been, perhaps it would simply have to be enough.

··· ➤ ➤ ···

The first night of the early September Philadelphia Orchestra concert series was an evening of sizzling musical offerings. The grand hall was filled with enthusiastic concert attendees, many of whom had come specifically to see the new concertmaster. Backstage was abuzz with anticipation, too, and Amelia was delighted to greet Nicola Hannevold, who looked healthy and energetic. Many from the orchestra were anxious to talk with Nicola, and Amelia obligingly slipped away from the crowd, her black tiered chiffon gown rustling around her ankles.

As she observed the well-deserved adulation for the guest soloist, Amelia found herself reevaluating what she had given up to fulfill her new role. *I love what I'm doing,* she thought. *And satisfied with the new challenges I've set for myself.*

And she was . . . at least professionally speaking.

True, her social life was rapidly improving, as well, although the most interesting young men were merely good friends, like caring brothers. But no one had emerged who fulfilled her must-have list. Amelia wanted it all—a lifelong love with a best friend husband, a kind and caring man who worshiped God and loved life and music . . . and who wanted lots of children. *Lord willing, as Joanna likes to say.*

Life was good, but the yearning to be a part of a family of her own continued to linger in Amelia's heart.

Nicola Hannevold played the Mendelssohn violin concerto superbly, and with more gusto than Amelia expected. Had the astute maestro stirred up the fire? He was known to have a flair for challenging young soloists to supersede their own benchmarks. Amelia supported Nicola with her own playing, just a few feet from where the guest artist stood facing the vast audience.

The concert hall brought back memories of Amelia's earliest years of performing, playing with all the joy in her soul. Tonight as she led the first violin section it was no different; she was enjoying herself immensely.

Later, during Nicola's encore, Amelia's mind raced back to her first-ever visit to the Oberlin Conservatory. So tiny and timid, she'd reached for her father's strong hand as they walked the hallway to meet the remarkable Ms. Malloy—sixteen years ago this week. In her short life, Amelia had never experienced a more encouraging instructor than Dorothea. Silently, she dedicated tonight's first orchestral concert to Ms. Malloy . . . and to Dad.

Thank you, God, for the gift of music!

After Nicola had taken her final bow at the sweep of the maestro's hand, the orchestra stood to acknowledge the crowd's applause. Amelia fell into step behind Miss Hannevold and the maestro, heading for the wings. There, she shook hands with Nicola again. And the maestro, too.

"My dear Miss Devries, your face simply glows," he said.

Amelia did feel flushed with the excitement; she had so enjoyed the cooperative effort.

Confidently making her way backstage, Amelia put away her violin and bow, closed the case, and slipped on her elegant cashmere wrap, then walked through the maze toward the back entrance.

She turned and noticed a strikingly handsome man standing near the exit. Aware of his intense gaze, she looked away decorously.

But, wait . . . there was something familiar about him. She moved closer, her curiosity piqued.

Can it be?

Chapter 42

The young man's smile and blue eyes were arresting—and unforgettable.

"Michael?" She hurried over to him. "Is it you?"

His face lit up as his eyes swept down her long gown. "You look just beautiful, Amelia." His deep voice brought back a rush of memories.

"Thanks . . . you're quite dashing yourself." She searched his face, still shaken by how very English he appeared in his fine heather-gray suit and colorful tie. His blond hair was also cut in a sleek modern style—gone were the bangs and shaggy-dog look. She laughed softly, suddenly giddy. "I almost didn't recognize you." How clearly she remembered Michael's Amish attire and demeanor . . . in all of her thoughts of him.

Michael stepped closer. "I've been searching for you . . . following your performance schedule. I wanted to see you again."

She smiled up at him. "What took you so long?"

He winked at her and reached to carry her violin case. "May I?" he asked and she nodded. "I hope you're hungry," he said. "On a whim, I made reservations at a restaurant not far from here."

On a whim! It sounded like he'd planned this.

"If that's all right," he added.

"Sure, wonderful." She followed as he led her to the door and opened it. The cool air hit their faces as they stepped into the light of the streetlamps.

"I have a lot to tell ya, Amelia."

"Yes, so much has happened since . . ." She paused. *Should she ask?* "I thought you'd decided to stay Amish. I thought that's why you stopped emailing."

He shook his head. "After I went to visit you in Ohio last December—to surprise you—I made the decision to leave the People for *gut*."

"So . . . it *was* you!" She stared up at him, incredulous. "Right before Christmastime—was that when you came?"

He nodded.

"Why didn't you ring the bell and come in?"

"I did, but your agent sent me away."

She groaned. "Oh, I'm sorry! I had no idea."

"I didn't want to interfere with your career . . . as he seemed to think I had." Michael explained that Stoney had indicated strongly that he—or Amelia's time in Amish country—was responsible for her lack of focus.

So that's what happened! It was becoming painfully clear in her mind. To think Stoney had sent Michael away! "Which must be why I didn't hear from you after that."

"Jah," he said, the Dutchy word seeming out of place with his new look. "I had to respect what I thought you wanted." He stopped for a moment. "I honestly thought it was for the best."

"But you're here now." Her heart beat too fast as she moved ahead to ask the burning question. "May I ask why?"

"Can we talk 'bout that over dinner?" His eyes searched hers. "All right with you?"

She nodded, amazed—and delighted—at this surprising turn of events.

As they walked toward his car, Michael shared more. "You know, the really important stuff came so naturally for us, Amelia . . . that night the storm blew you into the cabin."

She hadn't forgotten. "Yes."

"But you were spoken for then." He admitted humbly that Joanna had told him about her breakup with Byron. "Of course I had to pry it out of her. And I was glad to hear it. . . . I honestly kept thinking of you," he admitted.

Since saying farewell to Byron, she had done the same, comparing every guy she'd met with Michael.

They walked together across the parking lot, their strides in perfect sync.

"By the way, whatever happened to the fiddler?" he asked, a note of humor in his tone.

Amelia patted her heart. "Oh, believe me, she's right here."

"Amy Lee . . . Amelia." He paused and stopped beneath the streetlamp. "I have a confession to make."

"What's that?"

He smiled down at her. "I've missed you . . . something awful."

He reached for her hand, and Amelia sighed as she laced her fingers with his. Hadn't she dreamed this scenario countless times before?

"I'm glad you found me, Michael."

His gaze lingered and she held her breath, thinking he might kiss her. But just when her heart felt like it might beat right out of her chest, he stepped back and walked her to his car. There, he opened the door and waited for her to get in, then placed her violin in the trunk.

The moon cast a white glow as they drove. The music in the CD player came on softly—a dreamy violin rendition of "Somewhere Over the Rainbow."

It was the last song Amelia had played for him before their lovely sojourn at the cabin came to an end.

"I've nearly worn out this CD," Michael confessed, his eyes filled with longing as he reached for her hand again.

Not only was Amelia impressed with the scrumptious cuisine, but the restaurant's romantic ambiance was perfect. She listened with astonishment as Michael shared his earlier disappointment as his heart pulled him between what he wanted and what he had mistakenly believed was Amelia's desire for her career. "It definitely made for a long winter," he said, eyes solemn.

Listening to him, watching him . . . she found everything about Michael appealing. From the first, her heart had felt at home with this man. And even more so now that he was no longer Amish, although his quaint turns of phrase still recalled his Plain roots.

"Now that I'm sitting here with you, Amelia," he said, eyes alight suddenly, "I'd like to tell ya what I plan to do . . . to win your heart." He reached across the table for her hand and held it tenderly. "With your permission, I'm going to court you like you've never been courted before."

She blinked back happy tears. "Oh, Michael, I'd love that." *Dearly*, she thought, trying to keep her emotions in check.

"Wonderful-*gut*, then." He winked at her again, and she blushed. And while they enjoyed dessert, he asked her to catch him up on her life and work. "So you're much closer to Lancaster now," he observed.

"Absolutely. And to beautiful Hickory Hollow, too!"

He let her know he was still in touch with his parents—and Elizabeth—and that would never change. Amelia was relieved to learn that he could never be shunned for his decision not to join the church, and that he was still regarded as family. "Just as you will be, too, one fine day," he said, a twinkle in his eyes. "Lord willing."

She smiled, enjoying this beginning of their courtship. "You know what? I suddenly feel like playing a lively fiddle tune," she told him.

"Right here . . . right now?" he teased.

"Well." She looked around the dining room, white linens on each candlelit table. "Um . . . not exactly."

He squeezed her hand and offered an affectionate smile, as if to say, "*I look forward to you, and your music, for the rest of our lives.*"

In that moment, she knew there were certain precious feelings that could never, ever be explained or shared with anyone . . . not even her good friend Joanna. This night, this amazing moment, was one of those times. *One of many*, Amelia hoped with all of her heart.

Epilogue

Since courting my darling Amelia, I find myself becoming
more and more English in my thinking, while she admits
to embracing many of the Plain ideals—*the simple gifts*, as Ella
Mae says.

Amelia and I plan to marry in early May next year, when the
pink and white dogwoods and red azaleas are in full bloom. For
now, we see each other as often as our individual work allows,
and we fill in the gaps between visits with many emails and
phone calls.

My bride-to-be seems to enjoy helping plan the blueprint for
the house we're building. I welcome her input—Daed wisely
taught me that incorporating a woman's perspective is always
mighty smart. And do I ever believe it, especially when Amelia
suggested how many bathrooms we'll be needing, considering
the number of children we hope God will bless us with someday.

"*Lots of little fiddlers,*" she says with the prettiest smile . . .
and a tender kiss.

We also talk about what kind of wedding might best mix

the Plain with the fancy—a wedding pleasing to God. Amelia believes it's even possible to merge the sophisticated with the down-home, the modern with old tradition. She sees a long white wedding gown and a black tuxedo, as well as little barefoot flower girls holding daisies. And there will be music!

And I . . .

Ach, but what do I know? I'll be happy to leave the planning to the bride! " *'Tis wiser that way,*" says Ella Mae with her jovial laugh.

Of course, if everyone who loves Amelia shows up, there won't be a big enough place to hold the crowd. My extended family alone will require more than two hundred chairs at the reception. Thank goodness there are plenty of months to decide all of that!

For now, it's a joy to spend time with my sweetheart-girl as I come to appreciate the many facets to this special young woman who rediscovered God's peace and contentment in the very Amish country I was fixing to leave. I love everything about Amelia, including her serious playing and her fiery fiddling. This beautiful young woman the Lord allowed to burst into my life on a stormy summer evening, whose heart will join with mine when we say "I do." Each for the other, and both for the Lord.

When we can, we take brisk jogs around Hickory Hollow, and play some very competitive chess, too. We share our goals and dreams, as well as individual past struggles, blending our hearts ever so slowly as we get happily lost in conversation. And, oh, what laughter! I've taught her to ride a horse, catch a fish, and to lay out a vegetable garden, at least on paper. And Amelia's taught this former Plain boy a thing or two, as well: how to hold a violin correctly, and more recently, how to play a two-octave scale—the latter with my earplugs handy . . . for her sake!

I was privileged to meet Amelia's parents before her father passed away late this fall. We attended the memorial service together, Amelia weeping softly by my side.

Little by little, Amelia is saying good-bye to her old life in Columbus. She has a buyer for her townhome and will move in with her mother, a soon-to-be published novelist. That is, when Amelia is in Columbus and not playing in Philly with the orchestra, where she will continue to be concertmaster.

Jah, it won't be too long and we'll be blending my Amish family with her English one. We look forward to having my parents meet her mother sometime soon, once the weather gets warmer. Needless to say, there's plenty of curiosity all around!

Amelia and I often pray together as I hold her in my arms. I reach for her hand and offer thanks for God's great gift of love, our hearts made new . . . knit together by divine grace. Despite our vastly different backgrounds, we are much better together than apart. Like a fiddle needs its bow.

Author's Note

In this book, my passion for music, as well as the Plain community of Lancaster County, where I grew up, came together like a patchwork quilt. I've been waiting nearly a lifetime to write this book!

I'm forever grateful to my parents, especially my mother, who instilled in me the incredible joy of making music at the piano, with the violin, and vocally. Beginning in fourth grade, I studied violin. I enjoyed it so much, I played all through high school and college, after which I taught beginning violin students in my home-based music studio. While I was never as proficient a violinist as my protagonist, Amelia Devries, I'm thankful that my copy editor, Helen Motter, plays professionally. Thanks, Helen, for catching anything I may have missed in the details of Amelia's musical life.

My deepest appreciation also goes to Julie Klassen, with whom I brainstormed my initial ideas for *The Fiddler*, prior to her becoming a full-time novelist. Keep those bestsellers coming!

Special thanks to David Horton, who faithfully cheers me on

and develops my most story-worthy ideas. And to my longtime editor and partner in fiction, Rochelle Glöege, whose amazing expertise makes my stories sing. I am so thankful!

The following consultants and research assistants were invaluable to me during the writing of this book: First of all, my Amish friends, who prefer to remain unnamed; Dale and Barbara Birch, David and Janet Buchwalter, Hank and Ruth Hershberger, Jake and Ruth Bare, Edwin and Marion Rohrer, Erik Wesner, John and Jim Smucker, and Brad Igou. Thanks very much!

The splendid Amish setting of Hickory Hollow—popularized by *The Shunning* and its HERITAGE OF LANCASTER COUNTY sequels, as well as the Hallmark movie—is a fictional one. Yet it continues to live on in my psyche somewhere between the Old Philadelphia Pike to the north and Route 30 to the south . . . just as it did when Katie Lapp and Daniel Fisher were first birthed in my heart. (Not so far from my childhood home.)

Many thanks to my devoted reader-friends for your ongoing encouragement and prayerful support. You are a joy!

I can't thank my dear Dave enough for his TLC—and experienced editorial input—especially as my first reader during the initial draft.

Most of all, I offer my grateful heart to the always amazing Source of life, light, and indeed beautiful music. *Soli deo Gloria!*

Beverly Lewis, born in the heart of Pennsylvania Dutch country, is the *New York Times* bestselling author of more than one hundred books. Her stories have been published in twelve languages worldwide. A keen interest in her mother's Plain heritage has inspired Beverly to write many Amish-related novels, beginning with *The Shunning*, which has sold more than one million copies and is an Original Hallmark Channel movie. In 2007, *The Brethren* was honored with a Christy Award.

Beverly has been interviewed by both national and international media, including *Time* magazine, the Associated Press, and the BBC. She lives with her husband, David, in Colorado.

Visit her website at www.beverlylewis.com or www.facebook.com/officialbeverlylewis for more information.